THE NIGHT SEASON

PAUL BOWDRING

ALSO BY PAUL BOWDRING

The Roncesvalles Pass 1989

THE NIGHT SEASON

PAUL BOWDRING

killick press
an imprint of Creative Publishers

St. John's, Newfoundland
1997

We acknowledge the support of the Canada Council for the Arts for our publishing program

THE CANADA COUNCIL | LE CONSEIL DES ARTS
FOR THE ARTS | DU CANADA
SINCE 1957 | DEPUIS 1957

This is a work of fiction. The characters and incidents depicted are imaginary. Any resemblance to real people and events is coincidental.

∝ Printed on acid-free paper

Published by
KILLICK PRESS
a Creative Book Publishing imprint
A Robinson-Blackmore Printing & Publishing associated company
P.O. Box 8660, St. John's, Newfoundland A1B 3T7

Printed in Canada by:
ROBINSON-BLACKMORE PRINTING & PUBLISHING

Canadian Cataloguing in Publication Data

Bowdring, Paul.

The night season
ISBN 1-895387-89-2

I. Title.

PS8553.089945N54   1997   C813'.54   C97-950220-9
PR9199.3.B6285N54   1997

FOR JULIA

Acknowledgments

The author would like to thank the Canada Council, the Newfoundland and Labrador Arts Council, the City of St. John's Arts Jury, and the Canada-Newfoundland Agreement on Cultural Industries for their support.

Special thanks to editors Anne Hart and Ed Kavanagh. Thanks also to Ann Anderson, Don Austin, Peter Gard, Anne Marie Granter, Frank Holden, and the Thursday Collective.

Drafts of parts of this novel have been published in *The Fiddlehead, TickleAce,* and *Canadian Fiction Magazine;* other parts have been broadcast on CBC Radio.

My bones are pierced in me in the night season:
and my sinews take no rest.
                    —The Book of Job

And hark! the Nightingale begins its song,
"Most musical, most melancholy" bird!
A melancholy bird? Oh! idle thought!
In Nature there is nothing melancholy.
But some night-wandering man whose heart was pierced
With the remembrance of a grievous wrong,
Or slow distemper, or neglected love,
(And so, poor wretch! filled all things with himself,
And made all gentle sounds tell back the tale
Of his own sorrow) he, and such as he,
First named these notes a melancholy strain.
And many a poet echoes the conceit;...
                    —Coleridge, "The Nightingale"

The hearts of men have such blind darkness in them.
                    —Ovid, *Metamorphoses*

CONTENTS

As always in sieges, the bakers were the most troublesome group
of tradesmen.
—Eversley Belfield, *Sieges*

It had begun to snow again. He watched sleepily the flakes,
silver and dark, falling obliquely against the lamplight.
—James Joyce, "The Dead"

THE CONSOLATION OF PASTRY

Mother discovered the croissant late in life—I remember it
was on her sixty-fifth birthday, when my sister, Ruth, and I
took her down to the Newfoundland Hotel for brunch. And
after a lifelong loyalty to the lemon cream cracker, brief affairs
with the bagel and the English muffin, and an abiding, if
intermittent, affection for the jam jam, the tea bun, and the
apricot square, the croissant was now her absolute favourite.
As Ruth said, it was nice to see her being enthusiastic about
something, even if it was only a piece of pastry. After Dad's
death just before Christmas the year before, she had lost interest
in just about everything, and for a while seemed to live only
on tea and toast.

After I'd started high school, Dad had taken me aside one
day and asked me if I'd like to call him "Des." Without giving it
any thought, I said yes, but after a few attempts, the bald and
unfamiliar diminutive had (if you'll forgive me) desiccated on
my tongue. Like distances at sea, from "Dad" to "Des" had been
much farther than I thought.

I'd settled on "Desmond," which was what Mother had
always called him, though the rest of the world knew him only
as Des. Before that I had experimented with "Father Des" and
"Father Desmond." Being a lapsed Catholic, he'd got a great
kick out of that. I spoke his name, however, only when I had to,

and always found it hard to avoid a comic and ironically formal tone.

"Desmond obviously deplores the present government's tendency toward largesse," I would intone in response to one of his occasional, but loud, anti-welfare barks, from which the bite of conviction was so obviously lacking. Despite the relative prosperity—admittedly hard won—of his later years, he had grown up too poor himself to be able to deny a few crumbs of subsistence to anyone else.

"What's he on about now?" he would reply, addressing my mother.

"Eat your food, dear" was all she would ever say.

Ruth had continued to call him "Daddy," though we were just a year apart and she had received the same invitation. For a while, though, during a brief but intense love affair with the noble and handsome Adam of "Bonanza" fame, she had taken to calling him "Pa." Although I had expected him to flare up at this, he had shown only the slightest hint of distaste, looking at her sometimes and moving his mouth as if he had just licked a postage stamp or had something stuck between his teeth. Nor was he much bothered by "Sugar Daddy," which she had adopted for a time during our university years.

But he had never been that sweet, and now that he was gone, the formality of "Desmond" sometimes felt just right. Once in a while, however, "Father Des" would slip from my tongue, perhaps because it recalled the smile that had sweetened his face whenever I had used it. It wasn't often that I'd seen my father smile.

After Mr. Jackman's space heater had exploded early one cold fall morning and almost burned his house to the ground, Mother, whose row house was attached to his, decided to move out of the downtown. Mr. Jackman had escaped through a hatch onto the roof. He hadn't been outside his house in years, and a fireman found him hiding behind a chimney with his arms around his head, perhaps more in fear of that blinding ball

2

of fire rising in the eastern sky than the smoke and flames that were rising through the open hatch.

"Just a skeleton in a singlet" was how Mother had described him, having watched a fireman carry him down a ladder. She used to rap on his door and leave plates of food on his step, but he was almost deaf, and most of the time it had been left there only to be eaten by dogs or cats.

She was now living in an apartment on the outskirts of town, and on Christmas Day the taxi driver entertained me en route with a half-baked history of the croissant delivered in a St. John's brogue so well preserved it might have been buried in a peat bog for the past two hundred years, like half the artifacts in the museums of his ancestral homeland. He'd been inspired by the large plastic bag of croissants sitting on my lap, beneath which was Mother's Christmas present, a copy of Bing Crosby's *White Christmas* that I'd found in a Woolco record bin downtown. It was her all-time favourite album, and if the mood struck her, she might play it at any season of the year. During the Terrible Two's our daughter, Anna, had remoulded the original record into a serviceable concave kitchen platter by inserting it into an electric heater, and Kate had been unable to find a replacement.

We drove through the suburban wasteland of northeast St. John's, through Centennial Meadows, Eastmeadows, and the perversely named Spruce Meadows, where trees, it seemed, had been feared more than triffids, and had been just as heartlessly dispatched. To replace them, fortress-like fences had been erected as buffers against the heavy traffic on the main streets. I imagined wary suburbanites stationed behind them with anti-triffid weapons: flame-throwers and mortar-bombs.

Between two sections of a strip mall, a fluorescent OPEN sign shone optimistically in one of the drably curtained windows of the forlorn facade of a Chinese restaurant and take-out. There seemed to be one like it in almost every part of town, a mythical chain whose links were only in your head. It was probably the area's original eatery, but was surrounded now by gleaming and gilded competitors.

In a car that didn't seem to have a single shock remaining, we negotiated the frost heaves and hollows, the ruts and potholes, in the winter pavement. The cab driver informed me that the croissant was Austrian, not French, as most people believed, and had been invented in the seventeenth century during the Turkish siege of Vienna to strengthen the people's resolve. Turkey, he reminded me, had a crescent on its flag, so every time a loyal Viennese citizen ate a croissant with his coffee, he was symbolically gobbling up another Turk. He had once worked under a pastry chef in a Montreal hotel. He had very cold hands, he said. Perfect for pastry.

The driver was still talking as we pulled up in front of Mother's apartment building in Vinland Villa, a seniors' complex of dreary brick blocks whose aging exteriors matched the facades of their residents. In the fading afternoon light a rusting replica of a Viking longboat was listing to starboard in the common courtyard. It sat upon a crumbling concrete pedestal floodlit by high-intensity lamps.

This man knew more about pastry than I had the inclination or cash to find out. With the meter running, I waited patiently while he licked the last few flakes of his story from his perfectly cold fingers and then finally got out of the car to open the door to let me out, as there wasn't a single door or window handle on either side of the back seat.

I laid the croissants and the record on top of the cab as I searched through my pockets for my wallet.

"A little on the dark side," he said, peering through his dark glasses at the pastry in the plastic bag. In the eerie blue light of the mercury-vapour lamps, the croissants gleamed Daliesque.

"Merry Christmas," I said, handing him two tens.

He smiled and nodded his black watch cap at me, which had a dreadlock tassel in Rastafarian red, yellow, and green.

"You're not dressed properly," Mother said predictably, having given me the once-over through the security eye in her apartment door. "The radio said it's five below."

And the gifts I had come bearing were no distraction. She

took them without acknowledgment and stared severely at my bare hands and head, my raglaned body, my sneakered feet. I removed the coat and sat down on the wooden bench in the hallway to take off what she always called my sad excuse for boots.

"Why are you still wearing this get-up in the middle of winter?" she said, hanging the offending piece of khaki in the closet, out of her sight.

"It's not that cold, Mother," I said, in my useless defence. "Anyway, I didn't walk way out here. I came in a cab."

I pictured myself hobbling in here at seventy-five, when Mother would be one hundred and four, and having this very same conversation. What seemed fanciful, even absurd, at twenty seemed merely inevitable at forty.

There were three clocks in Mother's apartment, but none of them were working. They hadn't been working for a long time.

"What does it matter to me what time it is," she'd said to me the last time I mentioned them.

Under a glass dome on the dinette sideboard, an ornate brass-tone clock with black spade hands and a pendulum of rotating carousel horses said eleven fifteen. Dad had given it to her on their fortieth anniversary. The carousel wasn't rotating now because the battery probably hadn't been replaced for years. Beside the clock, in a gilt-wood frame, was an out-of-focus photograph of Ruth and me that Mother had taken at Ruth's university graduation.

On the wall in the living room, a large electric clock with radiating wooden arms alternating with metal spokes—a stylized sun—said twenty to seven. When it was plugged in, it made a sound like a fast-moving locomotive, but the hands of the clock didn't move at all.

On the kitchen wall a clock with a red plastic frame, a miniature hula hoop, said half past four. It too was unplugged, but in ten minutes it would be right for the second time that day.

There seemed to be some minor profundity here, some soft philosophical currency that my mind tried hard to negotiate as Mother and I sat at the chrome table beneath this clock in the windowless kitchen of her one-bedroom apartment, drinking King Cole tea and eating Purity partridgeberry jam and croissants.

She said she didn't want to eat too much because she was going over to Aunt May's for Christmas dinner. But as I hadn't had any lunch, and as this was probably going to be my Christmas dinner, I ate, as Mother remarked frankly, like a horse. Or perhaps like a loyal Viennese. I might have been trying to rally my own resolve.

The croissants were a sensational distraction, so to speak, and before you could say thesis-antithesis-synthesis, my philosophical fog had dissolved into dew. The pleasure, the power, the consolation of pastry was not something to be taken lightly.

Mother's problem, however, was getting her hands on it. Mr. Bowman, the downtown grocer whom she had dealt with all her life and who still delivered, free of charge, her meagre carton of groceries once a week, did not carry the croissant. And in the outrageously expensive deli in the strip mall across from her apartment building, the only source of pastry in the neighbourhood, the owner, who was also the baker and the cashier, was in the habit of intimidating his customers by correctively echoing their requests and then repeating them audibly over and over to himself as he filled them.

Mother had enough trouble with the pronunciation of the word as it was, having little flair for foreign tongues, but this man's repetitive hissing of the word "croissant" had so unnerved her on her first visit to this deli that she had never gone back again. She had refused to settle for more pronounceable but more pedestrian alternatives, though I had armed her with "puff pastry" and "crescent roll."

And so it was that I became her lifeline for these unobtainable delicacies, which she savoured almost as much as Antonio Salieri, his Nipples of Venus. They were no small solace to her in her later years, when she was besieged by sorrows I could hardly name. And whenever I called her to see how she was getting on, she would always request a fresh supply—a large secure fresh supply—enough, indeed, for a sizable hoard. She stored them in her refrigerator in wide-mouth Masons.

Mother had always been a big fan of the Mason jar, and her kitchen cupboards were chock-full of them—the wide-mouth Mason being her favourite. Up until a few years ago, she had used them only for homemade jams and pickles; but she didn't bother with that any more, for, as she said, "Who's going to eat them?" Now she was using her large stock of jars to store her entire food supply, meagre as it was, and into them went everything from lemon creams to kippers—and, of course, when she could get them, her entire cache of fresh croissants.

After finishing our tea, we went into the living room and sat side by side on the sofa to open our Christmas presents. On the coffee table was a miniature Christmas tree in a green plastic pot covered in cheery red tinfoil, a present from Ruth via one of the local florists. Three Styrofoam ornaments hung from its cilia-like branches—a Little Drummer Boy's tiny white drum with drumsticks attached, a red bell with a green ribbon, and a child's alphabet block with coloured letters. Between the tinfoil and the plastic pot was a small rectangular card that said, "All my love, Ruthie." Sticking out of the soil was a narrow plastic strip on which was stamped "Norfolk Island Pine."

Besides the few greeting cards on the sideboard, this was the only sign of Christmas in Mother's apartment. Next to the tree were copies of the *Sacred Heart Messenger* and the *Fatima Times*, which her childhood friend, Sister Perpetua, had been sending her faithfully every month since I was a child. Beneath these was a large and official-looking *Reader's Digest* "Super Grand Prize Sweepstakes Certificate" with Mother's name inscribed on it in computer-generated, inch-high, bold capitals. It informed her that it had been "duly recorded" that she had passed through the first two stages in a selection process and that her further participation was "herewith requested"—a prompt reply and a subscription renewal check for twenty-five dollars, which would make her eligible for Stage 3, a chance to win ONE MILLION DOLLARS.

I had given Mother a one-year subscription to the *Reader's Digest* as a birthday present about five years ago, but she had let it lapse, probably because Ruth had done me one better—given her a three-year subscription to the *Catholic Digest*. The secular digest, however, had not lost faith in her; after five years they were still trying to persuade her to renew her subscription. Unfortunately, the effect of this most recent and impressive-looking solicitation was undermined by a hot rose plastic packet stuck conspicuously to the back of Mother's Sweepstakes Certificate. Labelled, appropriately, CONFIDENTIAL, it looked exactly like a condom. If Mother had noticed that, she would have made a special trip to the garbage chute. Inside was a "Prize Validation" stamp to be stuck to the postage-paid envelope enclosed for her prompt reply.

Mother, who was a sock artist of some renown, with a broad and unusual palette, had somewhat surprisingly knit me two identical pairs of grey wool stockings. Upon this conservative canvas, however, she had designed a colourful configuration of three intersecting diamonds to be displayed by the outer ankles. Two smaller diamonds, formed by the intersection of the blue figures with the central yellow one, appeared to be a shade of green, but the colour kept blurring in and out, and I couldn't tell if it was in the wool or in my eye. She was borrowing tricks from the Impressionists, juxtaposing primary colours instead of mixing them, and letting the eye of the beholder blend them itself.

Inside one sock was a small rectangular tin of Erinmore pipe tobacco, the brand Dad had always used in his Peterson pipe. I didn't bother to tell her that I'd given up pipe smoking. The Christmas before he died he had given me an identical briar and a soft brown leather pouch filled with Erinmore tobacco. He had also given me duplicates of all his pipe-smoker's paraphernalia: beechwood filters and hemp pipe cleaners, scoops and picks for scraping dottle out of the bowl, a tamper for pressing fresh tobacco in, a clip-on perforated damper for windy days, and a lighter whose flame shot out the side instead of the top, so that you didn't scorch your fingers while lighting up. You almost needed a small suitcase to cart all this stuff around.

That, and the fact that I could never keep the thing lit, damper or no damper, had discouraged me from becoming even an irregular pipe-smoker. Not to mention my chronic self-consciousness about having that Sherlock Holmes sheep-crook hanging from my lip. And being a heavy cigarette smoker at the time, I didn't have the meditative temperament required to go through the smoking equivalent of the tea ceremony every time I needed an infusion of nicotine.

Crowned with the traditional Santa Claus cap, Bing Crosby's disembodied head was prominently displayed on the cover of his *White Christmas* platter. Set in an eternally youthful face, a pair of unnaturally blue eyes and teeth whiter than any white Christmas shone upon Mother, his loyal and adoring fan of forty years. His face was artificially tanned with make-up for the flash bulbs and the TV lights. Beneath his chin was a bow tie made of holly leaves and berries attached to a white fur collar that matched the trim and tassel on his cap.

Mother beamed back at this boyish face for several minutes. At one time she used to call him Harry, having discovered his real name in a movie magazine. It was beyond her, she said, why anyone would want to call himself Bing.

She struggled in vain with the tight plastic wrapping before handing the record to me to open. As I laid it on the turntable of her tiny record player and lifted the tone arm to remove a belly-button bushel of lint from the needle, it struck me that I didn't know whether or not Harry was still alive.

"Is Bing dead?" I ventured, but Mother had quietly left the room.

9

Bing himself replied unequivocally, or unequi-vocally, with a sprightly rendition of "It's Beginning to Look a Lot Like Christmas," but followed that with a somewhat solemn "God Rest Ye Merry, Gentlemen."

To put it mildly, he had never been one of my musical favourites. Perhaps it was simply because my parents liked him. At a certain age you stop listening not only to your parents but also to whatever they're listening to. At any rate, the song arrangements certainly didn't help—the thin, tinny-sounding orchestras that always backed him up, the bloodless mixed choruses and chorales, and especially the chirrupy chipmunk sister trios that seemed to pop up out of the holes of every song. But when Bing himself got a chance to sing . . . well . . . on this Christmas Day I began to warm to him, I had to admit.

He was singing a very silvery "Silver Bells" when Mother came back into the living room. She had taken off her sweater and slacks and put on a semi-festive plum red dress with a white belt and matching orthopaedic shoes. She sat down in the rocker and put her feet up on the humpty.

"Why don't you come on over to May's with me," she said. "You know how much they love to see you."

"I don't think so, Mother," I said. "You go on, I'll just sit around here for a while."

"They like to eat a bit early. May's always asking about Anna. 'Baby Anna,' she still calls her. I says, 'May, she's almost seven years old.' 'She was a baby the last time I saw her,' she says. It's too bad that woman never had a child of her own."

Mother's face darkened, and she picked up several magazines from the end table.

"I don't suppose you heard Silas Keough died," she said.

"No."

"Poor Elsie, I should call her up. I didn't know about it until he was buried. May saw the notice in the paper but that was about a week after the funeral. She's got papers lying around for weeks before she reads them. She got on the phone to Mrs. Kenny—my God that woman knows a terrible lot of things. She was talking to Elsie on the phone and she told her she was in the hospital when Silas died. She'd been phoning home all morning to tell Silas they were letting her out and when he didn't answer she said she was afraid to go back home. They took her home in the ambulance and she asked them to go in ahead of her and check. They found him on the bathroom floor.

"They brought him home to bury him but she went right back after the funeral. I don't think I seen them since they went away. That must have been twenty years ago."

Her voice trailed away and she began browsing distractedly through copies of the *Sacred Heart Messenger*, the *Catholic Digest*, and the *Fatima Times*. And as I sat watching her and listening to Bing begin a spooky but seductive rendition of "I'll Be Home for Christmas," I had a sudden fantastic thought.

In *The Secret Life of the Unborn Child*, one of the many baby books I had read before Anna's birth, there was a story about a man who had been a musical prodigy. He had become a conductor at the tender age of thirty-five—mere infancy for conductors, many of whom are still waving the wand well into their nineties—and though he had received his musical training on the violin, he discovered to his surprise that he knew the cello parts of certain scores by heart, sight unseen. The mystery was solved when he informed his mother about his strange gift. She herself had studied the cello and played with an amateur orchestra in her younger years. It turned out that the pieces he knew by heart were the very ones she had been learning to play when she had been pregnant with him—and, I suddenly realized, Mother had been playing Bing over and over when she had been pregnant with me.

Jesus, Mary and Joseph, as Mother would say. Bing by osmosis? Insidious croonings rippling through the amniotic fluid as I floated innocent and inert? A biological programming that I was no longer able to resist? And it was a sad measure of my present emotional state that by the time he had reached the end of "I'll Be Home for Christmas," the syrupy old crooner had me by the heartstrings. My secret life was no secret any-more—but thank God it was osmotic and not aesthetic.

For Mother, though, it was a different story. Hers was a real emotional bond. She had first heard "White Christmas" in the fall of 1942, in the middle of the war, and she and Dad had danced to it at their wedding. He had been home on leave, and they got married on Christmas Day—not the whitest, but the coldest, Christmas in memory.

He gave her the record, along with a phonograph, as a combined Christmas and wedding present. On the flip side, appropriately enough, Bing sang "Let's Start the New Year Right." It was a new 78 rpm single that he'd bought from a soldier at Fort Pepperrell, the American forces base in the east end of St. John's and, as Mother had told me many times, she had listened to it all through the following year while she waited for him to come home for good.

Not that he was very far away. He had enlisted in the Newfoundland Militia in 1939 and was stationed about twelve miles away on Bell Island, manning the guns of the 1st Coast Defence Battery on the cliffs overlooking Conception Bay. He came home on leave just about every month.

From "overseas," his brother-in-law, Joe Kelly, used to say, tormenting him incessantly during his visits to the house after he'd retired and come back home from B.C. He'd gone there to work as a logger in 1949. Joe spent most of his visiting time at loggerheads with Dad. They seemed to be prolonging some lifelong dispute that they had never been able to iron out.

Joe himself had actually served overseas, with a sort of paramilitary unit called the Newfoundland Foresters. "Logger" Joe, as Dad had always referred to the man whom Ruth and I liked to call "Uncle Mary" (but that's another story), had cut trees for the war effort on one of the great estates in Scot-land—or, as Dad liked to describe it in defending himself against Joe's merciless needling, lounging on his arse in the heather while he and his comrades back home fought off

German U-boats in Conception Bay. Joe would counter by characterizing this heroic activity as merely terrorizing the farmers in Broad Cove, on the other side of the bay, who, he claimed, used to harvest more shrapnel balls every September than turnips or carrots or Broad Cove blues.

Overseas or not, every time Dad left home Mother was convinced he would never come back. And her fears were not unfounded, for in September of 1942, and again in November—just a few weeks before their marriage—German submarines had sunk ore carriers anchored off the loading pier on Bell Island, ships that were loaded with iron ore for the Allies. They also torpedoed the pier itself, shocking the islanders from their sleep in the early hours of the morning and sending an aftershock of rumour that a German invasion was imminent. Though this, of course, had never occurred, Bell Island had been the only place in North America to have been attacked by the Germans during the war. The torpedoes had claimed four ships and sixty-nine lives. And it was a postwar sore spot with the old man, and additional ammunition for his tormenter, that the commander of one of those German submarines, Captain Friedrich Wilhelm Wissmann, had what Joe called the "Kraut version" of our family name. And not only that: Joe once wondered aloud if I had been named after him.

I had drifted into a dreamy and languorous repose due to the extreme thermostat settings in Mother's apartment. When I opened my eyes, I saw her standing at the window in her coat and scarf. She was waiting for May's husband, Ewart, to come and pick her up. Her hands were folded across her stomach, and her white purse hung from the crook of her arm. The purplish black fingers of a leather glove protruded from the open mouth of the purse like a multi-forked tongue from the jaws of a serpent.

Large shadowy flakes of snow were falling through haloes of bluish light in the courtyard. Bing had almost reached the end of side two and was well into his signature tune, "White

Christmas," when Mother put her hands up to her face and her shoulders began to shake with silent sobbing.

"What's wrong, Mother?" I said, sitting up, but knowing full well what was the matter.

She shook her head and exhaled a long sigh. Just then Bing began a foolish little whistle. Though I'd heard this tune a hundred times, I couldn't recall ever hearing that.

"Oh, Will," she said, right in the middle of it, "why did you have to go and leave that lovely girl ... and what's going to become of Anna?"

I hadn't expected that, and said, wearily, "Now, Mom, please don't start on that.

"It's Christmas," I added, with cheerless conviction.

She stopped crying, but continued to stand with her back to me, looking silently through the window at the snow falling before her eyes, upon the listing ship, upon the empty courtyard, upon the dead who were never really dead, and upon the useless grief of the living.

God, you get so fed up with speech.

Just the idea of telling anybody anything is enough to make you sick, every word weighing tons more than it did the last time you said it—or saw it—or heard it—or wrote it—or thought it. Who's got the energy? Who's got the strength? That's why the apple falls off the tree—from such a heaviness from life, from what's holding it getting weak.

But silence is a tiresomeness, too.
—Gordon Lish, *Mourner at the Door*

We must never, never make a virtue of our lonely burrowing.
—John Berger, *A Painter of Our Time*

PART I—*UNNATURAL HISTORY*

Ah, distinctly I remember it was in the bleak December;...
—Edgar Allen Poe, "The Raven"

THE BLEAK DECEMBER

Christmas again, but unlike Irving Berlin I was dreaming of something like Kafka's burrow to escape into until it was over. Live turkeys named after city councillors were on display in the downtown raffle-shop window, looking alternately outraged and astonished at the surge and swirl of gawking shoppers, an undertow of guilt sucking you into the all-consuming sea. Patient and smiling Christian soldiers, veterans of the soliciting wars, were waiting inside the doors of all the liquor stores, their transparent collection globes suspended from poles like unlit swag lamps or half the Scales of Justice. In the local rag, the rising Christmas suicide rate was reported daily, along with the highs and lows, the tides, sunset and sunrise. Castrati chorales sang the same timeworn carols on every radio and TV, and on the Muzak machines in the overcrowded stores. And Old Marley's face stared at you from every door knocker, from the reflective shallows of every plate-glass window, urging you to walk abroad among your fellow men, or else, on the next turn of the wheel, you just might have to come back and go through all this again.

Who didn't wish for a warm burrow to crawl into—at least until this wearisome round of getting and spending and laying waste ourselves was over. I would emerge with the groundhogs on Candlemas, and, if there was any shadow of a doubt, I would go back inside for the rest of the winter.

But it's not Christmas so much as the days leading up to it—the Only So Many Shopping Days, which now stretched all the way back to Halloween. The pumpkins are hardly out the door before we're lugging home the turkey and the Christmas tree, stringing lights along the privet hedge, making lists. Only fifty-four shopping days left till Christmas. Armistice Day speeches about a lasting peace are drowned out by the West End Baptist Handbell Choir floating along in the Santa Claus Parade. Christmas cards arrive before the first snowfall.

But I'm on Old Marley's side nonetheless. Every year I've watched him struggling with his chain, leading Scrooge down the road to repentance and rebirth; leaving him, finally, surprised by joy and the possibility of love, looking as nakedly astonished as Dorothy and John, prancing about in the sawdust and shit of the raffle-shop window beneath the barking loudspeakers waiting to have their heads chopped off; and leaving me, as always, with an astonishing lump in my throat, as amazed as anyone else that my emotional dew line had been infiltrated once again.

Anna and I had watched "A Christmas Carol" every year, and last December I tried reading the story to her. It was a cold snowy Saturday, about a week before I moved out. We lay under the duvet in our naturally air conditioned heritage house while Kate was off being mauled by the Christmas crowds at the Mall. She thought that the story was too long and difficult for a six-year-old, and that I really only wanted to read it to myself.

Though the book held some of the same fascination for Anna, I had indeed ended up reading to myself. About a third of the way through she became restless and distracted and started asking for *The Rock*, which was now her favourite. This book had been passed on to us by Kate's art-patron psychiatrist friends, the Rust D'Eyes, who had probably bought it as a warning for their *enfant terrible* son, Ramon.

The Incredible Thrilling Adventures of the Rock is a story with an unhappy ending—and an unhappy beginning and middle as well. In fact, there are no incredible thrilling adventures at all. At the start we find the Rock alone in the forest—alone as a stone, as Mother would say—presumably abandoned, though we never learn why or by whom. He waits and hopes, hopes and waits for someone to come and find him and take him home—if there ever was a someone or a home. But no one ever does. End of story; a sort of *Waiting for Godot* for kiddies. I had read it to Anna a dozen times, and she had read it to herself a dozen more. She was a tearful and imaginative child, and I think she had already begun to imagine the worst.

On Christmas Eve, when I was a child, we would leave pieces of fruitcake for Santa on a white plate on the dining room table, and I would wake up on Christmas morning to find the cake gone and the plate covered with sooty fingerprints. This plate of soot always amazed me more than anything I ever found under the Christmas tree, and I would always check to see if Santa had found his treat before I looked for the gifts that he had brought me. But this year, like last year, there would be no tree to look under—just a plate of soot, sans cake, for me.

In September the house I had been living in for the past eight months had been sold. I had moved from the west end to the east end of the downtown, and into another rooming house—though "booming house" might be a more appropriate description. Every morning around nine o'clock, since the first week of December, a three-piece heavy metal band had been mercilessly rehearsing in the basement beneath my first-floor room. They were probably preparing for their big New Year's Eve gig, when any three-chord outfit formed for the occasion could make a thousand bucks playing to rabid revellers in one of the hundred or more bars downtown, or in the Bayviews, Seaviews, and Oceanviews lounging around the nearby coasts, or in the festooned halls of Lions Clubs and Legions in the purlieus of Outer Suburbia.

I never thought I'd see the day when rockers would be rising at eight o'clock and going to work at nine like everyone else. Things sure had changed since my rock and roll days, when we were lucky to get to bed before eight o'clock. But the eighties had long been icumen in, loud sing goddamn. What music had crept by us upon the waters? Almost twenty years had passed since the Summer of Love and now we were limping toward the next millennium. The thought struck me that this bunch might have been conceived in the Summer of Love. So much for pedigrees. That time didn't seem so long ago to me, but perhaps I had drifted into a time warp. Upstairs the house reeked of dope and patchulie, and the rooms on all three floors were filled with ageless fellow travellers from the sixties—perhaps the progenitors of those lads banging away in the basement.

It was a house full of ghosts, and I was haunted enough as it was. Drifting off to sleep, I would be awakened like Scrooge on the stroke of one by Janis Joplin dragging her ball and chain across the ceiling—screeching and rattling her chain like Old Marley; by Jim Morrison trying to break on through *from* the other side; by the squeal of Jimi Hendrix's guitar; and by the knife-point sadness of "California Dreamin'," "Woodstock," and "San Francisco," the signature songs of my lost youth, which filled me now only with a hopeless nostalgia.

But though I had come of age during that time—and was happy that I had—I didn't want to live through it again. I just wanted to remember it fondly. And over a beer, preferably—for even the mildest weed now made me nervous—with some old friends back *from* the land, other orphaned forty-year-olds with ex-wives and ex-lives and children they saw only once a week.

And with all the rooms in the house humming as hard as ever, it was at least a consolation to know that we all still had our shit together, man, and weren't into Christmas. Last night, through the walls of my neighbour's room, our expatriate First Lady of Folksong, Joni Mitchell, author of our Woodstock anthem, had wailed her Christmas wish in her pained sopranino—a long river to skate away on. The Yangtze, I thought, or the Amazon. Something very long and far away. Though I wondered if either one of those freezes over. The Danube, perhaps, with the "Skater's Waltz" lilting all the way to the Black Sea. That seemed like an appropriate destination. I might even settle for the Rideau Canal.

But my fellow travellers had already skated away on a river of smoke that wound from here to California, and, at the thought of spending Christmas in this house, I was more than tempted to drift away with them.

Why stop fasting at this particular moment, after forty days of it? He had held out for a long time, an illimitably long time; why stop now, when he was in his best fasting form, or rather, not yet quite in his best fasting form? Why should he be cheated of the fame he would get for fasting longer, for being not only the record hunger artist of all time, which presumably he was already, but for beating his own record by a performance beyond human imagination . . . .
—Franz Kafka, "A Hunger Artist"

NOSEWORTHY (EST. 1929)

I was clearing my head in front of the display window of Noseworthy's, a confectionery cum deli cum secondhand furniture store on Water Street, a minimalist convenience or a maximum inconvenience, depending on how you looked at it. A "found gallery" was the way Kate once described it. You never knew what you might find in the place.

Mr. Noseworthy was minimizing even further, if that was possible. The store had been painted long ago and was now a weary shade of red—the colour of one of those ancient sheds on long-abandoned fishing stages. Above the windows a home-made sign had been repainted and no longer said "Noseworthy's Store," or even "Noseworthy's." He had dispensed with the possessive altogether, underlining his obvious desire to own or sell little or nothing. His shop was the mercantile equivalent of a monastery, and on its way to becoming just a thought in his head. Soon he would run the whole business—what there was of it—at home, lying on his back. It was a great place to rest your head and turn your back on the Christmas rush.

I examined this season's Christmas display cum exhibit, though there was little that could be called Christmassy about it. In fact, it was the same one that he had year round, but with

25

subtle variations that only the regular observant window shopper or gallery hopper would notice. Sundry items of second-hand furniture appeared and disappeared, and were replaced by others of the same timeless vintage. Sometimes things reappeared weeks or months later. Whether they had been through the hands and houses of shoppers, it was impossible to tell. Perhaps all the items were from Mr. Noseworthy's own house, and he simply liked to shuffle them back and forth.

In one window were what I had come to think of as his perennials: three tall chrome poles with signs on top, a grouping that, from a distance, looked like a miniature Crucifixion. The two shorter poles had terraced rectangular bases; the base of the middle one was sloped and circular. Atop this pole a backlit plastic Pepsi sign sometimes flashed on and off, depending on whether or not he had bothered to plug it in. The other two held rough-cut cardboard signs with heavy black hand-printing, one advertising hot dogs, the other, coffee and cigarettes. But something new had been added. The central pole was now encircled with empty soft drink cans, like an ancient Stone Circle, adding to the religious—or pagan—aspect. This was Mr. Noseworthy's Christmas message perhaps—an anti-Nativity scene, or the Nativity fast-forwarded to its inevitable and foretold conclusion.

Tacked to a side wall was an unseasonable soft drink sign—"Pepsi Beats the Others Cold," a beach scene with a frosted border. The back wall had a small grey door, or hatch, which was surrounded by red-brick wallpaper. On the floor was a black patent leather and chrome swivel chair with matching footstool. It was the sort of chair I imagined Mr. Noseworthy sitting in, gazing into the gloom somewhere at the back of his shop as far away as possible from the Christmas rush. He would be humming some old standard perhaps and swivelling a semiquaver every now and then, his feet set into the soft footstool.

On a display shelf in the other window were a pair of ice tongs, a bar jigger, an empty Hostess chip rack that looked like a spinal column, and a modest-looking chandelier, circa 1955. Behind these, on a square of parquet tiles, were a grey Arborite chrome table and a pilled and faded red sofa chair. Inside the shop itself there seemed to be nothing at all.

Though I had been observing what I had come to think of as Mr. Noseworthy's spiritual project for years, I still could not decide whether his business ethic was merely an eccentric personal statement, an unconscious asceticism rooted in some profound whim of his private nature (someone once told me that he used to be a tailor), or a deliberate avant-garde mercantile metaphysics that some member of the corporate elite might soon spot and develop into a franchise operation with Mr. Noseworthy at the helm. Minimalist inconveniences from St. John's to Saint John, then on to Toronto, Calgary, and Victoria by the sea.

I would not have been surprised, however, to come down here some day and find the place closed, the windows caged, and Mr. Noseworthy himself on display behind them—like Kafka's hunger artist, a professional faster, performing for passers-by, wasting away in his cage.

Standing there on the sidewalk of the oldest street in the oldest city of the oldest colony, et cetera, looking into the display window of what was now, perhaps, the oldest store on the street—established, appropriately enough, in 1929; standing there with cold wet snowflakes falling on my head, with the ghostly reflections of centuries of shoppers, their arms full of bags and boxes, rushing east and west behind me, the bells of forgotten streetcars echoing in my ears; standing there in the cold I warmed to the thought that Mr. Noseworthy was single-handedly and single-mindedly shepherding us all in the right direction.

Clear out, pare down, jettison, minimize. The past was a sad and wearisome weight. There was just too much history here to think about. Layers and layers, centuries of salt and sediment, had settled upon us, weighing us down. And no rusty rhetoric or golden arrows on bunting pointing toward the bright mirage of a future were ever going to get us out from under it. But it helped to stand in front of Noseworthy's and inhabit for a few pure and peaceful moments the uncluttered space that hung like a magnetic field around his shop. Headroom, to borrow a term from the audiophiles.

And as I stared into the empty shadowy space beyond the display windows, and for the hundredth time only *imagined* myself going in and actually buying something (somehow that seemed what he would prefer me to do), I had two not uncomplementary thoughts. One: John Cabot and his maggoty crew may have started all this by bringing up fish in hand baskets, and the rapacious fishmongers with their deep sea draggers may have inadvertently put a temporary stop to it, but it was Mr. Noseworthy who was finally going to put the Flemish Cap on the whole sorry misbegotten enterprise, exorcise its greedy wasteful consumptive spirit, jettison the cod merchants and Cabot, and perhaps very soon set sail in a handbasket. Two: If Kate and I could only come here for a Pepsi and a hot dog (sans condiments, to be sure), or a black coffee and a cigarette, our own burdensome history might be lifted from our shoulders, and our too too sullied flesh that had once been one might resolve itself anew. *O flesh, flesh, how art thou fishified!*

But the bare truth was, I had never spoken to, or even seen, Mr. Noseworthy. I had never been inside his shop, and neither had anyone I knew. He was even more retiring than his merchandise. Perhaps there was no Noseworthy at all.

I turned and stood on the edge of the sidewalk looking through the falling snow at the "The" building across the street—a three-storey structure with a clothing shop at street level and the definite article above the windows on the second floor. It was followed by the indefinite impressions of two words that I had never been able to figure out. All of a sudden a bus—I would have been less startled by a streetcar—pulled up at the stop I hadn't noticed I was standing at, and its front and rear doors *hissed* open. The driver gave me a businessy and expectant look, and I got on without a moment's hesitation, as if I actually had been waiting for it.

The bus was even emptier than Noseworthy's store. As I tend to do when being driven around in buses or cars, I drifted into a drowsy reverie as it proceeded on its route west along Water Street. The shabby storefronts beneath the new crosstown arterial overpass drifted by, then the old train station, the barber shop where I had once lost my shoulder-length hair, and the sign pointing to the road to Cape Spear. At some point along this route—though I had no recollection at all of the bus stopping or the doors opening—a woman with longer than shoulder-length hair had got on and sat down directly in front of me and thrown her tangled locks over the back of her seat almost into my lap.

Though the bus was warm, large unmelted snowflakes hung like stars from her long black hair—mesmerizing in their intricacy and seemingly imperishable. Perfect hexagrams and hexagons; hexagrams inside hexagons; hexagrams with other stars at their centres; mandala-like hexagons within hexagons, receding into infinity. It was as if I had awoken with lidless eyes under a low-domed planetarium. After the restful emptiness of Noseworthy's store, my head was filling up too fast.

At the Crossroads we left Water Street and began the long climb up Old Topsail Road. I felt a hollow nostalgic ache as we passed the old house, gentrified now almost beyond recognition, where Kate and I had once lived, where we had first made love, in a bedsitting room with a view of the Waterford River. And as the house fell from sight and my eyes fastened once again on the glittering tangled fall of hair inches from my face, burning with regret and desire I had an overwhelming urge to touch it, to kiss it, to bury my face in it. Surely it was being offered to me—a gift of balm. Had she not chosen this seat over all the others in this empty bus, where she could have kept a safe distance from needy lovelorn strangers?

"Man on bus sobs into woman's hair," said the next day's *Daily News*.

"Pathetic," flashed the *Daily Mirror*.

And as I entertained these thoughts, the hair was drawn up; it disappeared through an open door, which closed with a *hiss* and a rubbery *clunk*. And the bus with its driver and his lone companion laboured up the steady incline of Old Topsail Road.

"Kate!" I shouted at the back of his head, and he instinctively hunched his shoulders and let up on the gas. He looked at me in his oversized rearview mirror. I got up and stood facing the rear exit with both hands clasping the chrome pole that ran from ceiling to floor. It felt colder than metal had ever felt before.

He let me off at the next stop. I looked up and down the street, but there was no sign of anyone. Large snowflakes were still falling, drifting down through the bare branches of the elms and maples, but melting almost as soon as they touched the sidewalk. Though it was only four-thirty, it was getting dark, and the street lights were beginning to flicker on. I began to walk back down the hill, but I didn't meet a soul until I reached Water Street. A woman was waiting at a bus stop beneath a streetlight, holding a black umbrella studded with stars.

The news is sad but it's in a song so it's not so bad.
—Leonard Cohen, *The Favorite Game*

ANCIENT MUSIC

This morning at the crack of nine once again, the band that
lived beneath my bed was up and atomizing "Heartbreak
Hotel," fusing heavy metal and rockabilly in wondrous ways. I
lay in bed until I could stand it no more, then took a pillow
and a blanket up to the bathroom on the second floor. I bolted
the door and climbed into the old claw-footed, cast-iron tub,
which was as deep as a well. It was also as cold as a well-digger's
ass, and I wrapped the wool blanket around me like a sleeping
bag. Though the bathtub was several inches off the floor, I
could still feel the vibrations from the din in the basement. As
I lay there trying to sleep, half-expecting at any moment to hear
someone rapping on the door, I began to feel other vibrations,
from deeper and more distant subterranean spaces.

I was born in '56; I was ten at the time. I can hardly recall a thing
before then. It was in the spring, on my birthday, that I first
heard "Heartbreak Hotel." From that day on, I became im-
mersed in what had been called "the Devil's music," listening
for Elvis on all three stations on our old vacuum-tube Crosley
radio, which looked like a huge block of Baker's chocolate with
knobs. In the summer came "Hound Dog," "Don't Be Cruel,"
and "Blue Suede Shoes."

Every Saturday morning without fail I would be awakened
by the Devil's own internal alarm just minutes before the Big
Top Ten. I would rush downstairs and bring the radio up to my
room. Inside a jerry-rigged studio of patchwork quilts, I would
sing out the words of every song, and even the notes of the
guitar break on "Heartbreak Hotel." I was a human Fender

31

electric just waiting to be plugged in. But first I would have to perform unplugged on the Hawaiian guitar, the bane of all beginners.

It arrived that Christmas as a gift from my parents, the Simpson-Sears mail-order catalogue deluxe cardboard model, with catgut strings and hula dancers gyrating round the sound-hole. In my mother's photo album there is a black-and-white picture of me that she took that Christmas with our old Kodak Brownie Hawkeye camera. I am dressed in a fringed cowboy shirt (my other Christmas present), and both arms are locked around that white Hawaiian guitar, clutching it to my primitive breast as if it were my very soul, a soul that the hawk-eyed camera might steal.

I spent the holidays locked away in my room trying to learn the raunchy guitar solo that I thought Elvis himself played on "Heartbreak Hotel." What I would learn, eventually, was to accept the fact that lead work was not my forte. Perhaps playing the guitar was not my forte; in any event, I settled for rhythm, chopping and strumming, or, as John Lennon was to call it, "driving" a band. What was good enough for Lennon was certainly good enough for me.

But just *having* an electric guitar in those days was enough to get you into any pickup band. In a few years I would be strumming one in a high school group, spitting out rock and roll at church hall dances on an old Fender Broadcaster, circa 1949. It had actually been given to my old man by an ex-serviceman friend of his, an Oklahoman, who had once visited the house and had demonstrated convincingly—at a point in my budding playing career when I really needed convincing—that a Hawaiian guitar could indeed play American rock and roll.

He himself had played in pickup bands during his service stint at Fort Pepperrell during the war. After the war he married a Newfoundland woman and settled in St. John's. In 1960, however, the marriage broke up, and he returned to Oklahoma, taking nothing with him but the gunny sack with which he had arrived. He left Dad a few mementos in addition to the guitar, which he told him was "for your boy," though it was some time before the old man gave it to me. I'm sure he had actually considered selling it, as I was now fourteen and, in his view, "getting a bit too old for that sort of thing." This piece of flotsam from a wrecked marriage remained in my possession for almost twenty years, though for the second ten I hardly ever played it. In fact, I had forgotten that I still owned it until I discovered it when I was clearing out the basement of my mother's house the year she moved from the downtown.

At university this prestigious piece of gear got me into a band called Stubble. We tried to cultivate a bristly r & b sound, though there was little more than peach fuzz on our faces at the time, and our finger callouses were far more advanced than our playing. We just didn't have the time to give to it, though the music meant a lot more to us than just an escape from the books. We lived for that music and had a blind faith that it would all come together on stage.

On stage, in front of an audience, was the only place we wanted to be. Merely working it out in some dreary basement, away from that admiring sun, was like being exiled from a mother's love. And, fronted by the lovely Lynda Lambswood, we were better than most weekend outfits playing the sock hops, high school dances, and downtown bars. We couldn't believe our good fortune when she showed up at our door after she'd seen our ad in the *Muse*. She had that "Sad-eyed Lady of the Lowlands" look about her, just the sort of singer we had in mind. She was a part-time student who worked nights serving tables at a bar downtown. Five years older than the rest of us, she had, as she said herself, been around.

Lynda played the piano, but never on stage. Her voice was enough to drive a band. Though deep and throaty, it could soar. She excited us, as well as our audience, and made us do things with the music that surprised even us. She loved to sing "Unchained Melody," and it always got such a great response that she sometimes sang it twice a night. Whenever she did, she electrified the place, made the hair stand up on the back of my neck. We knew it only as a mid-sixties Righteous Brothers' hit, though the song had been recorded ten years earlier. She'd learned it from the 1955 Al Hibbler original, one of hundreds of 45s that she had in her collection. They hung on her walls on two long strips of plastic clothesline attached to coat hooks, like the beads of two giant necklaces.

Lynda knew her early rock and roll, and could toss out names we'd never heard of—like Big Boy Cruddup, Big Mama Thornton, Otis Blackwell, and Al Hibbler—as casually as she tossed back her long black hair. But she didn't sing "Unchained Melody" like Al Hibbler, whose original version sounded like a hymn, despite the fact that he uttered the Lord's name in the line "God speed your love" as if it left a very bad taste in his mouth.

Lynda sang it, it was clear to me, the way the song was meant to be sung. Not even the Righteous Brothers had wrung such feeling from it. Standing behind her, chopping out the rhythm, I loved to watch her belt it out. Legs wide apart, hands around the mike, at the emotional high spots she would tear into the upper octaves and clutch handfuls of her hair. She looked as if she might pull it right out of her head.

Nothing convinces like pain, and it was clear that Lynda had known her share. She knew what that song meant, if we didn't, and though we tried to take it where she wanted to go, when she sang, "Are you still mine?" and "I need your love," she was out there on her own, beyond all measure, beyond all pain, a cappella ecstatic, beyond the bars and chains of time.

Lynda lived in a dismal apartment in the basement of a house on Hamilton Avenue. Its sole attraction was a rent of ninety dollars a month. The only source of heat in the place was a network of hot water pipes that crisscrossed the ceiling on their way up to the radiators in the apartments on the first and second floors. Most of the pipes were at eye level, so there was a constant danger of cracking your head against them. Any medic peering in the window at that frequently stoned group of stooped adolescents trying to avoid being stunned by a pipe might have diagnosed premature osteoporosis.

The bathroom was in two sections, neither of which had a bath, but in the furnace room section was an enamel sink almost as big as a bathtub. The toilet was on a landing at the top of the stairway leading to the landlord's first floor apartment. As there was no door or curtain at the bottom of the steps, anyone strolling down the hallway from the bedroom, or after performing a quick toilette at the furnace room sink, had a clear view all the way to Tipperary.

The door next to the toilet could be opened from inside the landlord's apartment so that he could have access to the furnace room without having to go outside in the ice and snow and seek admittance through Lynda's basement door. The furnace looked as if it might have been installed not long after the first fossil fuels had been refined. The whole thing was encased in asbestos and looked more like a kiln than a furnace. As it was constantly on the blink, and the landlord was not in the habit of knocking, using the toilet for any serious business was a thing to be avoided if at all possible.

The apartment was furnished with a conglomeration of mismatched odds and ends—handmades, family castoffs, fourthhand furniture from secondhand shops, and proud pieces liberated from Church and State. There was an old upright piano with several dead sharps and flats, a long rough pine table with two pews that served as chairs and chesterfields, and a ratty old Newfoundland smoker whose straw stuffing kept falling out the bottom and making a bird's nest on the floor. Despite appearances, it was the most comfortable chair I'd ever sat in. In the bedroom there was a king-size mattress that took up most of the cold linoleum floor. On each side was a large wooden spool that served as a night table, compliments of one of the public utilities. A complementary piece was used as a coffee table in the living room.

Lynda's on-again, off-again boyfriend at the time, a lunatic errant Dutchman named Schyler van something-or-other, had made the pine table, and had stolen the other tables and the pews. Their love-life seemed to be in constant turmoil, and Lynda spent a lot of time in this freezing apartment, wrapped in an old muskrat coat, sitting at the pine table pining away—chewing her fingernails, chain-smoking, consuming practically nothing but coffee for days on end, and waiting for Schyler to show up. Once, on one of his trips to the furnace room, her landlord had found her semi-conscious on the floor, and she had been taken to the hospital in an ambulance and found to be suffering from dehydration and oxygen deprivation.

We were all sitting around this pine table smoking up late one Friday night after a gig, depriving our own lungs of oxygen for as long as we could, when the apartment door flew open, and what to our wondering eyes should appear but Schyler in his black leather biker's outfit, carrying a stone angel, pedestal and all, in his arms. His face was obscured by the opaque glass of the helmet, and he looked like some featureless extraterrestrial. He walked over and stood the angel next to Lynda in the pew. Then he stepped back, looked at the two of them as if he were arranging a photographic sitting, and, without saying a word, turned and stalked out the door. None of us had much to say either. We just stared at the angel as if we were witnessing an apparition of the Virgin or something and were wondering what the message might be. One of its wing tips was touching Lynda's shoulder.

A woman like Lynda was hard to forget, even for someone like Schyler, who had tactics the rest of us could only imagine.

The first time he and Lynda had split up, he had been arrested after a late-night, high-speed chase on the TCH, which had earned him, he told us proudly, the province's first citation for insane driving. Drivers who thought they were simply seeing the Come By Chance oil refinery's burn-off flame on the horizon were terrified to see a ball of fire coming straight towards them. It was Schyler, barrelling down the centre line of the highway on his motorcycle with his helmeted head on fire, a la Arthur Brown.

My own head was on fire that night, alone with Lynda and the angel in the cold hard pew. I still think of it as the night I lost my virginity, though I'd had sex several times before. But it had only been with girls—never with a woman—and it had always been such a shy and self-conscious affair.

I'd stayed on after the others had left, though we didn't seem to have much to say. I put my arm around her and kissed her hair, as the angel gazed with hooded downcast eyes. And though she seemed reluctant at first, finally she took me by the hand and led me to her bedroom. We made love that cold December night beneath her blue sleeping bag and her muskrat coat on the large mattress on the bedroom floor.

Lynda was tall, big-boned, and strong. When she came, she arched her body and lifted me up and grabbed her hair just like on stage. I wouldn't have been surprised if she had begun to sing, but high on the rim of that wild horizon, I heard only a terrifying desperate moan.

Afterwards she pulled the fur coat up over my back. She held my head in her arms, held it tightly between her breasts, and began to sob like a baby. She sniffled and sobbed between catches of breath as I looked through a forest of muskrat fur and out upon a host of linoleum daffodils.

Oh, Lynda, where are you now? We could talk the night away. That night, I couldn't think of a thing to say—it was all such a great mystery to me. Perhaps it's just as much a mystery to me now. In the bathtub I finally drifted off to sleep, filled with a longing that no sex could satisfy.

For though Jerome and his company knew the desert at first
hand, they put style on it: they are men of letters, cursed with a
feeling for prose.
        —Helen Waddell, *The Desert Fathers*

            yet there the nightingale
Filled all the desert with inviolable voice . . . .
        —T. S. Eliot, "The Waste Land"

DESERT FATHER

Perhaps I should have been a Father rather than a father, a
monk instead of a married man—a Desert Father, with hair to
my heels, living on barley bread and brackish water. Not some
paunchy dewlapped cleric living in a rectory the size of a hotel,
tended on hand and foot by a faithful housekeeper, but a hermit
priest, a sheepskinned ascetic in a small hut of stones, with a
thin reed mat for a bed and a single dry loaf hanging in a basket.
No early morning Masses in an empty church or nodding over
my breviary in even emptier afternoons, cheerlessly counting
the canonical hours. I would plait palm-leaves all day and tend
my herb garden, acquaint myself with nettles instead of rattles
and bottles.

But all in all I became quite good at it. Mastered the
multi-panel, environmentally correct cloth diaper and the
multifarious swaddling clothes Kate devised that first winter to
keep the Bunting from freezing to death in her crib. Abandoned my friends and the bars, and for a time became an
in-house, hands-on, full-time father while Kate went off to
work in the world of Art. All I asked in return was that no one
ever talk to me about Quality Time, or refer to me as the
Primary Caregiver, at least not while I was within earshot.

Read all the books that had been recommended, and many
that hadn't, and while Anna was napping planned in detail the

first two decades of her physical, spiritual, moral, intellectual, social, and financial life. Spent my share of sleepless nights communing with her at four in the morning over a bottle of expressed milk and a makeshift espresso. At that dread and silent hour, a child's face can look so innocent and wise you have to turn your eyes away. None of the books I'd read had said anything about that. Not even Lonesome Willie's great "Ode" had prepared me for that.

The first room that I moved into did look like a monastery cell. The ad said "Furnished Room," but the only furnishings were a hot plate, a lamp, a fold-up cot, and a handmade night table with a lacquer thicker than the mattress. There wasn't even a curtain at the window. The one-piece plastic lamp on the night table glowed like an exotic pink mushroom. Its large rubber plug, hanging loosely from a plateless socket, had indentations like teeth marks. By the bed was an ungroomed shag terrier of a rug. The hot plate was on a shelf that ran the whole length of the room. Above it a hand-lettered sign said "No Cooking."

My first impulse was to rush out and buy things to fill it up, search the secondhand stores and the antique shops for some old and inexpensive furniture—perhaps some practical "double-duty furniture," the sort of stuff that I remembered had been recommended in a book called *Entertaining with Elegance*, which Kate's mother, Dorcas, always eager to smooth out our social rough edges, had given us as a Christmas gift. It had entertained us for the rest of the winter; in fact, it became our favourite bedtime reading. We dug out choice bits in advance and read them to each other.

Our favourite parts included "the Ten Commandments" for husband-hosts, a list of the indispensable books in the library of the perfect hostess, and advice for dealing with servants and spongers ("generally bachelor and male") and for entertaining "authentic eggheads" ("reconstitute a menu described by Flaubert"), bores and snobs.

The double-duty furniture recommended by the author

included such things as hybrid bookcases—half shelves for "books and bibelots" and half cupboards for the Capo di Monte and Porcelaine de Paris dinnerware; desks with lots of drawers—half for papers and stationery and the other half for silverware and table linen; a cabinet that was both dresser and sideboard; and a coffee table with telescopic legs that changed into a combination bridge table and dining room table.

Equipped with such versatile pieces, single-room dwellers with entertaining in their hearts need never fear becoming hosts or hostesses manqués, though they were advised to stick to small cocktail parties, informal one-dish dinners, or cold suppers after the theatre, buffet style, rather than hot, sit-down meals.

But after only about a week the ascetic in me, rather than the host, began to emerge, and I came to like the bare walls, the empty space, the absence of *things*—even the fierce light coming in through the uncurtained windows in the mornings. And because there was more space and light, there also seemed to be more time. Not that I needed or wanted more of that.

As the days went by I discovered that there were very few things that I really needed. I ate out, borrowed books from the library, and made do with only one change of clothes. I moved the hot plate and the No Cooking sign out into the hall lest I succumb to the urge to equip myself for teamaking. Then I would have to acquire a kettle, cups, spoons, sugar, milk, and tea; then perhaps a teapot, a tea strainer, a milk jug, and a sugar bowl; then a small fridge for the milk, a tea cozy for the pot, a tea tray, and tea biscuits for guests; and then some exotic, high-grown teas from the Himalayas and, yes, why not, a tea trolley and a silver tea service with china cups and saucers. You never know who might drop in for tea. And after a successful tea or two, thoughts of a tea room, a coast-to-coast tea-room chain ... You can see where this tea tendency might lead.

Instead, I bought a bottle of Irish whiskey, being unable to afford my favourite Scotch malt. I kept it on the bedside table along with a bottle of spring water from the Alps.

"*Myman* will meet you there at two," the landlord, a Mr. Priddle, told me on the phone the day I moved in, fusing the two words and accenting the "my," as if he supposed I might have a lackey as well. I imagined meeting a new evolutionary type—a sort of domesticated Piltdown man—the ultimate non-cognitive cog in the capitalist wheel of misfortune. But Myman gnashed and gnarled instead of yessired, grinding his words into a sort of frothy syllabub, though he exuded a comic friendliness and a warm casual dignity.

He arrived an hour late and didn't seem at all surprised to find me asleep on the iron cot. I had walked on in, as I'd been instructed, and, as I'd just had lunch, I'd been lulled to sleep by the greater-than-gravity pull of a hot roast beef sandwich with chips, dressing, and gravy that I'd just downed at Bird's Family Restaurant and Bakery.

I was dreaming of Jeanie Hanlon, my favourite waitresss, who was offering herself to me at my corner table. It being a family restaurant, she had discreetly pulled a white curtain around us, as if she was a nurse and I was in a hospital bed. She was wearing nothing but a translucent white pinafore, and she pushed her hands down into her waist pockets and lifted her chest. Between her shoulder straps her areoles were rising like suns; and then her nipples popped over the top of her pinafore; and then her large breasts, white as milk, poured forth.

"Go on, they won't hurt you," she said to me, as if for some reason I needed encouraging, as if this was my daily medicine.

I could hear a jingling, like sleighbells, in the distance, and I awoke to find Myman standing in the doorway and bending over to tap the soles of my shoes with his keys. He seemed unwilling to come inside, as if I were already renting the room.

"Mr. Wiseman?" he inquired.

"Yes," I said, heaving myself up.

"I'm Mike," he said. "Sorry I'm late."

He remained on the threshold, didn't come forward to offer his hand.

"How do you do," I said flatly.

It was a common enough greeting, but perhaps because I had just woken up, it seemed to me that I was speaking some kind of rhymed gibberish. It went foolishly around in my head, each monosyllable receiving the accent in turn. HOW do you do, How DO you do, How do YOU do, How do you DO.

"It's the only room left," Mike broke in, doing his salesman's duties. "One hundred and fifty dollars a month."

I began to walk around the room, pretending to scrutinize every nook and cranny. Mike said nothing about the hot plate or the No Cooking sign.

"How long's the house been for sale?" I asked him.

"Years," he said. "All Mr. Priddle's houses are for sale. He bought 'em all during the Hibernia boom."

He was still standing in the doorway, hadn't once taken a single step inside. Outside, a truck as long as a train went past and the whole house, which was just a few feet from the street, began to reverberate. A rack of empty hangers in the closet tinkled. On the other side of the room Mike's feet, nestled in a pair of black leather brogues, seemed enormous in proportion to his modest weight and height, and his gold pendant caught the light of the low winter sun.

He led me upstairs to show me the bathroom on the second floor.

"Explore a celestial body tonight," someone had scrawled on the wall beside the mirror and illustrated it with a penis-arrowed male symbol entering the female.

"Explore Yeranus," someone else had replied.

The flush box was hissing, and the sink and bathtub faucets were dripping onto rusty-orange stains. Three clawed feet of the old porcelain and cast-iron tub were visible, and though it probably weighed a ton, it had an animated look, as if it might have a secret life. Doing bit parts with Disney or the National Film Board, perhaps, after we were all scrubbed and sound asleep in our beds.

We went back downstairs and stood in the hallway. When I told him I'd take the room, he pursed his lips into a smile, put his little finger in his ear, and nodded his head slowly up and down. With difficulty he removed two keys from an over-freighted keyring attached to his belt and handed them to me with a practiced semicircle motion of his hand.

"The square one for the outside and the round one for the inside," he said. "Rent's due on the first of every month."

After Mike left I lay down on the bed again and looked up at the bare lightbulb with its rippling rosette. As I was drifting off to sleep, another large truck went past, shaking every atom in the house. In the silence after the room stilled, the hangers in the empty closet shuddered—a tintinnabulation that echoed inside my head, and I remembered another room, long ago, in Amsterdam, a room Kate and I had spent all day looking for. We had collapsed on the bed and made love with half our clothes on. In the evening we were awakened by the sound of bells: some joyous Bach chorale, the notes ascending like a flock of Escher's birds, sweeping in over us through the open window, then fading as we fell into each other's arms again and into the deep silence of sleep.

It is, let me stress, an unnatural act to compose a poem or write
a story.
　　　—Robert Alter,
　　　　The Pleasures of Reading in an Ideological Age

Come, and take choice of all my library,
And so beguile thy sorrow.
　　　—Shakespeare, *Titus Andronicus*

UNNATURAL HISTORY

A library is not a home, but it's better than the home I have
these days. Patrons, as the public librarians refer to us, are few
and far between at this time of year. It's warm and quiet; there's
no Christmas Muzak; and, best of all, it's the only place in town,
besides church, where you're required not to talk to anyone.
I've probably spent more time in libraries than in all the homes
I've had put together. And if, in the end, I am to be put in a
home, perhaps some peculiar endowment to my alma mater
can secure me some out-of-the-way space in the library there.

But I avoid the university library, as a rule, though I have
my own private collection there, which I like to dip into every
now and again. Dispersed, I grant you, but at least all on the
same floor. One of the perks of the academic ministry was the
opportunity to order handsome hardcover editions of books for
which someone else paid the outrageous prices. But, as always,
I paid for them in the end.

Though it's a big library, and I can usually go there without
being noticed, I sometimes run into former colleagues or
students. Up among the stacks, sandwiched between walls of
books looming high above us, they are apt to question me. And
when, like poor Prufrock ... *I am pinned and wriggling on the wall*
. . . .

Yes, that's my last lecture there behind you on the shelf—a

45

broken-record recitation of uncanonized supertramp William Henry Davies' poem "Leisure" (you know the one: *What is this life if, full of care* ...) performed intellectually and physically prostrate on my desk with a paper bag over my head. I almost put myself to sleep. As usual, no one asked any questions. *The lecturer is a man who must talk for an hour.* And I'm off to the Learneds for a remount this summer.

No, you should not deduce any significance from this for your own career-path, tenure track or manure track, for it's clear, as my other-mother, Dorcas, is fond of reassuring me, that I had temporarily lost control of my faculties. No doubt the Faculty had also lost control of me.

But in the dead dusty air and dim light of those narrow aisles, in those intimate anonymous spaces, I am sometimes stricken with a helpless longing and remorse. But what can I tell them, after all? They who want to know what really happened and the wherefores and the whys, who want me to give them some sign, who want to siphon some strength from my empty tank for some wild and wayward notion of their own.

Kate was not fond of libraries. If you saw her inside one, chances are it was an emergency and she was trying to locate me. She was not a reader; she got little pleasure from books—even books on Art. Once in a while, if she was unable to sleep, she would transport a particularly heavy biographical tome or volume of art history from the study to our bedroom, perhaps with the thought in mind that the sheer weight of it would be enough to summon the sandman.

But she certainly wasn't a screen-gazer either, and she did everything she could to keep Anna away from the TV. Our 14-inch, black-and-white RCA had been turned on so infrequently its voice had atrophied. The evening news-reader always sounded as if he were battling laryngitis, or whispering gossip for our ears only. Nor was Kate a doer. Walking was the only exercise she engaged in. Slow walking, in a daydream. You could cover more ground out strolling with your three-year-old.

Kate liked to look at things, indoors or out—the inflorescence of plants, frost on a windowpane. The texture of stone could hold her attention for hours. And though she gave the impression of being shy, of always turning her eyes away from you, she never missed a detail of people she met only once. She would remark later on their fine long lashes or the smallness of their hands, and could swoon over luxuriant lunulae.

She could gaze at the embers in a fireplace longer than any addict could stare at a TV, or at silver thaw gathering on the maple outside our window, or at a pool of sunlight on the hardwood floor. But none of these things found their way directly into her work, which, except for a few portraits, was abstract and impressionistic. She was especially attuned to the textures of voices, and once did a series of abstract portraits inspired by the taped voices of strangers. She used her own voice so infrequently it could sound like a stranger's, but she sometimes vocalized at the oddest of times; in the supermarket she would utter small amorous moans while lifting and feeling melons, avocados, and limes.

I spent all of today in the public library uptown. I even stayed in the building for lunch—mock-chicken on mock-bread in the mock-cafeteria in the basement. Just a canteen, really, with a wicket and a wicket-keeper and a few chairs and tables under high-intensity lamps. Feeling mock-heroic, I finished with a cup of mock-coffee with mock-milk before going back upstairs.

The librarians looked restless and unfestive, scowling like gendarmes. Only four more shopping days till Christmas, and they obviously did not want to be here. They did not want to descend again to the closed basement stacks, as I had asked them to do several times that morning, looking for decade-old issues of periodicals that were so obscure they weren't even aware that they carried them. Besides browser-in-residence Harry Normore, I seemed to be the only patron. On my next approach to the librarian closest to my table, on whose desk was a flowerless dwarf of a Christmas cactus that showed no sign whatsoever that its due date was nigh, she saw me coming out of the corner of her eye and rushed off to a room behind the circulation desk.

Perhaps it was Harry, not me, who was annoying her. Today he was tearing through beefy back issues of *The Sunday New York Times*, never stopping for a second to read a word or look at a picture, his good eye cast down on the pages and his glass eye looking out, directionless. He performed this purely physical task with a noisy flourish, his lips and chin black with ink from licking his fingers to turn the pages, drooling ink back on to them as he went.

"I'm Harry Normore," he would whisper into your ear in a conspiring tone, sneaking up behind you while you were reading and risking eviction for disturbing the patrons yet again. Then he would look you right in the face with his one good eye, but my own eyes were drawn to the other one, which stared somewhere else altogether. It was unnerving, the look in that expressionless good eye, which was even glassier than the glass prosthesis. There was a desert behind that eye, and Harry had spent many more than forty days out there. Perhaps the better part of forty years. I could tell he had thoughts he felt no need to share.

A wink and a nod would usually bring a smile to his face and unglue that look, but, if it didn't, I'd sometimes have to make an unnecessary trip to the bathroom or the magazine shelves on the pretext of locating something or other. For what I didn't want to see again was Harry popping his eye out into his hand, revealing that raw red gash for my viewing pleasure.

Sometimes my mind would reel off cinematic fantasies of Harry and me—prisoners in some Orwellian bureaucratic bee-hive, assigned to rifle through old newspapers and magazines day and night, but never knowing what it was we were looking for. Though forbidden to speak to one another, Harry and I would finally conspire to escape.

As there wasn't a single librarian in sight, I decided to forgo my request. I felt like getting as far away from Harry as I could, so I walked to the back of the library and sat at a table from which I could look through a tall window that fell almost to the floor. A few brown leaves still clung to a large grey tree outside. The sun had just gone round the corner of the building. On the table a fellow patron had left a copy of the *Journal of Personality and Social Psychology*.

"Please do not re-shelve periodicals. We are doing a survey," said a taped-down and inked-up sign.

"How you like to survey this?" one graffiti writer had proposed, though he had not drawn the object of his pride.

On opening the pages of the journal, I discovered a toothpick, on which said patron had been seriously ruminating. It was at the beginning of an article entitled "Conflict Between the Sexes: . . . " But even the second part of the title spelled trouble. After the colon—or out of the colon, so to speak—came the language, or "guidge," as Ruth called it, of social science: "Strategic Interference and the Evocation of Anger and Upset."

I tried browse-reading a few pages and out it slopped: "domain-samples . . . act nomination procedures . . . upset elicitors . . . pair-bond formations . . . presumptively monogamously pair-bonded mates . . . ."

As far as I could make out, our researcher, armed with a "broad-gauge research strategy," was galloping off in pursuit of empirical game that might shed some light on why it is that men and women find it so hard to live with one another, what it is they actually do that causes so much trouble, "because little knowledge currently exists" on the subject.

Well, good luck to him, I thought. I might even have ridden along with him a while longer, sharing some of my own intimate upset elicitors as we loped along; but after only ten minutes I felt as if I was developing the mental equivalent of saddle sores. And, sadly, I knew that, regardless of what new empirical evidence our researcher might bag, what grand theory he might construct, what palatial system of "upset composites" he might erect, all the particular and bitter halves—and the particularly bitter halves—of the nameless and faceless pair-bond formations would still end up living alone in cold dreary basement apartments or bedsitting rooms alongside it.

I checked out *The Life Story of the Fish, His Manners and Morals; The Soul of the White Ant;* and *The Primordial Slime.* I'm trying to learn about the natural world—sister Ruth's domain—or natural history, as we amateurs like to call it. As she once said to me, trying to broaden my horizons, when you get right down to it, slime can be just as interesting as anything else.

On my way out, though, not wanting to withdraw cold turkey from my narrow but comfortable path, I picked up two pieces of unnatural history from a display table beside the door—a book on my adolescent heartthrob entitled *Kim Novak: Reluctant Goddess,* and *Tales from the Thousand and One Nights.* I thought I might like to reread my favourite childhood story, "Aladdin and His Enchanted Lamp." But, after browsing through the contents, I became enchanted instead by "The Historic Fart," a very brief story that had obviously been excluded from my childhood collection.

In this story a man lets out a long and resounding fart at his wedding feast, just as he is about to depart for the bridal chamber. He is so embarrassed and ashamed that he immediately leaves the house and rides off alone into the night never to be seen again. But after ten years of self-imposed exile, he is overcome with longing—not for his wife, but for his native land—and returns in disguise hoping that all will be forgotten. He wanders about the town listening to people talk and discovers to his dismay that not only do people remember his transgression, but are now recording time by it.

"On what day was I born?" he overhears a young girl asking her mother.

"You were born," her mother replies, "on the very night of Abu Hasan's fart."

And upon hearing this the man flees once again and remains in exile until the day he dies.

Now there's a marital upset elicitor for you—one not likely to be caught in any social scientist's net. But no more airy a transgression than countless others, and all with a local habitation and a name. Would that we could so easily whiff or sound our own. For my part, if I may take liberties with the immortal words of one Friedrich Klopstock: God and I both knew what they were once; now only God knows.

The term "Science" should not be given to anything but "the aggregate of the recipes that are always successful." All the rest is "literature."
—Paul Valéry, *Moralités*

Literature is news that STAYS news.
—Ezra Pound, *ABC of Reading*

NEWS

Coming out of Lar's Fruit Mart, where I had gone instinctively to gather some Christmas nuts like a squirrel programmed against the scarcity of winter, I ran into Kate's brother, Bill, going in. He held a fat manila envelope in one hand and a bloody handkerchief to his mouth with the other. On his head was a maltlike confection of a tuque. Beneath it Lar's whirligig light display revolved in the glass-bottom lenses of Bill's glasses. He looked like some deranged and penniless shopper intent on an all-at-once Christmas heist. Mumbling something about losing his molars, he put his arm in mine and led me back into the shop.

"I need to talk to you," he said. "Hang on just a minute. I got to get some aspirins."

He was at the counter before I had time to reply, pointing one of his blackish talons at the boxes of painkillers on the shelf. In his black stovepipe pants and suit jacket, Bill looked stylishly New Wave, though he had been wearing this type of outfit since the fifties. On his feet was a pair of short black leather boots marbled with salt. With their studded and unbuckled wraparound flaps, they looked like winged boots of the gods, talaria of Hermes or Mercury.

After rooting around conspicuously in all his pockets, he turned and gestured me over to the counter.

"Can you lend me a couple of bucks?" he said. "I must have left my wallet at the dentist's . . . along with my teeth."

He grinned, exposing several more that looked as if they should have been left behind as well.

I took out my wallet and found a two-dollar bill.

"Great," he said, snipping it out of my hand with a long-nailed finger and thumb and passing it to the cashier.

A short bristly-looking woman who had been standing behind us moved forward and lifted a large crowned pineapple onto the counter with an angry thump. At the sound of this heavy bass note, Bill wrapped a handkerchiefed hand around his mouth and let out a mock moan, as if the vibrations had rumbled right through his aching gums. Two bristly heads looked up at him from exactly the same height, the bodiless one with perhaps a slice more sympathy.

Bill Hawley wrote poetry and edited and published a little magazine called *news.* He was the black sheep of the family, the mote in his mother's eye, and I had always felt a secret pleasure in knowing that he was the exact opposite of what Dorcas wanted him to be. Dorcas saw poets—and all artists—as common cowhands who thought they were herding sacred cows. But though she'd succeeded in dampening Kate's desire to paint and in herding her into the corral of more conventional work as an arts administrator; though she'd managed to shepherd Kate's younger sister, Lydia, into the fold of the civil service; though "the girls" had been more malleable in her hands, Bill kept right on doing only what he wanted.

Dorcas sometimes referred to this as "writing for a living"—an oxymoron in more ways than one—though even she was not moronic enough to believe that, for a poet at least, this was remotely possible. We had also heard her refer to him as a journalist, a publisher, even a professor—depending, of course, on whom she was talking to.

The reality was that Bill survived on odd jobs that mostly had nothing to do with writing—or with living, for that matter.

He sorted mail at the post office during the Christmas rush; he edited unreadable reports by government engineers and technicians on such enticing topics as sewer systems and waste management; he reshelved books and magazines at the public library; he wrote reviews of books he never would have read for pleasure; and he worked the odd term as a sessional at the university. Between jobs, of course, he had to fall back on that unofficial patron of the arts, the UIC. The official government patrons had never been kind to him, though he had secured some funding for the magazine. When he was really in dire straits, there were always friends ready to lend him a few bucks, local bars that offered tabs, and neighbourhood grocery stores where he could get things on credit.

The title of Bill's literary magazine was a reference to one of Uncle Ez's many charmingly dogmatic ABC's: "Literature is news that STAYS news." This quote appeared as a running line of text on the cover, filling the entire space, each word typographically different, with the black letters of the title resting on a single rectangle of blue near the centre. Except for the issue number in the bottom right-hand corner, this cover had not changed at all in the ten or more years of the magazine's existence. There was no artwork or fiction; there were no articles or reviews. He published only poetry, and not much of that.

The magazine came out once or twice a year, and Bill did all the work himself. The small grant from the Arts Council barely covered printing costs. No one got paid for contributing, least of all Bill, who sometimes ended up paying the printing costs himself while waiting for the grant money to come through.

But *news* was the little magazine that grew—at least in reputation—against all odds, all expectations; against the tide of ordinary news; against the grain, the die, of literary history. For "die" was what they usually did, and without significant issue; but *news* had beaten all the odds. Unfortunately, it seemed to have beaten Bill as well, for the last time I had spoken to him, he had asked me if I wanted to take it on.

"Send it to Bill" had become the town's refrain, for even if he refused a piece of work, he would always take the time to return it, to the new and the gnarled alike, with some kind of encouraging word. It was a full-time job, but one with no pay, at least not the kind that was negotiable at the supermarket. The worst of it was that his own work had taken a back seat to everyone else's. Though his poems had been widely published in magazines over the years, at forty he was still trying to organize a manuscript and get his first book out. I knew this bothered him more than he let on, and even he was beginning to suspect that the magazine had become an excuse to avoid doing what he really should be doing.

Bill had an uncommon warmth and charm, and a spirit magnanimous beyond his means. We had always been able to talk, and even after the break-up, nothing changed. He never once questioned me about it, though I didn't see him all that much. He was very solitary, and would disappear for months at a time. There would be rumours that he was drying out. He was, to be sure, a serious drinker.

He was now living in the suburbs with a masseuse. But for years he'd been living off and on with someone Dorcas used to refer to as "an older woman." Her name was Nadine, but Bill called her Noddy. She owned a small house on Signal Hill—a house so small it looked as if it had been built for dwarfs. And it seemed to be sinking into the ground.

This ancient house had been declared a heritage building, but on Bill's insistence Nadine had resisted all overtures from the Historic Trust. First they'd wanted to mount a large plaque on the front; then they offered to buy it and restore it with funds from the Heritage Foundation, though Nadine and Bill would still be allowed to live in it.

But Bill cherished his privacy more than anything else, and didn't relish the prospect of living in a museum and being gawked at by day-trippers on Sunday drives up Signal Hill. He was adamantly opposed to restoration and gentrification, which he saw as leading to the destruction of real neighbourhoods and the resettlement of their residents.

In the previous decade, most of the downtown had been declared a Heritage Conservation Area. Developers had bought houses for ridiculous sums, restored them with government money, and sold them for twice the price. Property values had doubled; taxes had tripled; poor people had moved out and rich people had moved in. The Heritage Conservation Area had become a yuppie garrison, its southern perimeter a wall of tall ugly buildings that blocked out the harbour, the city's most beautiful natural feature. People who had been told what colour their houses could be painted, what type of siding to use, what kind of windows, now stared through these windows at a wall of brick and glass towers that City Council had allowed developers to erect right along the waterfront. In fact, these buildings even displayed signs saying Heritage Conservation Area. The centerpiece was a brick shithouse and parking garage known as Atlantic Place, in Bill's view one of the ugliest things, both inside and out, ever conceived by the human mind.

The gentrification of George Street was especially galling to him. Before he had moved in with Nadine, he had rented a palatial space there for a mere $200 a month. He had a whole four-story building all to himself, referring to it as Hawley Hall. He lived on the third floor, wrote on the fourth, which had a view of the Harbour from the dry dock to the Narrows, played pool on the second floor on an enormous billiard table that he had persuaded the owner to leave there in storage, and used the entire ground floor as a porch. There was hardly a stick of furniture in the place, and on all four floors mortar dust fell from the cracks of the bare brick walls and got into everything.

But the dust didn't seem to bother Bill in the least. He would always be making a joke about it, inviting me in after a few beers for mortarburgers, pâté de mortar, or, his specialty, the mortarboard, a lightly dusted smorgasbord for those with minor mineral deficiencies.

In the end, someone bought the building and opened the first bar on what was to become the George Street Strip. Unlike the more generous souls at the Historic Trust, however, the new owner had not offered to let him continue to live in it. It might have given him a whole new perspective on restoration if he had.

Before long, almost every building on George Street was turned into a bar, with names such as Swallies, Dickie's, Christian's, Gropers, and Bounders suggesting a veritable circus of possible human activity within a licenced setting. Bill moved out of Hawley Hall and in with Nadine.

After we left the fruit shop, Bill took me to an off-off George Street tavern—off Water Street, to be exact—where he said he had a tab. The place didn't even have a name. I'd never noticed it before, though in the past year I'd done a lot of walking around downtown. On the outside it looked like an aborted Mies van der Rohe—a small dirty brick bunker with no front window or sign of any kind.

It seemed the epitome of the sort of anonymous place that Bill was most comfortable drinking in. He hated hobnobbing with other writers and sitting around talking about Art. Once in a while, though, when he really wanted a pint of Guinness, we would go to a place he liked to call "Ye Olde Ersatz," as it had been tarted up to look like Ye Olde Englysshe Pub.

Inside, the place was freezing, and the only natural light came through a small barred window at the back behind the bar. There was no music, just quiet talk. We sat at a small round Arborite table in a roomful of men dressed in dark overcoats and caps, who, though it was December, looked as if they all might just have walked off a sealing ship.

But the pictures on the walls were not of seals but of sheep—on hills, in valleys, on meadows and marshes, in farmyards, and even one inside a house. Dignified and alluring-looking specimens, the one above our table had an almost philosophical expression on its face, a look as enigmatic as the Mona Lisa.

Bill brought back two beers from the bar and laid them on top of the large manila envelope on the table. As he'd remarked to me on the way here, the envelope was thick with news—or at least with what he always hoped would be news. The bottles stood off balance, and Bill was eyeing the angle with his head to one side.

"A bad sign," he said, taking out his bloody handkerchief and blowing his nose. He folded it and rubbed at some dried blood that had collected in the corners of his mouth.

"I've got this goddamn flu on top of everything else," he said. "How much mucus can a man hold? That's what I'd like to know. Not whether the universe is contracting or expanding."

He expelled another quantum of the vile substance into his handkerchief and looked at it with narrowed eyes before folding it all together into a neat ball and pushing it down into the top pocket of his jacket.

"Cheers," he said, and we clinked our bottles. A Newfoundland dog, mascot of the Happy Province, smiled at me from the label of my India Beer.

Bill's free hand was reaching for a corner of the envelope as I heard myself say, "So, how's Kate?"

"Right . . . right . . . I forgot . . . I was supposed to tell you."

He left the envelope on the table and took another mouthful of beer.

"She was trying to get hold of you the past few days. She decided at the last minute to go out to Corner Brook and spend Christmas with Lydia. Anna wanted to give you your present."

"When did they leave?"

"What's today? Wednesday. Monday, I think."

He lit an Export 'A.' "She's taking some extra time off work. They're going to be gone till after New Year's. I think she said they'd be flying back on Old Christmas Day.

"You should go back and look after the house while they're gone," he added. "Kate tells me you're living in a dump."

"It's not that bad."

"I got the key if you want it. I told Kate I'd keep an eye on the place and check on the cat."

"I still have a key, I think."

"Let me know if you do. It's a long ways in from my place."

He reached for the envelope again and retrieved a smaller one from inside it.

"You remember that long poem I gave you to read a few months back?" he said. "Blood Pudding."

"Yeah, I really liked it."

"I know. I sent it off to you-know-where just as it was. Listen to what someone wrote back."

He read without any difficulty through a thicket of long-hand on a blue rectangle of paper attached to the poem with a paper clip:

" 'Sensitively aware of the confused perceptions at the surface of life and the strong undercurrents of feeling beneath that surface. Unfortunately, the piece does not meet our current needs. Thank you for your submission and your interest in our magazine. Please try us again.'

"Can you believe it? The old brush-off again," he said. "No strong undercurrents of feeling this month, please. I've been trying to crack that goddamn magazine for years. It's the only one in the country—except my own—I haven't been able to get into."

"They did like it," I said. "It's a great poem. I'm sure anyone else would have taken it."

"It's the best fucking poem I've written in years," he shouted, waving it in the air. The bartender, a tall tattooed hulk who probably doubled as the bouncer, was looking over at us. Bill was a quiet and humble man, except when it came to his poetry.

"Fuck it. I'm going to publish it myself," he said. "Valedictory issue, by the way."

"You mean it?"

"Goddamn right. May as well get in there before it goes.

"Fuck it all," he added, throwing the poem down on the table.

He eased the words out of him like a sigh, like one of Kate's signature sighs, indicating the key for the rest of the afternoon. And it struck me then—for the first time, really—how their marked physical differences disguised just how much alike they really were.

The sigh, the sigh. It seemed to follow me throughout the house. It would reach me regardless of where I was, floating up the stairs to the study on the second floor, sifting in through window screens from the garden, drifting in like a scent on the evening air, broadcasting on some secret frequency above or below the everyday household sounds of the refrigerator, the dishwasher, the furnace and the radio, beating its small moth wings at my ear as if its canals and cavities were filled with light. And I had begun to take it almost as a reproach, this bad breath of the spirit, this soul's heaving.

Bill was looking grim. "No *news* is not good news," I said. I don't know why I thought this would cheer him up.

"It's good news for me," he replied. "Anyway, let's not talk about it. It's making me bitter."

"Have another beer," he said, finishing his own.

"No, I better not. I got some things to do."

He was settling in gloomily for the afternoon, and I was in no frame of mind to commiserate with him. I made some excuses about looking for gifts.

"Only a few shopping days left," I said, but he wasn't listening.

"Come out and see us, then, over Christmas," he said. "You haven't met Dona yet, have you?"

"No."

"Come out, then. Why don't you come out Boxing Day."

I said I would, and I got up to go.

I waved to him as I went out the door, and he nodded and raised his empty Blue Star in the air.

Do not reheat coffee that has been allowed to cool. The temperature changes will chase away the aroma and taste components will break down. Bitterness will be the end result.
—The Second Cup Newsletter

What do you see when you look back? Not a thing. And when you look ahead? Even less. That's right. That's how it is.
—Jakov Lind, *Soul of Wood*

THE WEISER

I wandered along the waterfront in the fog for a half hour or so, breathing in the sweet scent of salt air, then made my way up Baird's Cove to Water Street for supper. In Bird's Family Restaurant and Bakery I was staring at a picture of the ring-necked pheasant on the previous diner's gravy-stained place mat when Jeanie Hanlon rolled her trolley up to my corner booth at the back and began to remove cups and saucers, knives and forks, bowls, and plates that looked as if they'd been licked clean. Wings, chips, dressing and gravy, I'd say, but you'd almost need a forensic food chemist to make a case.

"The characteristic sound of the ring-necked pheasant is a double loud squawk followed by a silent beating of wings," I read, before Jeanie crumpled up the stained place mats and replaced them with new ones with a picture of the mountain goat kid. I wondered what had happened to the Christmas motifs—pictures of Frosty, Rudolph, and Santa framed with wreaths of mistletoe and holly. Like the other waitresses, however, Jeanie was still dressed in the spirit of the season—a cheery red-and-green ensemble with a sprig of holly over her heart—instead of the black slacks and white pinafore that she usually wore.

"Steep rocky slopes present few problems to the surefooted mountain goat kid. Much of its life is spent on such slopes, so it

63

has cupped hooves, which act as suction cups," read our text for today. I considered "cupped hooves" as Jeanie laid out a cup and saucer on an identical place mat for the absent guest across the table. Then she clopped off in her wooden sandals and raised a finger in my direction as she did so to indicate that she would be right back.

I ordered the special—pea soup, Jiggs dinner, and figgy duff for dessert. I asked for an extra scoop of pease-pudding. In times like these I revert to stodge. I've been a regular here for almost a year. The waitresses all know me and give me a big smile when they come to my table. "Yes, my love, yes, my duckie" is their motherly refrain. I've made it a point of learning all their names. I feel right at home here, to tell you the truth.

People come here to eat, not to stare into empty cups for whole afternoons and write poems on the snowscape neath the mountain goat kid, or deadline copy on their laptops. And when they finish eating they leave, so you can always find an empty table, even at mealtimes. But in the beginning I came here for one reason only: It was the sort of place that Kate and her friends would never think of coming to.

The restaurant was long and narrow, with mirrors along the entire back wall above the marbled Formica wainscotting, which made it seem almost as long again. Along the side walls were two rows of old-fashioned booths with red vinyl seats and green Formica tables. A row of square tables ran down the centre between red runners covering the aisles. Two inactive fans with helicopter-like blades hung high overhead, and two large seascapes dominated the walls. Both depicted sleek clipper ships in full sail. But in one of the pictures the ghost of a keen-eyed old sea captain was painted on the sky. He stood solemnly behind a ship's wheel, biting down on an enormous Peterson pipe and guiding his earthly ship from his heavenly home. He looked sternly and intently out upon the swell of diners, as if he was at the helm of this restaurant as well. At mealtimes it also was in full sail, and it negotiated the white-capped waves of customers as swiftly and gracefully as a clipper.

On a vacant building across the street, the face of an old clock, its hands stopped permanently at half past five, looked in through the wall of windows at the front. Ironically, this was the restaurant's busiest time, when its own well-oiled clockwork was really ticking. But Bird's Family Restaurant somehow seemed frozen in time, like someone's nostalgic hazy recollection rather than a real eating place.

None of the waitresses seemed to know just how old the restaurant was. Jeanie had worked there the longest—about fifteen years—and had begun about the time Mr. Bird had "wed" the place (as he was fond of saying) and changed its name to his. Before that it had been Snow's Sweetshop and Bakery, and Mr. Bird had once told Jeanie that he'd been a regular there for thirty years.

Mr. Bird was tall and spindly; he had a long neck and his head was always bobbing up and down. Whenever the waitresses spoke of him, however, it was always with a fond respect—never "Birdbrain" or "Birdlegs" or "the Old Bird," remarks which might very well have sprung to the mind of someone with ill feelings toward him. But with his long arms and legs sticking out of a raincoat several sizes too small for him, he seemed more harmless than Jacques Tati's Mr. Hulot—or at least capable only of an innocent bumbling kind of harm. During his visits he usually left this raincoat on, as if he had not really intended to stay.

He liked to sit in the restaurant and chat with the customers, and was always there for lunch and supper. He held their hands as he spoke to them—long after, it seemed to me, most of them wanted him to let go. When he ate, it always seemed to be pizza, though it was nowhere on the menu. I guessed that they made it especially for him.

A lot of older people liked to eat at "the Sweetshop"—as most of them still referred to the place. They probably came for the "home-cooked meals" and the "Sweets from Mother's Kitchen," Mr. Bird's trademarked baked goods, proudly displayed on the long counter at the front. People sometimes got up to admire them while they were waiting for their meals to arrive and, after having a taste of them for dessert, they would often buy more to take home with them on their way out.

The older we get, it seems, the stronger grows this yearning for the sweets from Mother's kitchen. Though Mother's croissant phase seemed to have faded—I think it reached its peak last Christmas—along with her hankering after other exotic (to her, at least) pastries and sweets, lately she had become obsessed with her own long-departed mother's cinnamon buns. She was convinced, it seemed, that if she could only duplicate this lost recipe, it would cure all her physical and spiritual ills.

Sometimes the square tables in the centre of the restaurant would be moved together to form a banquet table to seat a group of twenty or more. It would be covered with a long white tablecloth and, with a frame of silver grey heads, it looked like a large canvas waiting for a landscape or a still life. Complementing the silver grey seas and skies of the two large seascapes facing each other on the walls, it seemed to bring everything in the restaurant together.

But more often than not, the restaurant's older customers would be seated alone, gazing through a lace-curtained window at the front or lost in one of the large booths along the walls.

The ghost of Miss Nussey was a solitary regular here as well. She was an ex-nun who had lived a few houses up the street from us in a small squat bungalow with one centred dormer. With its dark blind always drawn, it looked like a single sleeping eye. Downstairs, the sun-yellowed Venetian blinds in the front windows were permanently shut as well, and there never seemed to be any lights on in the house. In one of the side windows of the front door, a permanent black-lettered sign simply said "NO." To what? I often wondered, on my frequent walks past her house. To junk mail? milk? To canvassers? solicitors? salespeople? snow shovellers? Perhaps to all of them ... perhaps to life itself.

She always wore one of those pink rainbonnets favoured by

women of her generation. She owned a stiff grey-faced dog of indeterminate species. His name was Sparky—a misnomer if ever there was one. She would turn and call to him in a whispering voice as he trailed behind her on their evening walks around the block.

His leash dangling free on the sidewalk, Sparky would sit by the front door watching Mr. Bird's customers come and go, waiting patiently for Miss Nussey to finish her meal. He did not wag his tail at strangers, and his face, like Miss Nussey's, did not invite a greeting.

She always sat at one of the tables by the front windows, where she could keep an eye on him, but I doubted that he even shifted on his haunches during the short time that she spent in the restaurant. She ate quickly, and always by herself, and sometimes even paid her bill in advance while she was waiting for her meal to arrive. Legs, chips, dressing and gravy seemed to be her favourite.

One fall morning about three years ago, on the sidewalk in front of our house, I had watched Miss Nussey being rolled onto a stretcher and lifted into an ambulance. While chasing after the usually imperturbable Sparky, who had made an unexpected dart out into the street in pursuit of a noisy crackie who had invaded his territory, she'd been hit by a car coming round a blind corner. Her raincap lay on top of the Silent Knight manhole cover looking like a pinkish beached jellyfish. Mrs. Higgins, her next door neighbour, picked it up and folded it with an ominous slow-motion finality. Next to the manhole cover was the stub of a cigar that looked like a dog turd with a manufacturer's band. Closer to the curb was the real thing, still steaming in the cool autumn air, but neither Sparky nor the crackie was anywhere to be seen.

Whenever I thought of Miss Nussey, it was that sad crinkled rainbonnet that always came to mind. She wore it on the coldest days of winter, as well as in the gentlest showers of summer, a thin translucent miracle membrane as protective as grace.

I had often wondered why she had left the convent, choosing instead to seclude herself in a nunnery of one. No one seemed to know very much about her—not even Mrs. Higgins, who, as Mother might say, knew a terrible lot of things about everyone. She seemed totally oblivious of everything when we passed her on the street, her eyes focused on the ground now, instead of on the heavens. In all the time we had been neighbours, we had not shared a single hello, though our eyes had half met once or twice.

There were times, walking past her house and looking at the mounds of leaves in her garden in the fall, or at her footprints in the deep snow on her walkway in winter, when I felt a strong inclination to ignore her NO sign and knock on her door. On the pretext of offering to rake her leaves or shovel her walk, I would get her to divulge those secrets of hers. After a hard hour's work, perhaps I would be invited into the house. In her small kitchen over tea in bone china cups, or in her dimly lit living room, which I imagined to be austere, cell-like—but free of crosses, holy pictures, and statues—we would talk of the spiritual life, of our lonely callings, our life on earth. We would have a secret spiritual affair. Across the light years of space and time, it was inconceivable that we should find ourselves sharing the same street, the same few hours and days, that our brief lives should brush so close, without even a word spoken in passing.

Miss Nussey had never come back from the hospital, and all of us had assumed the worst. A few months after the accident, the windows of her house had even been boarded up, though the dark blind on the dormer had now been drawn up and its lashed and scalloped hem looked like a raised eyelid. So I had got quite a shock one evening last winter when I entered Bird's Family Restaurant and came face-to-face with what I thought was Miss Nussey's ghost.

"That's her place, there by the window," Jeanie had told me with a smile. "Sure she's been coming here for years."

Miss Nussey was not in her regular place this evening; in fact, I hadn't seen her for a week or more. I thought of her small dark abandoned house, and of my own abandoned house, with the hall lamp probably still activated by a timer switch clicking on regularly at six, and Kate's voice on the answering machine—perhaps with some festive music in the background, something medieval with psalteries and fipple flutes—informing callers not that she was not at home, but that she was just too busy to come to the phone right now. On Miss Nussey's answering machine you would perhaps hear a silent beating of wings.

After I'd finished eating, I reluctantly ordered a coffee. Though the food was great, Bird's coffee always tasted like yesterday's brew warmed up again, and yesterday's coffee when just brewed tasted bad enough. Most of the customers here drank tea—loose tea brewed in ceramic teapots—and the coffee would be sitting in the pot for hours.

While waiting for it to arrive, I took out my key chain and looked at my motley collection of keys, most of which opened doors to rooms and houses and buildings I no longer lived or worked in. "Weiser," said the key to our empty house. "No wiser," I thought. Superimposed on the name was a stylized "W." The serifs projecting from the outside lines of the letter looked like two camel heads facing in opposite directions but sharing a single hump in the centre, which resembled a miniature inactive volcano. It looked like some weird Siamese camel about to pull itself apart and send a shower of hot volcanic fat into the air. I'd read somewhere that, contrary to popular belief, the hump contained fat instead of water, but the amazing creature was able to turn it to water simply by breathing air. And with all its fat in one place, heat easily escaped from its body. Thus it got neither hot nor thirsty during those long desert treks.

I ran my fingers along the serrated edge of the key and looked at the number stamped on the back. By a curious coincidence, it began and ended with our house number. I wondered why I hadn't noticed that before.

Jeanie delivered my coffee to the table, and I put the keys back in my pocket. As she bent over to clear the dishes off an adjacent table, I noticed an eagle-eyed old gent with a hatchet face stare at her ass and lick his lips. Raising his right hand, he began to shake salt on a black felt hat that lay on the table beside his soup bowl.

The characteristic behaviour of the septuagenarian ogler, or old goat, as he is commonly known, is an unbuttoned carnal look accompanied by the shaking of salt on the hat. I turned my gaze to the younger goat on the place mat in front of me. The "shaggy white ruminant," as they referred to him, seemed to have somewhat nobler thoughts on his mind. He was standing on an icy precipice ruminating and eyeing some far distant and much higher mountain peak. "Climb every mountain," said his thought balloon. I'm sure even the Mountains of the Moon weren't high enough for him.

Later, as I walked back east along Water Street, glancing in the windows at the shop displays, little bubbles of guilt began to rise to the surface of my mind. After several days of browsing distractedly through the stores, I had decided not to buy presents for anyone but Anna, and, now that Kate had snatched her off to the West Coast without so much as a fare-thee-well, maybe she wouldn't miss my not giving her one either. In the end, I would probably resort to a book, which was, as Kate always said, about the only thing I could ever think of.

A young lad dressed like an elf came out of the Christmas raffle shop holding a handbell. I stopped to look in the window at Dorothy and John. At the sound of the bell, John began to gobble madly. His featherless head and neck, all covered with warts and wattles and wrinkles, began to change from blue to purple to madder red, and the caruncle drooping over his bill began to grow as long as a trunk. He looked absolutely enraged, but Dorothy only moved her head nonchalantly from side to side.

He reminded me of a miniature Pompidou Centre, with its fittings and furnishings on the outside, its veins and sinews exposed to the world. I was transfixed by the rawness and ugliness of him, the cold hard eyes staring out of the naked red head. Perhaps he knew what was in store for him.

It was certainly one of the oddest creatures imaginable. I remember Ruth once telling me that they sometimes attacked—and even killed—one another for looking different, if they had mud or straw or shit on their heads, for instance. Deaf turkeys, hearing no gabbling from their young, might not even recognize them—and might peck them to death as well. She said it was generally agreed in scientific circles that they were quite low on the evolutionary ladder, for they could still hatch unfertilized eggs—"solitary reproduction," as she referred to it. But Ruth had ideas of her own.

In her view, birds were the most highly evolved creatures on the planet, and not because they had "slipped the surly bonds of earth"—but because they had broken free of the penis. Among our avian friends, apparently, plain old-fashioned copulation was becoming a thing of the past. The reason was that most male birds no longer had a *thing*, the wily females having contrived, over the long course of evolution, to get rid of it. Their reproductive system allowed them to reject eggs that had been fertilized by males with penises. Le voilà, the penisless male, who was now the rule rather than the exception. Most birds, she explained, mated by a method known as "the cloacal kiss," but solitary reproduction was obviously the next step forward.

Though this evolutionary turkey trot was less than convincing—the "how" was still rather murky, not to mention the "why"—and though I half suspected that she was just putting me on, and that this fanciful theorizing had more to do with recent events in the evolution of her personal life than with the evolution of avian life, it was not something to be dismissed entirely out of hand. Considering how combustible and unpredictable we humans could be, with a bit of mud on our heads or sand in our faces more than enough to get us going, with irreconcilable differences more the rule than the exception, maybe solitary reproduction would be the best thing for all of us.

One feels uneasy at night walking alone with a lantern! Alone, your boots rustling through the leaves, you are the only thing lighted up and visible; everything else is hidden and silently watching.
—Yurii Kazakov, "Autumn in the Oak Woods"

The thorns of reality being too sharp for my noble character—
I found myself nevertheless in my lady's bower,
A great gray-blue bird, rising
To the moldings of the ceiling
Trailing a wing in the shadow of evening . . . .
—Rimbaud, "Bottom"

THE LESSER NEWFOUNDLAND

I was surprised to find the house all decorated for Christmas. The customary wreath, handmade, as always, with branches trimmed from the base of the Christmas tree, greeted me at the front door. The lamp on the phone table, with its trusty timer switch, filled the hallway with a warm orange glow. Above it hung an orange nude, a small print by Modigliani.

In the living room the tree was strung with popcorn and cranberries and miniature lights. A few tasteful handmade ornaments, most of which we'd been given as gifts, hung from the branches. A brilliant red cardinal had been placed on top, and Anna's large brown owl sat unhappily on a bottom branch. Beneath the tree some opened gifts were lying in nests of torn wrapping and ribbons—a two-volume coffee-table book, *Birds of the Eastern Forest*, from Ruth, and a recording of Spanish music, *Guitarra*, from Kate's Spanish friend, Alicia. A note taped to the back said: "Dearest Kate, I wanted to thank you for your nice attention. Hoping you will enjoy listening to that tape. Narciso Yepes is really a good guitar player. He makes you vibrate to his rhythms. Un Abrazo, Alicia."

There were nuts and a nutcracker in a wooden bowl in a

copse of Christmas cards on the coffee table, a box of expensive Belgian chocolates underneath, more greeting cards on the mantle, a box of chemical logs by the fireplace, and real mistletoe over the archway between the living and dining room.

But despite all this, or maybe because of it, the house had an abandoned look, like one of those ghost ships sailors find becalmed on some flat sea in the horse latitudes, brigs and galleons that especially seem to haunt the pages of the *Reader's Digest*, the horse latitudes of the mind, where you sometimes find yourself becalmed in a doctor's or dentist's waiting room. Multi-decked ghost galleons with tables set and warm meals half-eaten, coffee on in the galley, not a thing out of place, but not a crew member anywhere to be seen or a single clue to explain their disappearance.

In the kitchen, though there was no warm coffee in the pot or food on the table, there was a stainless steel bowl of water and a plastic dishpan of dry cat food on the floor. On the table was a note for Kate's friend Sylvie, with instructions for looking after Miro.

As I was reading it, in she came through the cat door, looked at me as if to say, "Oh, it's you again," and immediately stuck her face down into the trough. She had on her long winter coat and looked as shaggy as a wildebeest.

I opened the back door and went out onto the verandah. It was a frosty night with a cold white moon; according to the weatherman this morning, it would be the longest night of the year. The sun was now wintering somewhere along the Tropic of Capricorn—Isla San Ambrosio, perhaps, or Mauritius, where Herb and Dorcas had gone on a cruise last winter—restoring its energies and taking a well-earned solstica before returning on its long trek north.

Wind-torn shreds of plastic flapped against the skeleton of the abandoned greenhouse in the garden, its white bones illuminated by the light of the moon. The moonlight also fell on the salt fish hanging on the clothesline in the Murphys' garden next door, an apparition of white faces in the darkness like Pound's "petals on a wet black bough."

I went down the verandah steps and out into the garden. Though the weather had turned cold, as yet there hadn't been any snow. The moon shone on the strawlike frosted grass that crunched beneath my feet. The garden was littered with broken branches and dead leaves; candy wrappers and soft drink bottles and cans had been thrown in over the fence. The dried stalks of dead plants hung their heads in the frozen flower beds. A solitary lawn chair with a broken arm sat underneath the lilac tree.

Back inside the house I found myself walking around and picking up things from tables, mantlepieces, and window ledges. They already looked like someone else's things, especially Kate's curio collection of camp-kitsch objects that she'd gathered at flea markets, secondhand shops, and downscale galleries during the first of what she began to call her "blue periods" (even worse than her red periods, I'd said to her one time), when she was unable to paint, when she began to question the whole idea of painting, of Art itself; when, trying to undo some kink of the imagination, she had curated this home horror show as if to ridicule the creative impulse, to "kill the Buddha," as they say in the East.

Looking at these objects in her private permanent collection—the hideous ceramic blue monkey, the "100 percent Virgin Acrylic" baby-blue poodle woven around a Purity syrup bottle, the varathaned tree branch ring-holder set in pitch in a blue jam jar, and her own signed and framed paint-by-numbers "Blue Sunflower"—I had doubts about the creative impulse myself.

I examined some of the more legitimate objets d'art: the Inuit soapstone owl, the hand-blown glass snail whose neck was so long it looked like a kangaroo, the stylized terra cotta bull from Mexico standing unsteadily on only three legs, and the volcanic stone sculpture from Paros whose decapitated head still rested precariously on its long neck.

Anna, unfortunately, had not been born with an innate respect for Art, or with the ability to discriminate between the good and the bad. Though she had battered the good stuff—we had found the head of the Greek statue in her sandbox but had never been able to find the bull's missing hind quarter—she had left the poodle, the monkey, and the ring-holder alone, in spite of my many attempts to make sure they were conspicuous and within her reach.

All the paintings and prints on the walls seemed to have taken on different aspects. In the Blackwood print from the Lost Party series, the stranded sealer with upraised arms, trying to get the attention of his ship, now looked to me like a seal pelt himself, or a human pelt, lying flat on the ice, seen from a great height. In Kate's drawing of her mother's maid, Veronica, the face now looked sullen and pouting rather than thoughtful. The black eyes of Modigliani's "Woman with Red Hair," once warm and welcoming, were now burned-out holes, or cold sorrowful cinders, and her head, like the head of the stone statue on the mantlepiece beneath the print, appeared to be perched precariously on her long neck. The amorphous shapes in the abstract painting "Single Father," which now might have represented something for me, looked even more meaningless and disembodied than ever.

I was re-experiencing Paul Klee's oil-on-burlap "Angst" in the dining room when I noticed an appropriate antidote raising its proud head on the sideboard below it—a 40-ounce unopened bottle of Glenfiddich, no less, towering above some lesser spirits. I carried the bottle and a glass over to the coffee table in the living room and poured myself a generous measure. I turned on the radio and the Christmas tree lights and lit a Firepower log in the fireplace. On the end table next to the radio was a brochure with a photograph of a Newfoundland dog that was so badly reproduced it could have been used as an item in a Rorschach test. "Consider the Mighty Newfoundlander," the caption proposed. Sipping on my single malt I sat back and did just that.

Of all the large breeds of dogs, none possesses a kindlier or more pleasant disposition and countenance nor is a more trustworthy and discriminating guardian for children and home than the Newfoundlander.

The Newfoundland's chief ancestor must have been that most beautiful of dogs whose conformation is identical with his own, the Pyrenean sheep-dog.

The descendants of these dogs today are straight and wavy-haired black, white or any combination of these colours. They are powerful dogs, stout of bone and tough of sinew, weighing seventy to one hundred pounds.

The Newfoundland is a most useful dog to our fisherman-farmer, having the intelligence needed for herding.

From the Newfoundland has been developed the retriever or Lesser Newfoundland, now called Labrador, probably to distinguish him from his big brother, the Newfoundland.

In order to grow full-sized and well-developed dogs, good feeding is necessary: house scraps, meat, fish, flour foods and milk, with a little sulphur twice a week. In winter a teaspoon of cod-liver oil every other day will aid growth.

The average full-grown male measures about 28 inches high; the female, about 26 inches. They stand between 5 1/2 and 6 feet on their hind legs.

Was this to be my replacement then? I wondered, poking the brochure under the coffee table. And maybe Miro's as well, whose skills as a trustworthy and discriminating guardian for children and home were about as good as a goldfish's. If it was, no doubt it was Dorcas's idea—an appropriate replacement in her view, I'm sure. Perhaps she would have a full-grown and well-oiled beast chained like an elephant by its foot to the newel post in the hallway waiting for Kate and Anna as a Christmas gift when they got home.

In a novel I can remember reading at Christmastime many years ago, but whose title and author I have forgotten, there was a character who, in late youth or early middle age, had been suddenly struck by the realization that everything he'd been nonchalantly spouting in his younger days about Death and the Void was grimly true. Though I'd never put much stock in the harridan stereotype of the mother-in-law and, frankly, had always been put off by all the glib disparagement that was commonly directed her way, I too had once been struck—or at least nagged—by the realization that in Dorcas's case at least this stereotype may have been made flesh.

Miro, perhaps sensing the possibility of rejection or at least demotion to second place, jumped up into my lap and insinuated herself between my thighs. I milked her ears to console us both, producing a contented drool that dripped onto the front of my pants and began to spread into a widening stain. She gave me an adoring look. This certainly wouldn't look good, I thought, for an unexpected visit from the Feline Inquisition. I pictured them bursting through the door, unrolling a furry scroll, and reading charges of zoophilia.

The Christmas tree lights twinkled, the chemical log glowed in the fireplace, the green Glenfiddich bottle shimmered, and the walnuts in the bowl seemed to swell in their shells. After a third unmeasured single malt, I was beginning to feel ashimmer myself. I pondered the possibility of my own canine companion—beautiful, wavy-haired, well developed, intelligent, useful, trustworthy, discriminating, with a kindly and pleasant disposition and countenance. And at five and a half to six feet on her hind legs, an ideal dancing partner for that lilting Strauss waltz that was now playing on the radio. What more could a man desire.

As if she'd been reading my traitorous thoughts, Miro jumped off my lap and bounded to the top of the faded rose wingback chair on the other side of the room. She looked across at me with one of those supercilious expressions that she and her kind have doubtless been refining since the dark days of domestication millennia ago, when they'd exchanged their freedom for food and shelter, shed their wildness and began to share our hovels. I put on my warmest empathetic smile, raised my glass, and wished her a Merry Christmas.

ONE FOR SORROW

Leafing through *Birds of the Eastern Forest* after breakfast the next morning, I came upon His Blackness, the much despised crow, or Common Crow, as he is known by those who supposedly know him best. There among the vivid coloratura—the orioles, finches, warblers, and vireos; the blue-winged and red-winged, the rose-breasted and yellow-breasted; among the cerulean, scarlet, and indigo; the golden-winged and golden-throated—was the bird for whose voice surely the word "raucous" was coined.

"The standard 'put-down' among birdwatchers," Mr. Livingston tells us, "is the question, 'Do you know the crow?'" But the Common Crow, he says, is a "thoroughly uncommon animal." It has not just endured its endless persecution, including the dynamiting of its communal roosts, but has thrived.

The crows of my childhood burned in their mysterious blackness against glaring frozen fields of snow or stiff white sheets hanging from clotheslines in the surprising suns of March. Mother would try to shoo them away with the flap of a hooked mat ravelling round the edges, retreating from both the dust and the crows like some fainthearted matador. They would caw defiantly and stand their ground.

Unlike Mr. Livingston, Mother was not an admirer of the crow. She saw him not only as a portent, but also as the juvenile delinquent of the bird world. "As hard as 'ignivite,'" she would mutter in crow Latin, as she banished him forever (she hoped) from the garden. It was her description as well for the equally brazen human delinquents in the neighbourhood, who would take it into their heads any day of the week to beat me black as a crow on my way home from school.

Ignivite, I believed, was the toughest thing in Creation, though I had no idea what it was, and it never even occurred to me to ask. Not that there was any point in asking, for Mother almost certainly didn't know either.

I had always imagined it to be some kind of rock; but years later, while studying late one evening in the university library, the word came blazing back to me when I came upon the Latin phrase *ignis vitae*, "the fire of life." His Blackness, the uncommon crow, was suddenly transfigured.

There was another bird in the crow, I thought, waiting to get out. Perhaps a scarlet tanager, about whom Livingston had written: "There is a definitely unreal quality about the colour . . . which seems fairly to glow and shimmer with some internal energy . . . ." And his partner, the painter J.F Lansdowne, had agreed: "It's impossible to paint that bird—there aren't the pigments to match it."

Or perhaps "the storied nightingale," as Livingston had labeled him. The crow was classified as a songbird, after all. Even with that curse of a voice, he tried to sing. But, contrary to the almost universal view, Livingston felt that the voice of the fabled nightingale was "more to be admired for the persistence of its rapid, disjointed, and extremely repetitive phrases than for euphony."

Even Kate, who had an empathy with all living things and a fondness for birds which might have equalled that of St. Francis (she brought bread out to the bird feeder on even the coldest of winter mornings), could not take to the Common Crow. "One for sorrow" was her constant refrain, as predictable when she saw one as "Nevermore." But never, ever, "Two for joy"; they seemed to be invisible to her in pairs.

Then came the day of the crow's redemption, a warm windy day in late June. We were driving out to the cemetery, of all places, and seeing a solitary crow on such an occasion might have prompted Kate to stop the car and turn around. In the back seat were some gardening tools, a watering can, and two trays of flowers for Kate's father's grave. On a stretch of road where tall deciduous trees almost formed a canopy, we saw what must have been a raven, that larger and more illustrious member of the crow family, that bird of the wildest solitudes, Poe's "grim, ungainly, ghastly, gaunt, and ominous bird of yore."

But maybe he only looked so large because he flew so close—right past the windshield and as if in slow motion, with a branch in his beak almost the length of his wingspan. He came so close I could see his nasal bristles.

"It's a crow," Kate said, in a tone of wonder, instead of her customary refrain. "I never thought he was that kind of bird."

"What kind of bird?" I said. She was smiling broadly. The car had slowed to a crawl; she was trying to catch him in her rearview mirror.

"A father, a mother—a parent," she said. "I never imagined him building a nest. I always saw him as a vagrant, a scavenger—robbing other birds' nests, living out of garbage cans."

"I think it was a raven," I said. "Ruth tells me ravens mate for life. Some of them live to be more than forty years old."

She was grinning fondly and looking through her open window into the trees. The thought of the crow family as monogamous homemakers seemed to amuse her no end.

Ruth once taught me how to tell a crow from a raven. The raven is a much larger bird, of course, but that's hard to tell at a distance with the naked eye. I think it had something to do with a "beard," or the cut of their tails. Or perhaps it was the wingtips, or the sound of their voices. Not by their colour, obviously, or their markings, as you can with most birds. Black, of course, is the absence of colour. Black is ... well ... if you'll forgive me, ravenous—it swallows light. Is it the absence of colour, then, or the home of all colours? Where the pretty pigments go to take a break from their wondrous work. Put their feet up and watch a bit of black-and-white TV. Or perhaps curl up for a whole week and sleep. Grey in its little institutional cot, orange and red in their twin beds, gold and purple in their burnished brass king, blue in its seabed, brown in its riverbed, mauve and puce in their futon, yellow in its chaise longue.

Kate parked the car in the rutted grass laneway that ran through the centre of the cemetery, and we got out and followed a well-worn path that weaved among the graves. Some were well tended, with freshly cut grass and newly painted paling and wrought-iron fences. Perennials were in bloom; vases and pots of fresh flowers had been placed by the headstones. Others had been long abandoned to bushes and weeds—Queen Anne's lace, mile-a-minute, wild rose, and alders.

Some graves were marked by simple white wooden crosses, others by elaborate monuments of the crucified Jesus or praying angels and saints. Purple and lavender lupins were everywhere. A blank space on the marble headstone of one double plot awaited the name of a surviving spouse. Another monument needed only a final number; the name and the year of birth had already been chiselled in.

One plot, bordered by a crumbling concrete enclosure, was overgrown with such a profusion of mile-a-minute that no gravestone could be seen. The plot next to it, however, was like a new-mown lawn; it was covered with brilliant lime green astro-turf and surrounded by a low gleaming white-enameled wall. It looked like a set or scene awaiting a presentation or ceremony of some sort. Or perhaps a game of mini-golf or croquet.

The epitaphs were timeworn and forgettable variations on love and memory: "Ever Remembered, Ever Loved," "Not Lost to Memory or to Love," "Love and Memories Last Forever," "He Is Just Away," and so on; but two stood out: the buoyant, "He Laughed, He Loved, He Lived," and the emphatic but ambiguous, "No More Pain." Whose pain were they talking about here? I wondered.

Kate's father had died suddenly when she was just thirteen, and though that was twenty-five years ago, talking about him could still bring tears to her eyes. They had been very close, and the years seemed to have sharpened rather than dimmed her memories of him. She still planted flowers on his grave every year, a few weeks before the annual memorial service, though no one else in the family visited the grave or attended the service any more. Kate avoided it herself, preferring instead to go out a few days before to see how the flowers were doing and to commune with her father's spirit alone. The one memorial service we had attended, standing for an hour among a chattering and distracted crowd of at least five thousand souls, had the festive air of a garden party and had left her feeling melancholy and unconsoled. She had remarked that it reminded her of a spectacular opening—but they had forgotten to display the work or, worst of all, had even forgotten the drinks.

Her father was buried in an unfenced single plot with a small granite headstone. She began to weed a small patch of ground at the base, revealing a concrete border. Then she removed a thin layer of sod, turned over the soil, and planted the pansies and marigolds she'd bought at the nursery. She seemed to need to perform this act every year, to kneel and put her hands into the earth that lay upon him. With the shears I cut the grass and weeds upon the grave. As we worked, she once again told me the story of the kingfisher. Perhaps seeing the crow had reminded her.

She is seven years old, it is mid-summer, and she and her father are fishing in a brook. They are sitting on a high bank with their legs dangling over the side. He casts the line and then he lets her hold the rod. They are in deep woods and it is very hot and still. In late afternoon, when the blackflies begin to swarm, she sits between his legs and he lights a cigarette and blows smoke around her head to drive them away. She is talking and watching the line in the water through a veil of smoke when her father makes a shushing sound in her ear, whispers "Look,

look," and points to a hole in the high pug bank on the opposite side. Suddenly, from out of the red clay, a winged and crested blue and white blur emerges and swoops down to the brook, catches a trout in its beak, and then rises and disappears over the tops of the trees.

It had all happened so fast, and without a sound, and it was so long ago that, listening to her, I felt that she was no longer sure that it had even happened at all. She told me this story again and again.

I took the green plastic watering can, along with a plastic bag full of grass and weeds, and walked over to the caretaker's hut where there was a garbage bin and a water tap on the outside of the building. When I got back, Kate was tidying up. She poured the entire can of water on the flowers, and we picked up the gardening tools and walked down the path toward the car.

As we drove slowly down the narrow paved roadway to the cemetery gate, Kate glanced into her rearview mirror and startled me with a sharp intake of breath. The hair rose on the back of my neck as I looked in my sideview mirror and saw the sidesweep of a long black limousine, the glinting metal of time's winged chariot, and not just hurrying near, but no more than a few feet from our backs. "Objects in mirror are closer than they appear," I read on the dusty glass. Read and ye shall be comforted, I always say. Kate pulled the old chugging Lada onto the grass shoulder of the road, and I caught the licence plate as the black-curtained hearse sped past. *ASH*-123, was what I read, though it might have been AZH or ASK or even HAS.

Dear gods, help us to bear the new sun!
Let our firm hearts pray to be orphaned!
—John Wain, "The New Sun"

TRUE GRITS

Before going up to bed last night I had dug out two dusty cases of empties from the recesses of the back pantry—they looked as if they'd been there since I moved out—and lodged them against the cat door to prevent a mangy-looking specimen of *F. catus* that Kate and I used to call "Sculpin" from getting inside and spraying his rank bodily fluids around the porch. During the day I had noticed him skulking around the verandah and doing his business against the balusters. The smell didn't blend too well with the comforting aromas of breakfast.

This morning, Miro was perched on the verandah railing outside the kitchen window with an expression on her face that said, "It'll be you out here in the freezing cold next time round the Ferris wheel, Buddy." Doubtless she was dreaming of her soft cushion on the warm radiator. I had forgotten to check to see if she was in before I had blocked off her door last night. She jumped down off the rail and began to scratch at the windowsill, standing on her hind legs and peering in at me. I went out into the back porch and pushed the beer cases aside, and she came rushing in through the small wood-flap door and into the kitchen, pausing for only a split-second to sniff at her cat biscuits before making a beeline for the living room radiator.

I had to make a special trip to the corner store to get bacon and eggs, toasted white-sliced, *real* tea and *real* coffee, but it was a welcome relief from this tiresomely wholesome storehouse of oat bran, cracked wheat, hominy grits, buckwheat mix, rice cakes, herb tea, Postum and Ovaltine. Why does ingesting this chemical feast of nitrites and nitrates, cholesterol, sugar and fat, along with an after-breakfast fix of tar and nicotine to complement my third cup of caffeine, make me feel so goddamn good? Kate would not have responded verbally to this rhetorical provocation, but would simply have drained her "Gandhi's Coffee"—a righteous concoction courtesy of her New Age friends, the Gibberts—and spooned toasted cracked wheat grounds into her mouth from the bottom of her oversized CBC Morning Show mug to emphasize her commitment to the good grainy life. Unlike her mother, she was not a sermonizer. Hominies without homilies was her approach. And though we fought about almost everything else, we rarely battled over our daily bread, piously grainy though it always was. I even helped her pioneer an authentic sourdough. Just like the prospectors of Klondike days, I nurtured that fermented dough in my armpit. For a whole weekend I nursed that fetid lump, and, I can assure you, the smell of an armpit in which fermenting sourdough has slept day and night gives a whole new meaning to the term "body odour." For someone more than content with white-sliced, this was service beyond the call of duty, I can tell you.

Looking out through the kitchen window after breakfast, I spotted Sculpin over in the Puglisoviches' garden next door. He was nibbling twigs and then rolling ecstatically beneath some of their exotic shrubbery. Then he appeared on the verandah, sniffing along the railing, looking for Miro, no doubt, and gazed in at me with an opiated, sleepy-eyed look on his scarred face. He had small pink eyes and hardly any ears to speak of, but a head as big as a bowling ball. I gave a sharp rap on the window, but he didn't flinch, just stared at me until his eyelids began to droop again and his white nictating membranes appeared. I wondered what he'd been into. What kind of shrubs were the Puglisoviches cultivating in that garden, anyway? His body was usually as taut as strung catgut, if you'll pardon the expression, but right now he looked saggy, vulnerable, almost approachable, the sort of cat you might say "puss puss" to and have him come curling around your ankles.

In the midst of my reflections on this tabby terrible, Dilly, the Puglisoviches' own cat, sprang—though "scravelled" might more accurately describe the movement of this denatured and declawed Siamese dumpling who ventured outdoors only a few times a year and probably hardly knew what a real cat looked like—scravelled up one of the fenceposts between our gardens.

It would be more than accurate, though, to say that Sculpin sprang—from our verandah railing some ten feet through the air right onto the fence post where Dilly was still trying to balance himself—and appeared to head-butt this pudding over into his own backyard. No need for pacing and padding rituals where a soft touch like Dilly was concerned. Then he turned his back on the vanquished intruder and sat on the post casually licking his mitts, displaying his sang-froid.

If, indeed, I thought, we do come back round on the wheel, and if I do return as a cat, I hope I come back as a Sculpin rather than a Dilly or a Miro, who had abandoned the alleyways for the fireside, the lap, and the warm radiator, and now relied on unreliable humans to look after their daily needs. Miro had, however, trained us to scour the supermarket shelves to find the one type of cat food that she would tolerate. She had been petted, feted, bathed in organic flea powder, and luxuriously toweled and groomed when she came in wet. She now demanded to be stroked, and sulked if she wasn't. She had been inoculated yearly against feline viruses, brushed thrice weekly to keep her from swallowing her silken locks, which might form fur-balls in her stomach, medicated to dissolve any fur-balls that did form and which might end up on the rugs, collared and tagged for identification in case she wandered off, and enclosed inside a six-foot fence to keep her safe from dogs and traffic.

Yes, I'd rather come back as a Sculpin anytime. I knew the perils of that other life too well. Human or feline, it was all the same. Sooner or later the fire goes out, the radiator turns cold, someone blocks off your door with a beer case and goes to bed and forgets all about you while you wait all night on the verandah in the freezing cold dreaming of the fireside and your biscuit bowl.

Sculpin, on the other hand, looked as if he'd never had a bowl or a home and didn't want either, was as lean and tough as an old leather bag, ate anything you gave him but looked as if he could live on leaves and twigs if he had to, probably ate fur brushes and fur-balls for breakfast, depended on no one, looked convincingly ugly and unapproachable and, when all was said and done, was probably downright unkillable. That kind of grits you can't buy at the health food store.

Perhaps if the future existed, concretely and individually, as something that could be discerned by a better brain, the past would not be so seductive.
—Vladimir Nabokov, *Transparent Things*

What more can life offer
than the longed for unlooked for event when it happens?
—Catullus

THE IMPENDING GLORIOUS YEARS

Someone wants to save me from the Universal Product Code. His warning was in the mailbox this morning, Christmas Eve, along with a Christmas card from Kate's cultish friends, the Gibberts, pap philosophers of the New Age.

"Beware! You are being brainwashed!" exclaimed the Reverend Winzel Pendergast of God's Blameless and Spotless Ministry.

"But you don't have to be on your way to Hell!"

Ruth once told me that Darwin discovered, after a lifelong study of the subject, that a common expression on all our faces—man, woman, and beast alike—is astonishment. I can believe that. But I for one don't need scientific evidence to convince me that the world is a strange strange place.

The Reverend Winzel claimed that every computer bar code on every product in the supermarket has hidden in it the number 6 repeated three times. This, he said, is the mark of the Beast, or Antichrist, and the number of his name.

"But do not be misled!" he warned. "The product code, used for convenience by supermarkets, is now being used by Satan's agents to get our minds accustomed to the hidden code so that the Devil can create the Antichrist and set up his kingdom. And the supermarkets probably do not even know this!

"But take notice when this computer code appears on our bank cards, because then it becomes personal and will lead to the mark being compulsorily tattooed on our bodies in order for us to buy and sell.

"Don't accept the fatal tattoo when it comes, but accept Christ and make sure now that your name is written in the Lamb's Book of Life. You don't have to be on your way to Hell!"

Certainly a unique evangelical pitch, but it's all there in the Book of Revelation according to the Reverend Winzel.

On the Christmas card from the Gibberts was the ubiquitous Bird of Paradise, mascot of the New Age, chirping some birdturd from the Basic Repertoire: "Divine Hope is like a dream that comes at the end of the night, bearing the promise that soon the day will dawn." This was sustenance for Kate in her time of trial? Hallmark had philosophical bite compared to this.

Curiously, it reminded me of poems I had once read in an anthology of modern Soviet poetry that bore the imprimatur of the People's Commissariat of Enlightenment. I had come across it while browsing through the Russian section in the stacks of the university library. Poems with lines like:

> *The Dawn Force of Creation brings to you an unprecedented flowering.*

> *Our accomplishments take us to magnificent heights.*

> *We and you, my native land, are the Masters of the Impending Glorious Years.*

Et cetera, et cetera.

I had checked the book out for comic relief and left it lying on my desk. My office-mate, Bernie Oudette, or O'Death, as we liked to call him, would sometimes plank himself there when I was working and intone parts of these poems aloud, interspersed with comments like, "Who the fuck ordered this?" and "Where's Joe McCarthy now that we really need him?"

I wondered if the Gibberts had actually succeeded in taking Kate under their paradisiacal wing. Somehow I doubted it. She was too strong for them, as she had been for me.

Kate had the oddest assortment of friends you were ever likely to meet. I don't know where or how she collected them, and I'd given up trying to figure it out. They included beeswaxed New Agers like the Gibberts, who did not contaminate their precious bodily fluids with anything resembling alcohol, coffee, or tea; who drank only purified water from taps that had been fitted with sophisticated filters, or bottled water from mountain springs, or herb infusions and natural fruit juice medleys with names so exotic that Kate could never remember them when she went shopping at the health food store; who were, of course, vegan, primarily for bio-spiritual and ethical reasons; and who had replaced the Welcome mat on their doorstep with a hooked rug that said, "Thank you for not smoking." You weren't even allowed to smoke in their garden.

But she also had friends who were still dropping acid as often as rabbits dropped buttons; friends who drank a bottle of Scotch a day, or a dozen beer, or both; friends who didn't eat for a week at a time and, when they did, went to fast food places for fish and chips cooked in two-week-old rancid fat, or charbroiled burgers from cows raised on DES, or sweet and sour chicken covered in a red-dyed viscous discharge.

She had friends who would have lived on a golf course if they could have, who mucked in the stock market and discussed nothing but market trends and accumulated investment portfolios; La-z-boy Marxist friends who could not even say the words "golf" or "stock" or "investment portfolio" without looking as if they wanted to spit; peace activist friends so full of zeal they looked as if they would even kill for peace; organic gardeners with eveningfuls of information about compost; beekeepers, barkeepers, barristers, and bureaucrats; and, of course, a small colony of artistes manqués who clung beseechingly to her curatorial robes.

But they were not friends, really, just overfriendly acquaintances. They attached themselves to her like iron filings—and no one could doubt her naiflike magnetism. But I sometimes wondered if she sometimes wondered just who she was among all those people. Not even Jesus had such a high level of tolerance—and certainly not his loyal follower, the Reverend Winzel.

As things became more difficult between us, she had, mercifully, stopped bringing them back to the house for nightcaps and post-opening analyses; or, mercy of mercies, inviting them over for dinner. She was not, thank God, a hostess manqué. I had reached a point in my life where sipping and supping through three courses of tedious talk with people I hardly knew was a divine comedy with three infernos. I'd become as solitary as a clam and, for the most part, she respected that; in her own way she was as solitary as I was.

I preferred to meet the few friends I still wanted to see in some neutral territory like a bar or cafe. And that was usually where I would see Kate's friends as well, when she and I were out together for a drink or lunch. She would inevitably have to reintroduce me to each and every one—and especially to members of her artistic clientele, for there were so many of those that I could never keep track.

I would confuse Ann the installation artist with Anne the "impressionist" photographer, who specialized in blurry portraits of legendary locals, but excelled in pretentious artist statements. "I want to awaken the viewer's own stored memory-image from its retinal sleep," her last exhibition catalogue had proclaimed. "Ban all artist statements!" I had proclaimed to Kate one evening after I had scanned it. "By their art ye shall know them" was her calming reply.

I would confuse Anne with Maude, the fabric artist; Maude with Maud, the beekeeper; and Maud with Maud, the conceptual artist, whose lifetime project was creating no art, and who had exhibited a series of framed artist statements explaining this in detail to the few who cared enough to wonder why.

The Gibberts, exponents of "New Brain Theory," had

wanted to save Kate from me and me from myself. They believed that we all have three brains instead of one, each working independently and competing for energy. Garland Gibbert told us all about it one evening over vegan cabbage rolls—his specialty—at a round picnic table in their back garden. The leaves looked like they might have been hacked from one of those giant Findhorn cabbages that we'd all heard so much about, and were stuffed with bitter dandelion greens, nuts, seeds, and brown rice, and served with cruel tankards of fortified soy milk. It was the same evening he had asked me not to smoke, though we were sitting in what seemed to be a crosswind and inhaling so much charcoal smoke from the orgy of neighbourhood barbecuing that he had to stop talking several times to catch his breath.

According to Garland, most of us still lived in the reptile and mammalian brains, our ferocity and vindictiveness barely restrained by self-interest and the law. But a third brain was developing—a New Brain for a New Age—charged with a spiritual energy that would save the planet. The supreme task of the New Age was to channel all our energy into this neo-cortex. It had actually been evolving for a long time, but was still little more than a shadowy ring around our old brains, a more complex grey matter that few of us ever used.

Well, I guess I was in no position to argue with that; and considering the imperiled state of almost all the relationships that I had any personal knowledge of—and these were the fit few that had miraculously survived—very few of my friends were either. Emotional and political minefields all. And in our autumnal phase, the Gibberts, evangelical corbies that they were, had perched in the bare trees among the last few dry leaves waiting to take advantage of Kate and me in our emotionally exhausted state. And o'er our bones when they are bare the wind shall blow for evermair.

They would have perched on the burnished beams of our refurbished heritage cooler watching us in our death throes had we let them, but my instincts—paranoia, they would have called it—had divined insidious intent, and where insidious intent is concerned, they're rarely wrong. Our Welcome mat had been taken in as well and, in my heart at least, had been replaced by one that said, "Thank you for not coming."

It had never been out, really, but Ingrid Gibbert was one iron filing who had been impossible to shake off ever since Kate had curated her first solo exhibit of New Age objets d'art, a display of hooked rugs and patchwork quilts with regulation Bird of Paradise and Dawn Force of Creation motifs.

Kate was the sort of person who found it hard to conceal her unhappiness, and she and Ingrid had had too many cafe au laits over the objets d'art. Ingrid was determined to help, to be there for her, and at one point she had gone as far as to advise Kate that I was beyond hope—though perhaps not beyond Divine Hope.

But we were not yet ready for the "New Age Wake-up Call"—the populace at large "called to praise" with some psycho-cybernetic named Godwin Gladtz at 6:30 a.m. at the Battery Hotel, or a "New Brain Encounter Weekend" at the Sunshine Camp. There was no telling how my overactive mammalian brain would behave in those circumstances. The Battery was an inadvertently appropriate choice of locations, it seemed to me, though it sounded less insidious than "Sunshine Camp," which had once been a recreational therapy centre for crippled children. Ads soliciting innocents for both these hurrahs had appeared in the weekend *Evening Telegram.* "If you are in any way connected with people," one ad had read, "this program is heartily recommended." I guess that left room for most of us.

A now admittedly crippled child of the sixties, I had once joyously sung "Let the Sunshine In" and, yes, our Woodstock anthem: "We are stardust, we are golden, and we've got to get ourselves back to the Garden"; but the Sunshine Camp was not the garden we'd had in mind. And now it was like offering wax wings to ratites.

And maybe we wouldn't ever get off the ground again, let

alone soar to magnificent heights; maybe we were hopelessly marooned in the Old Brain for good, the faded bloom of the Summer of Love having left us dozing under the bo tree among the tie-dyed rags of time with all talk of Divine Hope and the Dawn Force of Creation blowing over us like so much dust in the wind; you and I, my brothers and sisters in disillusion, slaves of the Impending Glorious Years, which for us shall be forever impending.

Maybe astonishment was the last high left—though I would be the last one to diminish it. This common cockroach of the emotions had been selected, naturally, for some good reason. Like a banana peel it always had a way of leaving us on our intellectual asses, mumbling and trembling on the verge of an assurance of something or other, we know not what.

So, like some metaphysical Boy Scout, I tried to be prepared. Waiting for it, expecting the unexpected, walking when I want to run; though full of care, standing and staring nonetheless; not cool, but humbly composed, slackly poised, like a hammock; the inner eye looking true north, away from the distracting magnetic objects of my desire; my bow on my back, arrows in their quiver, always expecting to come upon the bathing goddess instead of the hart and trying to avoid the fate of poor Actaeon, who, in blind pursuit of his prey, was turned by the goddess into the stag himself and killed by his friends or his own dogs, I forget which.

But, of course, nothing ever happens then. It's like planning a surprise party for yourself.

Garland and Ingrid Gibbert reeked of righteousness and, when all was said and done, their daisy-chain doctrines and non-sacramental extreme unction made me even more uneasy than the rabid defoliant voice of the Reverend Winzel Pendergast, spraying the heathen scrub on all sides of him to clear the track for his own train of thought.

I might very well have been beyond hope, but the Gibberts were beyond astonishment—an even more hopeless state, it seemed to me. Beyond astonishment, and not to be trusted.

... we are made for art, we are made for memory, we are made for poetry, or perhaps we are made for oblivion. But something remains, and that something is history or poetry, which are not essentially different.

—Jorge Luis Borges, *Seven Nights*

Look: no one ever promised for sure
that we would sing. We have decided
to moan. In a strange dance that
we don't understand till we do it, we
have to carry on.

—William Stafford,
"Introduction to Literature"

PART II — *BORROWED VIEWS*

God created man and, finding him not sufficiently alone, gave him a companion to make him feel his solitude more.

—Paul Valéry, *Tel Quel*

The mystery of what a couple *is*, exactly, is almost the only true mystery left to us, and when we have come to the end of it there will be no more need for literature—or for love, for that matter.

—Mavis Gallant, *Paris Notebooks*

A LOVER'S CANARY

"Scars don't suntan" was Ruth's response to Mother's suggestion that she take a trip to Florida to distract herself after her husband, Ron, had left her for "another man" in the winter of 1984, the year the clocks struck thirteen for Ruth. She already looked distracted enough, though Ruth had always seemed partly unravelled, even when her life was knitting and purling along.

Mother was in the Blue Zone of St. Jude's Mercy Hospital, a victim of another of her irregular but severe asthma attacks. From the front door Ruth and I had followed the visitors' spectrum guide-path through the hospital prism, and then the branching blue wavelength through the Blue Zone to Mother's semi-private room. The other bed in the room was empty. Mother had an IV in her arm and a Ventolin mask over her mouth and nose, which made it difficult for her to talk. Being a non-stop talker when she was nervous, she was bothered more by this than by her difficulty breathing.

"Florida's lovely at this time of year," she shouted at Ruth.

Her eyes glazed nostalgically, as she recalled, no doubt, the winters she and Dad had spent there—every single one—after his early retirement, until his death from an unexpected heart attack at sixty-four.

But Ruthie, as we still called her, was one tough cookie, and was the last person in the world to enjoy lying around in a bikini under the palms, reading some 1200-page James Clavell and turning bronze. And she was not just temperamentally disinclined toward sunbathing; she avoided it for health and aesthetic reasons, for she worried about melanoma and premature aging. "Doing the bronze age" was how she described it anytime she saw anyone sunbaking. She sometimes lectured me on the subject, though I spent most of my time in lamplit rooms, even in summer. I was a confirmed sedentary, and neither the heat of the sun nor the wild winter's rages had much effect upon me.

Ruth's response to the breakup of her marriage was to stuff Ron's herbal pillow down the garbage chute, sell all his records, mostly Broadway musicals, to a secondhand book and record shop, and replace Ron with a baby grand piano. She hired a thirty-ton hydraulic crane to lift it sixty feet into the air onto her balcony overlooking St. John's Harbour. Two men dressed in muscle shirts and Caterpillar caps managed to midwife it through the doorway of her third-storey apartment.

It was a grand gesture, even if it wasn't a grand piano, her answer to Ron's marriage-long objection: "You'll never get it up those narrow stairs." Ruth stood directly under the piano as the crane lifted it skyward, ignoring the operator, who was gesturing her to safety. I stood on the balcony between the muscle shirts, waiting to lend a hand, but their brusque manner made me feel like a fifth wheel, so I went inside to the waiting room and stayed out of their way.

Ruth had studied piano for years as a child, but had abandoned it, as had her two closest friends, during the agonies of adolescence. She had taught me how to pick out the first few bars of Beethoven's "Für Elise" and the *Moonlight* Sonata. Even as a child, it seemed, I'd worked the melancholy mode. Now she would stay up all night drinking brandy and coffee and playing mad things like Liszt's "Mephisto" waltzes (no "Consolations" or "Funerailles" for Ruth) until her unappreciative neighbours had her evicted from her apartment. That had taken three months, and then she left her job and St. John's to work in Terra Nova Park for the summer. In September she left Newfoundland altogether.

She was truly taken aback by the reason for Ron's departure, and for a long time afterward she wondered what his choice of her as a mate could have meant with regard to her own sexuality, her womanhood. She had taken to rereading the psychologists she'd rejected—"Havenot" Ellis, "Horney" Karen, and "Figment" Freud, as she called them—and even books of pop psychology, with such titles as *The Feminine Man and the Masculine Woman,* and *Lesbian Eros.* At university Ruth had moved on to natural science and had dismissed all psychoanalysts as charlatans or, at best, mere artisans with divining rods. She reserved even more contempt for the behaviorists, who had tried to adopt the rigorous methods of natural science and study only saliva.

Ruth had slogged through so much science and pseudo-science during her ten-year university marathon that she hardly knew what to call herself. At the time her marriage broke up she was working part-time as a biologist at the Marine Lab off Logy Bay Road, examining cadavers of rare giant squid. But she was also a knowledgeable botanist, zoologist, and ornithologist, and could be called upon to soothe your burns with the succulent leaves of exotic plants, to entice your cranky canary to sing, or to give your toddler an antidote after he'd eaten dumb cane.

I pictured Ruth's brain not as some lumpish doughlike fungus but as a luxuriant species of petaled plant.

"Is that true, what you said about scars?" I asked her, picking the petals as I sometimes did for interesting tidbits of scientific information. Though she was a scrupulous worker in the scientific fields, Ruth had antic, even fictive, tendencies, and had to be watched. That scars don't suntan, she explained patiently, was a physiological fact, if not an emotional one.

Sitting in the beige vinyl armchair at our mother's bedside,

I absentmindedly fondled an ashtray shaped like a kidney as Ruth revealed the mysteries of melanin, scar tissue, and pigmentation. For reasons that were also a mystery to me, I was becoming more and more fascinated by these little curiosities of nature, though Ruth's patient detailed explanations often went in one ear and out the other. My mind, for some reason, did not hold on to hard fact, physiological or otherwise. It was as hard to recall and reproduce as birdsong.

As Mother had drifted off to sunnier climes, Ruth and I strolled off down the blue-striped corridor of the Blue Zone to find somewhere to have a cigarette. The lights along the walls looked like large diamond lozenges. We found a lounge area at the end of the hall and sat in another pair of beige vinyl armchairs—these with imitation brass studs—facing a TV set on which was a sign saying "Thank You for Not Smoking." As there was no one else around, we lit up anyway and sat back in the armchairs, smoking and talking, quietly destroying the air of our Blue Zone lair. Ruth drew eagerly on an acrid-smelling Gitanne, quickly creating a low cloud-cover. In a corner of the room, looming through the smoke like a ship's figurehead in a fog, a large statue, some Mary-clone or other, stood on a globe with a snake beneath her feet and a coy, almost sexual, look on her face. We both noticed it almost simultaneously, and Ruth laughed all over herself, like Dickens's old Fezziwig.

"Now that I haven't lived at home in such a long time, all these statues and crucifixes and bleeding hearts seem downright bizarre to me," she said. "But I'm sure Mother feels right at home here. I mean, her family took Maryolotry to new heights. You remember that story about Uncle Joe and the time he went to get his birth certificate?"

"What happened?" I asked, looking around for an ashtray.

"He found out he'd been called Mary as well—just like his sisters. Besides Mother—Mary Jane—there's Maura, May, and Maria—and Joseph Mary Aloysius. He refused to take the certificate, denied it was him, told them that the year was wrong. And of course then he couldn't get his passport either, which was why he wanted the birth certificate in the first place. He was so embarrassed by the whole thing that he actually waited until we joined Canada—almost two years—before going off to British Columbia. You didn't need any documents after that—except, of course, your TB clearance.

"Bizarre," she added after a pause for a long drag on her stubby Gitanne. And then she was off and running once again—Le Theatre de Memoire night at St. Jude's Lounge.

"You remember that huge glass-covered picture of Jesus that Mom and Dad had hung over the bed. It had a varnished black frame and took up almost half the wall—and the bleeding heart of Jesus took up about half the picture. Imagine having sex beneath that—we were conceived beneath that for Chrissake!"

"Exactly," I said, and she sprayed herself with laughter. She laughed so hard she began to cough, and she douted her cigarette in a flower pot on the table between us. The flower had an inflorescence like candelabra.

"I don't think I ever told you this," she said. "I guess it happened when you were away in Toronto. When I first brought pagan-atheist Ron home to Mother, we were sitting around the dinner table in the dining room one evening and he looks up at another icon of the Sacred Heart on the wall alongside the old man's carpet carving of a codtrap or something and says, 'Is that a relative of yours?'

"I could have choked the son-of-a-bitch. I mean, I knew his mother was a witch and everything . . . but Mother sure doesn't like anyone joking about Jesus. She just slurped her soup and, as usual, pretended that she hadn't heard. Luckily, the old man was in the bathroom having a pee.

"But speaking of icons, you should have seen what I saw coming here in the taxi. On the dash between two skunk-strength lavender heart sachets with paper-lace borders was a gilded panda with pennies for ears swathed in baby-blue and pink plastic rosaries."

"The Gallows Cove Numismatic Panda Cult," I explained.

Ruth guffawed, displaying her modest overbite, and swung her head back against the vinyl upholstery. Recovering, she continued with her story about Ron.

"Now Ron's mother—there's a joyful woman for you. Forget everything you ever heard about witches. I mean, they're the most maligned species on the planet. She belonged to a coven when they lived in Vermont, in a place called Sleepers River. They'd meet in the woods beside the river every new and full moon—skyclad, as they call it—to worship Hecate and Apollo. They're deeply religious people, and they're happy as hell. 'Harm no one, do what you will' is their motto. All this stuff about hexes and spells is nonsense. There's more joy in Ron's mother than in all the Christians I've known put together. Isn't that what religion is supposed to be about?"

"I thought it was supposed to be about pain," I said. "Suffering, guilt, fear . . . "

"Fuck pain," Ruth said. "There's pain enough."

She stretched out her long legs and leaned her head back, yawned and looked up at the yellowed ceiling. She ran her hands through her long black hair.

"Should we go back inside or will we let her sleep?" I asked, seeing that she'd talked herself out.

"Maybe we'll just let her sleep," she said. "I think I'd like to get out of this place."

In the years ahead Ruth was to follow the trail blazed by Uncle Mary (as we now began to refer to him), working as a forester on the B.C. coast, walking the same paths that he and his lumberjack comrades had clear-cut through the cedar rain forest more than thirty years ago.

But in the spring of 1984 she signed up for a two-year stint with CUSO and left at the end of the summer to work in a rural village in Sierra Leone. Her sojourn lasted less than a year, however, for she contracted a strange tropical virus and was sent home suffering from what she called "brain fever."

While in Africa she sent me long feverish—practically

indecipherable—letters cataloguing the exotic flora and fauna. In one letter she described the vulva of a female gorilla in heat as having the appearance of a large pink blossom visible from a distance greater than the length of a football field—an invitation to all the males in the colony, who would then line up to copulate with her. In another she told me that the local women had taught her how to piss like a man. "True liberation," she called it. These two images fused capriciously in the smithy of my overactive imagination, and I pictured the six-feet one-inch Ruth as a wildly liberated Julie Andrews on an old "Sound of Music" marquee, alone on some high sierra above the village singing a mock-heroic rendition of one of Ron's Broadway favourites, "Climb Every Mountain," while drawing back the folds of her vulva-blossom and urinating from a standing position.

She returned the following spring with her unidentified virus and a black-faced yellow bird called a "lover's canary," an indigenous variation of the miner's canary. It was the answer to all her problems, she said.

As children Ruth and I had listened in horror as our grandfather told us stories about those poor yellow birds, no longer high up in banana tree but living on death row in the gloom of a mine, bright breathing jewels set in dark cages. His father had been a coal miner in Wales, and canaries had saved his life countless times; if dangerous gases were present, they were the first to die.

In the isolated mountain village where Ruth had lived, a couple would keep a lover's canary in their house during the first few months of a trial marriage. If the bird lived, the couple stayed together. If it didn't, they sought other partners.

Ruth wanted to be sure next time. But she was still living alone when the canary died.

This is thy hour O soul, thy free flight into the wordless,
Away from books, away from art, the day erased, the lesson
    done,
Thee fully forth emerging, silent, gazing, pondering the themes
    thou lovest best,
Night, sleep, death and the stars.
    —Walt Whitman, "A Clear Midnight"

... the poets seem always to be looking up at the sky.
    —Burton Watson, *Chinese Lyricism*

AT MALADY HEAD

I went out to see Ruth at Terra Nova Park that summer, just a few weeks before she left for her sojourn overseas. "Overseas" was the word Mother used when she talked about Ruth's trip, as if her child were going off to some foreign war. Little did we know that she would return a casualty in the end. She was an emotional casualty even before she left.

In early August she phoned to say that she wouldn't be leaving from St. John's after all. She wanted to avoid any tearful farewells. Her plane to London went through Gander, and as the airport was only fifty miles from the park, she had decided to catch her flight from there. From London she would fly to Freetown in Sierra Leone.

Kate and Anna had flown to Corner Brook for their annual summer visit with Kate's sister, Lydia, or Aunt Lyd, as she liked Anna to call her. It was a name that I would flip about with gleeful abandon whenever Kate and I got into one of those family arguments that degenerated into bashing our off-off-the-wall in-laws.

I had once gone out there for a summer holiday with them, but I would never go back again. It seemed to me that the citizens of Corner Brook, or Coketown, as I had taken to calling it since my visit, were in the forefront of some sort of evolutionary change, living as they did in an atmospheric crucible of toxic emissions from a paper mill that had been operating without restraint since the 1920s. "The smell of money" was how they proudly referred to it, and they were very sensitive about air-breathers coming in from the outside with their petty complaints.

Lydia's husband, Frank, who was a third-generation Coketowner and a foreman at the mill, was very very sensitive, and said to me that, if the smoke from the stacks was burning my "baby eyes" that much, in future I should probably think about taking my holidays with a large case of Jockey Club in a trailer in a gravel pit on the east coast—like all the other Townies that he'd known.

Frank was nothing if not frank. You never addled yourself wondering whether or not you were welcome in his home. And except for all the slurry particulars, I was more than glad to take his advice.

One sultry hot summer, when I was still living in Toronto, and the atmospheric Pollution Index had risen to some alarming new high, a cartoon had appeared on the editorial page of the *Globe and Mail* showing the evolutionary stages of man. The face of that year's model—what I now thought of as Coketown Man—looked like a combined death mask and gas mask. It was grim and distorted and had evolved new organic configurations for ears, nose, mouth, and eyes.

As Galapagos of the north, though, Toronto took second place to Coketown. Set in a bowl whose rim was a circle of high hills, the town filled to the brim with snow in the winter and with emissions from the mill stacks all year round. The stench of sulphur dioxide cut into your nose and eyes. Scientists would soon be flocking there like zealous Darwins to wait for the first signs of Coketown Man to emerge.

I left to drive out to Terra Nova at noon on a Friday and arrived at the park around four o'clock. Inquiring at park headquarters,

I was told that Ruth was not staying at the main campsite but at a smaller one called, appropriately enough, Malady Head, which was several miles farther down the TCH. The park attendant unfolded a brochure and pointed the site out to me on a small crude map. Though he pronounced it "Ma*laddie*," he wasn't fooling me. He handed me the brochure with a small sly smile, and I began to wonder what kind of shape milady's head was in.

I found Ruth about an hour later on a stretch of stony kelpy beach giving her Seashore Walk 'n' Talk. Dressed in a Ranger Rick outfit, she was sprawled along the crest of a wave of rock at one of the beach's tidal pools. A touristy-looking mix of about a dozen people were stooping, squatting and sitting around her—robust hikers in heavy boots and khaki shirts and shorts, older women in plastic raincaps and pink and baby-blue polyester suits, and two couples in matching multi-coloured Bermuda shorts, one of whom had a small boy who seemed to be called Barfin. Barfin kept running off into the woods. When the other couple's terrier saw him escape, he would yap fiercely and try to chase after him.

"Heel, Rascal," his master kept barking, tugging just as fiercely on the leash. "He's always running away on you," he grumbled to no one in particular.

None of this seemed to distract Ruth, who was now splashing salt water over a colony of barnacles.

"Look at them! Look at them! Look at their feathery little limbs!" she exclaimed as gleefully as a child.

"What are they *doing*?" asked an older woman who was holding a parasol.

Ruth glanced over her shoulder in the direction of the voice and noticed me hovering over the group. She gave me a small wave and a smile and mimed a very surprised "Hi."

"They're looking for food," she answered. "If you splash water over them, they think the tide's in."

"Ooohhh," said the woman, looking genuinely amazed.

"The intertidal zone is as tough as the Bronx," Ruth said,

perhaps aware that there were some New Yorkers in the audience. "You've got to be shore-smart to survive. There are two high tides a day and about seven thousand waves rolling in and out. If you don't use your head, you'll get washed out to sea. Now these barnacles here use their heads in a unique way. They've got them stuck to this rock with the strongest glue known to man. Snails hold on with a small muscular foot. Starfish use suction cups, and clams, of course, burrow into the sand.

"There's a dogwinkle," she said, pointing to a tiny snail-like shell attached to a barnacle. "If you ever had root canal work, then you know how that barnacle feels right now. That doggie has his drill right down into him, sucking out his insides."

"Eggghhh," said one of the Bermudas, shivering and shaking her shoulders and beaming two rows of teeth white as sea-washed stones.

Ruth grinned and hopped down into the trough of the wave of rock, her arms spread out for balance like a surfer.

"He's a carnivore," she said. "But his cousin the periwinkle is a vegetarian. Let's go see if we can find an urchin."

She put her arm in mine and we walked off down the rocky shore, trailing the group like straggly seaweed behind us. We found a sea urchin on a slimy green rock at the foot of a cliff. She turned the spiky shell over on its back, and everyone watched in amazement as the seemingly armless and legless creature righted itself.

"Wowwwww," said Barfin, back from the woods just in time to catch the performance.

"Look at that," chorused the Bermuda quartet, and even Rascal looked on in yapless awe.

We moved on down the shoreline, sloshing in unannounced on the homeless hermit crab, which had no shell of its own, the brick-red rock crab, the blue mussel, the bread crumb sponge, the razor clam, the tortoiseshell limpet, the bushy-backed sea slug and, my personal favourite, the sea cucumber, which could eject its guts, its entire entrails, when threatened by predators, and grow new ones.

Ruth pointed out coral seaweed, sea lettuce, sand dollars, moon snails, and—a bit risque for this lot, I thought—the horseshoe-shaped gonads of the moon jellyfish, which, she explained, was neither jelly nor fish, but 98 percent seawater. If the cupboards of the briny deep were bare, this creature, good-luck gonads and all, could shrink in size from a foot to an inch without suffering any ill effects.

"They can live without food?" said a woman in a plastic straw hat.

"All they need is love," Ruth said. "More die of heartbreak."

The Walk 'n' Talk was at an end. Ruth called for questions, and Young Barfin the Eager shot up his hand.

"Can we see a giant squid?" he asked.

"If you'd been here last summer, you could've," Ruth said. "One washed up on a beach just outside the park."

"How big are they?" asked Barfin.

"As big as King Kong," she said. "They can be sixty feet long. Ten times taller than me."

"Are you really six feet?" said Barfin, showing off his arithmetical skills.

"Yes I am," said Ruth.

"Wow," said Barfin. "That's tall for a girl."

Ruth went on to dazzle us with the range of her piscatorial knowledge, answering more questions about the giant squid, and others about the sardine, the electric eel, whales, capelin, neap tides, and slime.

I could still recall in detail, months later, Ruth's answer to the question, "Why are fish slimy?" I could, if called upon, recite a methodical, catechism-like answer to it, as if it were, "Why did God make slime?"—much as I had recited, as a good Catholic boy, the answer to the oft-repeated question, "Why did God make us?"

But though my brain, for reasons of its own, had now begun to store such details of the so-called natural world—Ruth's world—that fall I began to fear that I was losing my grasp of my own world—the unnatural world, the world of literature—mired as I was in the almost supernatural world of compulsory first-year literature studies.

Novels, stories, plays, and poems—indeed, movements, schools, periods, oeuvres, and ages entire—were slowly unravelling and, as it were, decomposing. It was probably some weird compensatory mechanism related to what Dorcas, in her menacingly matter-of-fact way, would later refer to as my "occupational crisis."

Yes, though I had once professed literature like a faith, and ministered dutifully to my captive congregations, that faith was obviously—to borrow a phrase from the Reverend Arnold—no longer at the full.

In the evening, on the brow of Malady Head, Ruth and I lay upon air-cushion mattresses on the seats of a picnic table and looked up at the stars from a campsite she was sharing with a hermit thrush. She could have had her own room at the lodge with the other park personnel, but she preferred to be alone in a tent. The others were all men, she said, and, when all was said and done, she would rather listen to birds than men. I recalled that she herself had once told me that only male birds sing, but I thought it best to keep this to myself.

For supper Ruth had whipped up a remarkably successful Coleman stove omelette. Then we had lain back at twilight time on our makeshift beds, our heads resting on large pillows of air, our hands clasping cups of real coffee painstakingly dripped through her brass-mesh, single-cup coffee maker. We were waiting for the hermit thrush—the North American nightingale, as some birders had christened him—to begin his evening recital. He seemed to be waiting for all the other birds to hush.

This plainest of birds—duller even than the common sparrow—whose sole distinguishing feature was a rufous tail visible only in flight and who, as his name suggests, was notoriously difficult to "sight," had, Ruth claimed, a voice sweeter than any other bird.

When he finally began to sing, it was indeed as beautiful as Ruth had said it would be, a song as pure and sweet as that of Keats' old-world bird, and just as deserving of an ode.

But he was not singing of summer in full-throated ease—no, what intrigued me, what I liked about it most of all, was the barely perceptible note, the undertone, of hesitation in his song. Perhaps not hesitation—more a note of surprise, astonishment even, that he was able to do this at all, that this beautiful song was actually coming out of *him*. But maybe he was only wondering if anyone was listening.

Ruth said she couldn't hear it, but I insisted.

"You're imagining things," she said.

And perhaps I was.

As darkness fell upon Malady Head and the stars began to emerge more clearly out of a black-blue sky, Ruth and I held hands beneath the picnic table, as we had done as kids, and she led me on a Celestial Walk 'n' Talk through the constellations of the Milky Way.

We found the three bright stars of the Summer Triangle. Hanging inside it from the apex was the Northern Cross; in its right-angled corner was Lyra, the lyre; Aquila, the eagle, hung from its third corner like a kite.

Above the triangle were the dippers, Little and Big—Ursa Minor and Ursa Major—and below them, Corona Borealis, the crown, which looked more like an ear with a bright diamond stud.

Ruth pointed out Sagittarius, the teapot, and Scorpius, the fishhook, just above the horizon. Here, she said, we were looking right into the centre of our galaxy, through a dense timeless mist of stars.

"This may sound like metaphysical mush," she said, still holding my hand beneath the picnic table, "but my problems all vanish when I look out there. I thought I'd be the last person to say something like that.

"All that shit Ron and I went through . . . I can't believe how I let it fuck me up. I'll probably end up like one of those women who go off to the country and live with a dog. A husky . . . or a malemute—a male mute."

She laughed, a nervous loony sort of laugh that sounded as if it might be coming from the trees. Then she fell silent for what seemed a long time.

"This is the best time of year to see shooting stars," she said finally. "Did you know that most of them are no bigger than a grain of sand? Comet debris . . . no more than an ounce at the most . . . they burn up when they enter the earth's atmosphere. We may even get to see a meteor shower."

I waited for some further explanation, but she was silent once again, and I felt her warm hand slip out of mine. I orbited my head slowly under our ceiling of stars. There were millions, it seemed, though, according to Ruth, a mere four thousand were visible to the naked eye. I was hoping to catch a falling star, a streaking incandescent world—a world in a grain of sand—burning itself up before my very eyes, but the sky was absolutely still, and voices that seemed as distant as the stars floated on the night air below the hill.

Happy families are all alike....
—Tolstoy, *Anna Karenina*

God setteth the solitary in families....
—Psalm 68

IL PESTO

How do you deal with a woman who once confessed to you that John McCormack used to be one of her *vulgarisms?* At a cold and constant 59, Dorcas, like some greying infant, was still exploring the world with her mouth. And though the emotional temperature between us had never been much more than lukewarm, a chill really began to set in that fall after Ruth's departure—and reached its nadir during the season of peace and goodwill.

One evening over a pre-Christmas dinner, I foolishly let slip my intention to resign my job; to give up my rutted manure-track position flogging belles-lettres at the career academy; to abandon my untenable and futile attempts to force-feed literature to young and restless jocks and jockesses, aspiring engineers, lawyers, doctors, business persons, and, worst of all, teachers, and, for a while at least, do absolutely nothing.

Dorcas drew herself up like a pouter pigeon, expelled several indignant puffing sounds, and then a really righteous bone-in-her-throat cough—which might have alarmed us if we'd been eating something besides pasta—before letting her fork rest for the longest time upon the best pesto I'd ever made. My repertoire is small, but not unadventurous, as Kate's stepfather, Herb, might have described it, in that patented litotesian lingo of his. I even surprised myself at times.

"You're not a bad cook, son" was what he'd actually said one time, after my Cod in Rose Petals fiasco, sounding like Ward

Cleaver consoling the Beaver after lambasting him for getting the family into yet another unforgivable mess. Herb liked to call me son whenever he felt I needed forgiveness. I would need more and more as the months went by. Herb, the good stepfather, and not a bad man, seemed to have plenty to bestow.

Unforgiving Dorcas, however, was not just unimpressed but downright annoyed by this "Latin" food, and her untouched mound of trenette noodles began to look more and more like a bed of kindling for her ire. She stared sternly around the table with a "Tell Cook I'm sorry but I have to leave" expression.

Cook gazed wearily at the sticky tines of her fork—the hollowware that he reserved especially for her—and replayed his scavenger hunt that morning: stalking the rare Genoese trenette noodle, the great grated Sardo, pine nuts scarcer than pine-clad hills, extra-virgin olive oil, and fresh basil in mid-December. No fettuccine, linguini, or spaghettini, thank you; no pre-pubescent Parmesan; none of your slivered almonds, flash-frozen spinach, rapeseed oil, or dried basil soaked in hot water.

To get the fresh basil I'd had to penetrate deep into the suburban hinterland of Wedgewood Park, where Kate's friend, Maud, a former back-to-the-lander, had come back to the lawn in the late seventies and now kept bees and grew herbs year-round in a sort of split-level greenhouse cum log cabin.

The paste had been produced with a fatherly patience in a marble mortar with a hardwood pestle—not in Kate's whirlwind high-tech blender—and now, after all that, it looked as if no one was going to eat it.

Dorcas had begun to verbiggerate. "Nothing" was a concept she also had trouble swallowing, being of a singularly unphilosophical temperament.

"Can I be excused?" Anna asked wisely.

"May I be excused?" Kate corrected, exhaling her characteristic sigh. "Not until you finish your dinner."

"I don't like it, it's gritty," Anna protested.

"There's dessert," Kate said, " . . . *if* you eat your dinner."

"How can *one* do *nothing?*" Dorcas demanded, spitting words like irritating bits of grit from her mouth.

How I hated it when Dorcas used the impersonal. It always sounded so much colder on her lips than on anyone else's.

"I don't know about *one*," I dispatched, as calmly as I could, "but after the last ten years *I* think I'll find it easy."

Caught in the gravipause between our fields of force, Kate sighed again, more deeply this time. Her sighs had a gravity all their own. She was not anticipating a scene, just a wasted evening, for Dorcas was not inclined to deal with me directly, no matter how upset she might be. She preferred instead to voice her complaints through Kate. In the weeks and months ahead she would pester her at every opportunity to try to convince me to come to my senses, to accept my fatherly responsibilities, my family duties, and not to let the burden of winning the bread fall on her. Mercifully, Kate listened but did not repeat. For this unhappy family, things were bad enough as it was.

And Dorcas herself would take advantage of every situation where she knew I would not be able to respond—in church, perhaps, or at a concert—to prod and pester me as well, to nudge me toward the high moral ground.

"I have to confess that John McCormack used to be one of *my* vulgarisms," she said to me that evening over our pre-pesto aperitifs as Kathleen Ferrier was singing "Kitty, My Love." Herb was somewhere behind a copy of the *Sunday Express*, and Kate was upstairs helping Anna into her new dress.

Listening to the record, I had been thinking distractedly that Kitty was the name of the horse that had fallen through the ice in "Tickle Cove Pond," an old Newfoundland folk song that the old man had always seemed to be whistling or playing on the accordion. With that one casual icy remark Dorcas sent all six of us—John, "the Lad of Athlone," Kathleen, "the Lass of Lancashire," the two Kittys, the old man and me—crashing through the thin ice of our vulgar *un*serious music.

There was an almost blithe heartlessness about Dorcas,

which always kept you on your guard. Sometimes you hardly knew that you'd been stabbed.

In an unguarded moment of tenderness one time, lifting the drooping chins of a sad parade of rain-beaten "Tickled Pink" daffodils in her garden, she said she would like to be reincarnated as a flower. If she comes back as a flower, I said to myself, more than likely it will be loosestrife.

For years she'd been a member of the St. John's Symphony Guild, tireless toilers in the field of serious music. She spent countless hours a week on publicity and promotions—selling subscriptions to the concerts, raising money raffling Audis and BMWs, selling tickets to the New Year's Eve Viennese Ball. She toiled away in an office at her Waterford Bridge Road home, which had, as she kept reminding us, a "privileged" view of the Waterford River—meaning perhaps that she was close enough to enjoy, from her bay window or her deck, the daily prospect of the evening sun glittering on its dark brown back, but far enough away to avoid seeing the toilet paper waving like ghostly white kelp along the bottom or smelling the sewage from the inflow pipes.

In return for her volunteer efforts, Dorcas received—for the whole family—a full season of complimentary tickets to the concert hall, where this member of the family would nod through parroted renditions of harmless classics patched together by a "resident" artistic director who, rumour had it, parachuted onto the podium for rehearsals only a few hours before the shows began.

But during the season of my admonishment, a hotshot young conductor was imported from the United States. According to Dorcas, he was a Bernstein protege. He actually came to live amongst us, walked around downtown in black leather jacket and riding boots, jogged the Rennie's River hiking trail with his Golden Lab. He seemed determined to whip this sleepy orchestra into shape.

There were complaints, of course, that he was moving too

fast, and he was advised to slow down—at least to Allegro. It was feared that the musicians were getting in over their heads—they were, as Dorcas reminded us, almost all amateurs—and that there was going to be some great public embarrassment.

I think it occurred one night that spring, during the second-last concert of the season, though all my senses couldn't vouch for it. Dorcas had us all in attendance for what was to be the season's highlight concert—Rossini's *Barber of Seville* Overture and Smetana's *The Moldau* in the first half of the program, and then, in the second, a foray across the border with Shostakovitch's *War* Symphony, a musical depiction of the Nazi onslaught on Leningrad.

Sitting between Kate and Anna, Herb stoically pursed his lips and looked defensively mock-attentive. He was wearing his sagging tweed jacket and a version of the necktie about which Oscar Wilde had once remarked: Only a deaf man could wear it with impunity. His large eyes, with their heavy lids drooping like laburnum, were lost behind a needlepoint tapestry of ceiling lights reflecting on his black horn-rimmed glasses. His newspaper was hidden inside his umbrella. He was a newspaper addict and didn't go anywhere without one. He was expert at reading it without a sound, even in the live acoustic of a concert hall. Anna sat on one side of me and Dorcas on the other, her large mink coat taking up half of her seat and half of mine. She would never risk checking it in at the cloakroom.

After Rossini's scintillating overture, the *Moldau* flowed by almost unnoticed; but after the intermission, the *War* Symphony raged for well over an hour, with casualties all round, especially among the orchestra. What we felt when it finally subsided was probably akin to shell shock. The audience was noticeably slow in applauding. I felt stunned; my brain, numb; and I couldn't be sure if a small sharp voice, doubtless inspired by the martial spirit of the evening, hadn't stuck it in my ear during a short pizzicato section in the final movement.

"The battle's not over yet," I think it said.

But the battle was over for the new conductor; he resigned after the final concert of the season, though the Symphony's Board of Directors claimed that they had already decided to dismiss him. Whatever the truth of the matter, I took some consolation from the fact that his resignation coincided exactly with mine. Surely there was some significance, I thought, in this conjunction in the lives of strangers.

The final concert was at the Basilica a few weeks later, a rare Easter performance of Handel's *Messiah* on the actual date that it had first been sung—April 13, 1742, in Dublin, with Handel himself conducting, according to the program notes. There, Dorcas shot out her lips and smote my ear again with her tiresome refrain.

"We're *losing* faith in you," she said.

The lame man shall indeed leap as an hart, I said to myself—taking as my text the mezzo's recitative—before I sing "Hallelujah" with this woman again.

Herb, who sometimes read the newspaper even at the dinner table, came to the rescue that December evening when the temperature inside threatened to get colder than outside. His mind worked in mysterious ways, as any mind probably would after thirty-five years at the Registry of Births and Deaths, and two, sometimes three, newspapers a day. And Herb didn't just read newspapers; he combed them, panned them, sifted through the gravel and grain until he found the news that had barely fit—which was usually the stuff that most intrigued him. I think he believed that they were trying to hide it from him. "Mississippi dwarfs allowed to hunt with crossbows" would be headline news if Herb were editor-in-chief.

But that evening he mercifully sidetracked all of us with one of his litotesian remarks, apropos of nothing whatsoever, about shit.

"Now this is no small problem," he broke in. "Twenty million gallons of raw sewage pumped into the Harbour every day. *Twenty million gallons.* It's a cesspool."

"Herb, not at the table," Dorcas protested.

Looking back, it seemed that a lot of my conversations with Herb had been about fecal matter. He was, as we used to say, *into* decomposition, putrefaction, decay, and, most recently, biodegradation. Since his retirement he had been swept up in a swell of environmental concerns—the rain forest, fossil fuel depletion, the ozone layer, the greenhouse effect, soil erosion, and waste disposal. He was a member of WREC, the Waterford River Environment Committee, a group that was trying to clean up the river. He'd started a compost heap and an organic garden. He'd become an amateur environmental sleuth and know-it-all—which fridges and aerosol cans didn't contain chlorofluorocarbons, which stores used recycled plastic bags, which suds didn't contain phosphates, and which toilet paper our anuses could safely be exposed to without being biodegraded by the deadly dioxin.

"Two hundred and forty gallons a second," he went on, shaking his head in wonder at the incredible fact that a mere tenth of a million people could produce that much excrement.

"Herb, for God's sake," Dorcas shouted.

She got up noisily, stamped upstairs, and slammed the bathroom door. Herb looked apprehensive, as if he expected to hear at any moment the painful sound of another flush. Anna helped Kate remove plates of uneaten pesto to the kitchen.

"Oxygen levels 50 percent lower than normal, coliform counts five times higher," he expostulated to his audience of one, as if I alone were responsible for this awful mess.

"Anoxic growth," he said solemnly, delivering a final fatal diagnosis. "There soon won't be any sea life left . . . or land life, for that matter. We're talking plague. The tides can't get it all out through the Narrows. It's like trying to flush turds through the neck of a bottle."

He disappeared behind the newspaper, leaving me to contemplate coliform counts, turds, plague, and anoxic growth while I awaited the arrival of my crème caramel. With *zest* from rare Seville oranges, it would be, I hoped, la pièce de réistance.

"They're thinking about running it out into the ocean through pipes beneath the Southside Hills," Herb continued as Kate carried in the dessert.

"Now that's certainly no unhopeful thing," I said.

Behind his newspaper he quietly nodded his head.

One of the most difficult things to do is to paint darkness which nonetheless has some light in it.
    —Van Gogh

Everyone wants to understand painting. Why don't they try to understand the singing of birds.
        —Picasso

EL SOL! EL SOL!

June, not April, is the cruellest month, but not for breeding lilacs out of this dead land. Maybe a few green leaves by then, a few lionhearted dandelion, a few pale crocuses showing their faces, stirring whatever memory and desire are still left in us after eight months of winter.

Yes, crueller by far than April or May, from whom we expect nothing but more *weather*—wind, rain, freezing rain, snow. *Blow, winds, and crack your cheeks!* Cold Junes breed desperation and despair, making us wait and wait and wait, and wonder if lilacs have ever bloomed here.

The June that Ruth returned ill from Africa was especially unwelcoming. For the second year in a row, a June 16 frost killed Kate's greenhouse tomatoes, and we began to refer to Bloomsday as Doomsday. Pack-ice blocked the northeast coast, and Arctic icebergs roamed Conception Bay and the sea-lanes leading to St. John's Harbour. A cold brown fog rolled in over the city every afternoon, chilling the air to wintery lows. We were still scraping frost off our windshields in the mornings. Kate abandoned outdoor gardening and began growing plum tomatoes on our south-facing windowsills.

But all things come to those who've given up waiting. On the 24th we awoke and it was summer—the St. John's Day holiday, appropriately enough. It surprised us with sunshine and 70 degrees, driving us out of our hibernacles to the parks and the ocean. Kate and I packed a picnic lunch and took Ruth and Mother to Bowring Park. Anna, who loved to run, had gone off to school for Sports Day, which had already been cancelled three times because of rain. Though school was officially over for the summer, and June 24 was a statutory holiday, some dedicated teachers and parent volunteers had agreed to put the show on for the kids.

Will it last? I wondered as we started out. My mind was still overcast with dark wintery thoughts: Even as it shines upon us it betrays us; it's already slinking south for its equinox rendezvous; our longest day is already over.

I was glad that we had another sun with us, one that wasn't able to get away. I glanced in the rearview mirror at Ruth's black-faced "lover's canary," El Sol, and drove sunglassless into the painful sunshine.

We sat on a bench beneath a tree on the highest hill in the park, near the Bungalow. We could see all the way to Signal Hill, and we seemed to be even higher than Cabot Tower. Today, as Mother had done on every visit here during the past five years, she expressed her displeasure at the fact that she could no longer go over to the Bungalow for a cup of tea. It had been converted from a civilized and relaxing public tea-room into something a sign on the door called a "facility for private functions." But not, unfortunately, for the sort of private function one was always called upon to exercise after having drunk several cups of barklike tea in the middle of a public park from Mother's oversized carafe-thermos. That sort of facility was always a mile or more away and cleverly camouflaged behind the park's bushiest evergreens.

Along with the thermos of tea, Mother had brought along her ceremonial bone china cups and saucers, nestled in a plastic shopping bag stuffed with tea towels and cotton wool. She absolutely refused to drink tea from the park's canteen. The sight of a tea bag stewing in a Styrofoam cup was enough to elicit a rarely used ejaculation. "Jesus, Mary and Joseph,"

Mother would retort. A cup of tea was almost as sacred to her as a font of holy water.

Mother sat soldier-straight on the bench with both hands upon the round brass-lipped mouth of her black vinyl purse. She pursed her own lips and gazed imperiously over the unfolding green of the thinly leafed trees toward Signal Hill, as if surveying the acres of her own private estate. This park, she informed us yet again, had been donated to the city by Charles "Tricks" Bowring. She had seen a display documenting the exploits of this famous St. John's mercantile family in the Bowrings' cafeteria on Water Street, which had long been her favourite eating place.

Ruth laughed her head off at this, telling Mother that it was time she started wearing those bifocals that her doctor had prescribed years ago. She had also seen the display, and "Tricks," she claimed, was not a nickname but a verb that had seen action in a bit of folksy family history. She was unable to tell us, however, what sort of mischief Mr. Bowring's rival, Mr. Charles, had been up to. But it was Sir Edgar Bowring, she said, who had donated the park.

Mother had grown up within a mile of Signal Hill and was content only when she could still see it. It was her Acropolis, her Mount Vesuvius, her Calvary. Though she'd ventured as far away as Florida, mainly to please Dad, she had no interest whatsoever in going anywhere in Newfoundland outside St. John's. One short trip around the Bay, out to Salmon Cove Sands, had been the extent of her Newfoundland excursions.

Since Dad's death, Lydia, who had a kind and generous heart, had tried many times to get Mother to come visit her in Corner Brook, which she portrayed in her letters as some sort of latter-day Vinland. "Lush" was a word she often used—and "otherworldly." But her effusions were understandable, having spent most of her young life wandering the glacial terrain of the treeless east coast, scouring the sparse vegetation under louring skies with Kate and their father in search of what passes in these parts for indigenous fruit—bakeapples, blueberries, partridge-berries, cranberries, and marshberries, berries whose bushes gave new meaning to the term "low lying" in their struggle for survival on the windswept cliffs and barrens. Their genetic make-up might even have military applications. The marshberry, to be sure, was more root vegetable than fruit.

Kate spread the red sleeping bag out on the thin grass and laid the blond wicker picnic basket, of which she was especially fond, down among the stylized game birds printed on the lining. I hung the birdcage from a low branch above our heads. El Sol had been brought along to practice his singing and to learn some new songs. He was what Ruth called an "open-ended learner," and he proved to be quite a game bird himself. In fact, once he started, he never seemed to stop singing, and was a real virtuoso performer. But there were stretches where there was neither rhyme nor reason to his song—just a lot of disjointed and atonal twittering, not too many whistleable tunes coming out of him. Ruth said that he was entering his "plastic-song phase," when his singing became really erratic, as he discarded the tired old tunes he had been warbling all year and began to master a whole new repertoire. Unlike other birds, he could change his tune from year to year; and, unlike us humans, she said, he could develop new brain cells in his "high vocal centre" to help him do it.

I imagined new neurons popping into being like fireworks. He was programmed to forget every year, to lay down his weary tune, to become a new bird with a new song. Granted, he would still be a caged new bird, but his cage was just a little more obvious than the ones enclosing the rest of us.

El Sol shone and sang as we spread out our picnic lunch of ham sandwiches, dill pickles, potato salad, corn muffins, and cranberry juice in the centre of the sleeping bag. Kate, Ruth, and I each occupied a corner, but Mother stayed on the park bench, being of the opinion that the ground was still frozen and we were all going to "catch our death." The ducks, geese, grouse, and partridge, all painted brown with green wingtips, swirled around us out of the painted reeds as we crunched our pickles and bit into our sandwiches and listened to El Sol's summer serenade.

Ruth was uncharacteristically silent, despite Mother's persistent badgering. She pointed out that her baby had "nothing on"—Mother's reading of a T-shirt, shorts, and sandals—and insisted that she was still very sick and that if she didn't get up off the cold ground she was going to get sicker. Though Ruth's face still bore the remains of a tan, it had a drawn and weary look. Her eyelids had epicanthic-like folds, and her large dark eyes were heavy and swollen. She sat with her long legs folded yoga-like beneath her, and her African *lappa*, a versatile piece of woven goods that could serve as mat, blanket, curtain, or garment, wrapped like a stole around her shoulders. She held her paper plate of food as if she were temporarily holding it for someone else, and stared absently into the distance. Her skin looked translucent, and was tinged iceberg green.

When she'd finished eating, Kate removed her sketch book from her large rattan bag and announced that she was going to limn our likenesses—do a *plein air* family portrait. This immediately made us all self-conscious, as if we were going to be captured and displayed in an instant in some embarrassingly artless Polaroid snapshot—though I've sometimes found the very artlessness of snaps, their come-as-you-are, cinéma vérité non-aesthetic, as reassuring in its own way as Art itself.

Even Ruth snapped to attention and began an informal perfunctory toilette. Not to worry, I reassured myself. Art was going to settle and part our hair, brush the crumbs from our clothes, wipe the mustard from our faces, *poof* the dandruff, powder our noses, pull up our zippers, and rearrange our clothes. And at the end of the day Mother Nature would shepherd us out of here with a gentle breeze at our backs and a still-warm sun on our shoulders.

But though I would be the first to admit that I have oft rested my weary head on Art's comforting breast, I would always be a little wary of Nature, living as we did on a cold hard rock out in the ice-packed North Atlantic. She could just as easily change this west wind into a southeaster, and chill us to the bone with a thick cold capelin-season fog. She might muss us up even worse and slap us around: undo our shoelaces, tie them together, and push us down this half-green hill. She might turn th:s warm wind around right now and pull this bright day down faster than a blind. She could be even more unpredictable than the Muses.

But not today, I thought. Not today.

Ruth and I smiled at one another as we made small adjustments to our clothes, our hair, our glasses, our profiles, and Kate began to transfer our features, a la chiaroscuro, to the large sheet of Arches paper. As she sketched, her expression became darker and more intense. I had always loved to watch her work. She hadn't done any of her own work for a long time, and this would be the last thing I would ever see her do. Perhaps she would paint me with the feathered head of this diviner.

Kate moved farther away from the group to get a better perspective and sat on her heels on the bare grass. Ruth's eyes were closed; her head had fallen forward, and her neck and chin had sunk into her shoulders till her face had the appearance of a swollen toad. Her neck muscles had been weakened by the copper coils she had worn in Africa, where they were successively fitted for the purpose of permanently elongating the neck. She had still been wearing them when she returned home, but because of her illness her doctor had ordered them removed. Ruth's neck, though long, was not quite long enough for her height, she said. Some African women she'd known had extended their necks to well over a foot. But there had been cases, her CUSO nurse had warned her, where women had died from asphyxiation when they'd removed the coils after wearing them for a long time. The neck muscles had atrophied and were no longer able to support the head.

Ruth suddenly shuddered awake and quite unexpectedly threw her head back and let it bounce and settle into its normal position. Mother opened her compact and began anxiously powdering her face with a round pink puff.

I began to feel the weight of my own head, and I leaned back against a tree and closed my eyes. I felt the sun warm my face and the first soft summer breezes stroke my hair. I could hear the distant sounds of children's voices. Farther off, the mournful sound of a distant freight sounded like a ghostly echo of the last passenger train—or a lament for its own inevitable demise.

El Sol fell strangely quiet, cocking his small head to one side and looking studious and alert, perhaps wondering if this could be a new tune to add to his repertoire. Or maybe he was just attending to the internal workings of his own neuro-fission. Or was he finally getting down to the more serious business of monitoring the interpersonal chemistry here, as Ruth claimed it was his mission in life to do? Perhaps he had already detected the dangerous vapours in the darkness that had long been gathering around Kate and me. I wondered what was going on behind that small black face; but on this day I had no desire to descend with him into the sunless shaft of a mine.

> "If there were no authority on earth
> Except experience, mine, for what it's worth,
> And that's enough for me, all goes to show
> That marriage is a misery and a woe; ..."
> —Chaucer, *The Canterbury Tales*

THE ART OF IFE

In late July, after the icebergs had finally left the coast, the weather became surprisingly hot. It was the summer carpenter ants almost ate the verandah, and wasps built a nest in its dentilled eaves. In the mornings we would sit outside drinking coffee among little haystacks of sawdust that appeared overnight, all along the railings and upon the floor. Ever vigilant for flying ants and wasps, after Kate had left for work I would sit reading for hours in the blue two-seater Adirondack lawn chair she had bought at the woodworking shop of the Waterford Hospital.

It was the summer the sawfly defoliated the mountain ash, leaving only the spines and mid-ribs of leaves; and the leaf-miner tunnelled into the leaves of the lilac, rolled themselves up, and turned every last leaf brown. The lilac hadn't bloomed at all because we had pruned it at the wrong time of year.

In June, Ruth had returned from her ill-fated mission to Africa on the day after our second annual Doomsday frost. The next day Bill came back from a trip to New York wearing the lime green suit jacket he'd worn at our wedding and a Three Mile Island T-shirt that said, "We All Live in Pennsylvania."

In the spare bedroom, a black suitcase lay on the bed for weeks, looking like a threat.

Surely some judgment, some revelation, some renting of the fabric, was at hand, but, as usual, we chose to ignore the signs.

One warm and windless summer evening around seven o'clock, acting on the detailed instructions of the Forestry Service, I went out into the back garden dressed to kill. Our neighbour, Mrs. Murphy, out examining some sun-dried cod hanging on her clothesline, did a double take and took several steps back when she saw an armed and masked figure descend the back steps into our garden. Dressed in a yellow plastic rain cape with, appropriately enough, a matching Caterpillar cap that one of the piano movers had left at Ruth's apartment, pink rubber gloves, and black rubber boots, I waved at Mrs. Murphy and called out a reassuring but muffled "Hi" through the large rectangles of the rusting wire fence that was our shared border. Unfortunately, the hydraulic spray gun, loaded with Malathion 50 EC, 4 ml per litre, was in my waving right hand, and she decided, perhaps wisely, to retreat into her house.

It was a perfect evening, meteorologically speaking, the very one the FS had advised me to wait for, though I really didn't have the heart for what I was about to do. Walking across the grass in my protective garb toward the infested trees at the back of the garden, I felt as alienated as Dustin "The Graduate" Hoffman tramping the lawn in his frogman suit, and as temperamentally disinclined toward this kind of work as he'd been toward a career in plastics.

As a kid I had secretly flinched when my friends, armed with "BB" guns, shot holes through fat spiders hanging like bull's-eyes at the centres of web-targets; or stuffed dry grass into jars filled with grasshoppers and cruelly cremated them. I'd covered my ears when they'd stomped blakeyed heels on the biggest beetles they could find, just to hear the crunch on the pavement.

These inhibitions I had inherited from my father, who, though he was quick enough to give Ruth and me a "flick" whenever he felt we needed it, kindly escorted insects out of doors, and would even labour to raise a frozen window in winter to let an errant housefly escape. Never mind that it was only going to freeze to death outdoors.

I laid the spray gun down on the grass and removed the Forestry Service pamphlet from my back pocket to read the long asterisked list of precautions once again.

* TOXIC IF SWALLOWED, INHALED, OR ABSORBED.
* PREVENT CHEMICALS FROM CONTACTING SKIN.
* DO NOT INHALE SPRAY MIST.
* WASH THOROUGHLY WITH SOAP AND WARM WATER AFTER HANDLING.
* WASH CONTAMINATED CLOTHING WITH SOAP AND HOT WATER BEFORE WEARING AGAIN.
* PROTECT GARDEN CROPS AND FLOWERS WITH WATERPROOF COVER.
* DO NOT SPRAY TREES FROM WHICH BERRIES ARE TO BE USED TO MAKE JAMS, JELLIES, OR OTHER CONSUMABLES.
* BURY EMPTY CONTAINERS AFTER USE.
* IN CASE OF POISONING CALL 911.

Clearly it was more than the asters that would be at risk. Christ, I thought, this stuff is worse than fallout. I dropped the pamphlet on the ground and pulled the white mask that covered my nose and mouth down under my chin. I lay down on the grass in my yellow cape and flung out my arms. The back of my right hand fell upon some fallen lilac leaves, and I turned it over and crumbled the dry brown shells in my fist. I looked up at the blue sky through the remaining blotched and defoliated leaves. A few luminous silver clouds drifted by. Several small brown moths fluttered above the lilac tree. And high above them, even above the clouds, higher, it seemed, than I had ever seen them, gulls hovered in the radiant blue air—as still as caterpillars in their cocoons. I closed my eyes and was soon wrapped in the cocoon of sleep.

Kate had packed the black suitcase late one night during one of
our silent rages. We raged quietly late at night so as not to
disturb The Child. I had accused her yet again, employing all
the authority of a Biblical motif, of burying her talents, of
betraying her art, of kowtowing to Momma. I was not totally
uncomfortable in this role of Grand Inquisitor, of persecutor
and prosecutor rolled into one, for I knew there was some truth
in what I was saying.

She nervously pinched her cowlick back from her forehead
and accused *me* of *writing* things in secret. I said I'd never written
a thing in my life. Did the world need another half-hearted
professorial proser?

Of course our arguments were not really about any of that.
Perhaps we no longer knew what they were about. The upset
elicitors for this pair-bond formation were not on any psycholo-
gist's scale. Our hearts had grown cold, and we were suffering.
About suffering they were never wrong, the Old Masters . . . .

One evening, when Kate was out, I emptied the contents of
the suitcase onto the bed. There was a small box of Maxishields
with a picture of a woman made of flames coming out of the
ocean; a telescopic toothbrush and a can of tooth powder; a bar
of non-allergenic soap wrapped in a blue face cloth and towel;
a travel iron and a travel alarm in a madras plaid zippered case;
a dainty black drawstring bag with sunflower appliqué contain-
ing a plastic yogurt container with a piece of masking tape
marked SEWING KIT stuck on the lid; a pair of Wilkinson
Sword Kitchen Cutters that Kate sometimes took to work and
which could cut anything from cotton thread to sheet metal;
and a worn paperback entitled *Picasso on Art*.

There were no clothes at all—not even stockings and
underwear. Apparently she was going to leave with just the
raiment on her back. Like the lilies of the field she would not
worry about the morrow; give no heed to what she would put
on. But the contents of the suitcase had their own secure
unhurried logic, and the practical, cool and calculating choices
surprised me, considering the emotional state she'd been in.

I constructed the probable sequence of events in her flight from home and hearth. A night alone in a hotel most likely, for she would not want to wake and upset Anna or deal with Dorcas's gloating inquiries. There, she would read herself to sleep, as she sometimes did if she was overtired or troubled.

I opened the Picasso at a dog-eared page to an underlined quote: "In the end, there is only love. However it may be. And they ought to put out the eyes of painters as they do goldfinches in order that they can sing better." Considering what his biographers had revealed about him, or at least what Kate had told me they had revealed, I doubted whether this New Master had believed any of that. Then again, maybe he had believed it, but had been unable to stop being a cruel bastard anyway. And who, except perhaps Pastor Pendergast's Blameless and Spotless Ministry, could heave any stones in his direction.

Perhaps Kate would reflect on this dubious Lesson from the Master as she lay reading late at night in her hotel room bed. On the edge of sleep she would imagine hearing, as if from a great distance, that blind bird's song.

She would wake early next morning to the travel alarm. In the bathroom she would ignore the unwrapped specimen-size bars of soap on the sink and the neatly arranged towels and face cloths on the rack. She would unwrap her bar of non-allergenic soap and wash and dry her sensitive skin with a face cloth and towel that had been washed in non-allergenic soap powder. Then she would extend her telescopic toothbrush, shake some tooth powder into her palm, and perform her usual languorous abstracted brushwork. While dressing, she would perhaps find a loose button on her blouse, snip it off with the Kitchen Cutters, then remove the sewing kit from the appliqué bag. After replacing the button, she would give her blouse and skirt the once-over with the travel iron on the small writing table, then step into the clean dry underwear and stockings that she'd rinsed out the night before and left on the shower curtain rod to dry; then into her clothes, her Birkenstocks, her cranky Lada.

Yes, Kate knew how to look after herself, though looking at her pale face and thin frame you would never say it.

Driving to work around eight o'clock, she would stop at a Tim Horton's, Cafe Canada, for a cup of coffee and—her weakness—a honey crueller, though it was always the pious date-nut bran muffin when with anyone else. She would phone to tell Anna that she'd had to go in early to work.

But, as I already knew, I would be the one to leave; Kate had yet to spend a single night without Anna.

I walked out of the house about a week before Christmas, taking that still-unpacked suitcase with me, after an absurd and wearisome argument in the early hours of the morning about where to place the Christmas tree. After Kate had stomped off to bed, I took the still-untrimmed tree and placed it outside, a vision of Anna's tear-streaked face filling my head as I did so. She had found it herself—in September when we had gone out to the barrens picking blueberries. At least Kate had been picking blueberries. While she was bent over her berry bucket, Anna had led me off into the woods looking for Christmas trees. Knowing that her mother had a fondness for them, she had tied one of her red ribbons to an anthropomorphous spruce.

Before I left I looked in on Anna, asleep in the top bunk of her bed with her forehead flush against the headboard, as she had done since she was a baby bunting. A copy of *Harry the Dirty Dog* lay beside her—Harry, white with black spots, who hated getting a bath so much that he buried the scrub brush his family used to wash him with and ran away. When he came back home, filthy black with white spots after a dog's-day tour of every mud hole, coal pound, and tar pit in town, his family didn't even recognize him.

Anna was now reading herself to sleep, and she alternated between the top and bottom bunks on a schedule that was strictly between her and her tea doll, Ragglan. When she was almost three, and had been climbing out of her crib and getting

into our bed for several months, we had finally gotten around
to taking her to some furniture stores to buy her first bed. She
had fallen in love with this bunk bed with its little ladder
leading up to the top and its three drawers with Pinocchio
nose-knobs along the bottom. The salesman, a rather taciturn
type for this kind of work, had simply stood by the side of the
bed and leaned on the top bunk, smiling like a pumpkin. Kate
and I had smiled right back at him and then at one another and
said ... well ... why not ... you never know. But we did
know—the frost was forming on the pumpkin even then. Anna
would have both bunks to herself.

On my way out the door I gathered up another useless
object to add to the suitcase's paraphernalia—a paisley umbrella
to protect me from the January northeasters. It had been left at
the house after a party years ago, and no one had ever returned
to claim it. Standing half-open beneath the coat tree, looking
like some pale winter flower, it seemed to be offering itself to
me.

On the wall behind the coat tree was a poster Ruth had sent
us, along with a catalogue, from the Freetown Museum in
Sierra Leone. It announced an exhibit called "The Art of Ife," a
collection of brass and terra cotta heads, their age and origin
still unknown, discovered in the Nigerian town of Ife. This
mysterious work had appeared, it seemed, in isolated perfec-
tion, being totally unlike any traditional West African art.

On a terra cotta background beneath the large blue letters
of the exhibit's title, the delicately scarified face of a young
woman smiled at me serenely from across the centuries. I raised
the umbrella and, with its metal tip, scarred an "L" on the
poster's earthy orange brown.

The Christmas tree, a small bushy spruce that shed worse
than the cat, was lying on the sidewalk beside the circular
concrete garbage bin in front of our house. Kate preferred the
spruce to the more popular fir, or var, as the old man used to
call it. Kate called it a "right-brain" tree. She liked its darker and
more secretive shades of green, its nonchalance with regard to

symmetry, and the fact that it looked *naturally* ornamental and Christmassy. The fir, by contrast, was a "left-brain" tree, too logically symmetrical, too aesthetically correct.

I picked up this asymmetrical bush and stuck its trunk down into the loose garbage, balancing it this way and that till it stood upright. I turned around to look back at it as I walked off down the street with my suitcase and umbrella. Under the streetlight in the fog, it looked as if it had been growing there all along, a giant ornamental evergreen in a large concrete pot.

No one here knows
which way you have gone:
Two, now three pines
I have leant against!
—Li Po

It is curious but true that the juice of the nettle proves an
antidote for its own sting.
—Anna Bond, *Organica*

THE DOCENT'S TALE; or, BORROWED VIEWS

But Christmas was still a long way away. In August Kate
suggested separate vacations; it was, as they say, an idea whose
time had come. I called up Stan Wilkie, an old friend who had
moved to Vancouver, and told him I was thinking of dropping
over for a visit. He said he had nowhere to put me up, and he
might even be gone when I got there, but he knew of a great
old hotel, and cheap, right on Stanley Park.

Kate was planning a trip to London with Lydia, who could
never get her husband, Frank, to go anywhere. All he wanted
to do, she said, was drink beer, and fish. Lydia reserved tickets
for "Cats" even before they left. Dorcas had agreed to look after
Anna.

I flew to Calgary and then took the train through the
mountains. In the dome car I met two newlyweds in their
seventies who had over a hundred years of married life between
them. They seemed to think of it as some sort of savings account
on which they'd be drawing interest for the rest of their lives.

They'd been remarried only a few days and were just
starting out on a year-long honeymoon. Their former spouses
had died within the same week. The four of them had known
each other all their lives, had lived on the same street, had

played cards together every Sunday. Thus Walter and Inez had fallen into the arms of the inevitable.

" '*Why not*,' I said to Inez," Walter said to me. "Isn't that what I said, Inez? '*Why not*.' I almost said it to the judge instead of 'I do.'

"The *four* of us had been married, really," he added. "We were that close."

He clasped a pair of hands with blue veins like rivers; but as he held them in the air in front of his face, the vessels drained and vanished.

"Maybe we'll go for another hundred," Inez said, closing her eyes and leaning into Walter as the train leaned into a slow wide turn, presenting us with a view of a deep river valley with thickly treed hillsides under a rolling mist. It receded into infinity through white-capped blue mountains.

Inez's eyes remained closed as the train rolled relentlessly forward, into the next one hundred years; the river appeared to flow backward, into the last, though it must have been rolling with us to the sea.

Stan had made a reservation for me at the old hotel near the park that he'd mentioned on the telephone, and on my first night by the sea I stayed in a hot, sea-breezeless room not much bigger than the compartment on the train. The defunct fan on the night table made me feel even hotter. Squatting in a corner of the room, an old floor-model TV set looked almost as big as an oil-fired furnace, and actually seemed to be giving off heat. I reached behind it and disconnected the plug.

I slept late the next morning and was awakened after check-out time by a loud rap on the door. Opening it, I was confronted by an embattled-looking woman with a small ar-moured vehicle on top of which was a battery of bottles and aerosol cans. Beneath this was a bucket of balled-up rags and several stacks of bed linen and towels. I checked out without having a shower or shave and took my knapsack down to the restaurant in the hotel basement, where I had a breakfast of poached eggs, bacon, home fries, and nasturtiums.

I bought the morning paper at a dispenser in front of the hotel and sat under a weeping willow in the park on a bench overlooking a lagoon. In the "Furnished Rooms for Rent" section at the back, I came across an ad that said, "Unfashionable East End. Not just another view of mountains and ocean." I called and a business-like voice said, "Mrs. Dancey speaking." She offered me a large room in a quiet house for $250 a month. I told her I'd take a taxi out there right away. Though I'd be staying for only a couple of weeks, it would be much cheaper than any hotel.

Mrs. Dancey looked much younger and her manner was much warmer than she had sounded on the telephone. But she was still very matter of fact and said she wanted to make it clear that she was not going to "look after me." She had looked after a son and a husband and that was the end of that, she said, emphatically, but not bitterly, I thought. I said I hadn't expected that sort of arrangement and was used to looking after myself.

We were standing in her kitchen, and she was wearing a sort of field labourer's frock, dirty gardening gloves, and a rice paddy sun hat. I could have the run of the house, she said. I had my own bathroom, and I could use her kitchen if I wanted to cook. She raised a muddy glove and invited me to sample her herb teas at my leisure. They were drying in paper bags hanging from string all around the kitchen. Nettle tea was her favourite, she said.

After showing me the room on the second floor, with its Ikea furniture and, as promised, its unique view of the northern mountains and the ocean all the way back to Stanley Park and the Lion's Gate Bridge, she led me downstairs to show me her gardens. Climbing plants covered the latticework on the front verandah, which overlooked an unmowed lawn with large clumps of ferns and stinging nettles. Blue forget-me-nots were growing everywhere. Huge yellow daisies crowded the walkway, backed by a terraced choir of lupins and lilies. A fiery rock garden sloped down to the sidewalk.

The rear verandah overlooked a garden full of fruit trees—fig, peach, pear, plum, and apple. The garden next door was a mini-vineyard, and the grapevines had even taken over the lattice-topped fence. Bunches of grapes drooped into Mrs. Dancey's yard. To a weather-beaten refugee from the solely spiritual vineyards of the harsh east coast, where autumn clusters of bitter dogberries hung in mock semblance of grapes, it looked like a Mediterranean paradise.

In the centre was a large herb garden, her pride and joy; all around the perimeter were cultivated beds of nettles. She pointed out some mushrooms drying on top of a shed—the poisonous red and white fly amanita, which she used to make her own flypaper. I had noticed several strips of it hanging from the kitchen ceiling.

When Mrs. Dancey removed her gardening gloves to tie up some purple-flowered vines climbing the latticework on the verandah, the sun caught the bluish translucent skin of her hands and the lacquered nails of her long fine fingers, on which all ten crescent moons were rising. The hands showed no sign of her daily toil among the flower beds, the herb gardens, and the fruit trees. I looked at the bony knuckles of my own hands, with only the crust of a moon visible on the thumbnails, and hangnails that grew like weeds on my fingers.

Stan worked part-time at the post office—a four-hour shift starting at four in the morning—and was waiting to be transferred to Toronto. Three afternoons a week he worked as an orderly in a nursing home for veterans. He and his wife had split up about a year ago, and he had given up the expensive apartment they'd been renting in Kitsilano. He was now living in a bare bedsitter on what he called "the Lower East Side," close to Chinatown, and above a thrift shop called Tik Tak Buy Sell, which now displayed his test pattern chesterfield set, his coffee table, lamp, bookcase, magazine rack, and hassock like a stage set in the front window. As we walked past, he stopped and looked at it thoughtfully, as if he weren't quite sure where he had seen this scene before, or, given the right cue, as if he just might march right in and buy it all back.

He went up to the window to take a closer look. Hanging from his hand was a fool on a stick, complete with cap and bells, which he'd bought on a whim on our walk through Gastown. In his plaid shirt, multi-coloured braces, and herringbone pants that hung about two inches above his red sneakers, Stan looked like a jester himself. He let out that mad laugh of his and jangled the fool's bells against his leg; then he stepped back and shook them at the window like a priest shaking an aspergill of holy water on a coffin.

Next door was a meat market called Freddy Friendly Meat. "Come in, we'd love to meat you," said a sign in the window. In the recessed doorway between the two shops, which led up to Stan's room on the third floor, a man in a stained brown suit was curled up asleep with his head resting on a bag of garbage and his legs inside a cardboard box. Stan bent down and shook the fool's bells at him, and he covered up his face and let out a sleepy groan.

Stan was trying to fit his key in the lock. "That's my namesake, Stanley . . . Stanley Park," he said. "He grumbles and he disobeys the Word. The Word of God and the word of my landlord. Say hello, Stanley, and stop grumbling."

"That's not his real name?"

"That's what he calls himself. Easy to remember when you've drunk several bottles of lotion and the dregs of a few aerosol cans. After a few years of that, you forget a lot more than your name."

As Stan opened the door, Stanley groaned again and shifted onto his other side so that he faced into the street. We stepped over him and Stan locked the door.

"I'd let him sleep in the hallway, but he pisses on the floor—sometimes he even shits on the floor. The landlord told me if I let him in again he'd throw us both out."

We walked up the stairs to Stan's room under the proverbial bare light bulb hanging from a long frayed braided wire. He hadn't bothered to lock his door. Besides his furniture, he had jettisoned practically everything he owned—his books, records, plants, even most of his clothes. All that remained were a foam mattress and a blanket, a table and chair, a few dishes, a concertina, and a large succulent aloe vera plant in a terra cotta pot. Stan stuck the fool down into the pot, laughed his fool's laugh, then went into the bathroom and closed the door.

On the counter was a box of Pop Tarts and a bottle of Nescafe. On the table was a dog-eared copy of Auden's *Selected Poems*. I removed the bookmark—a yearly pass to the Dr. Sun Yat-sen Classical Chinese Garden, which Stan had altered to read, the Dr. *Stan* Yat-sen Classical Chinese Garden. I flipped through the pages and began to read "Musée des Beaux Arts."

> *About suffering they were never wrong,*
> *The Old Masters: how well they understood*
> *Its human position; how it takes place*
> *While someone else is eating or opening a window or just*
> *walking dully along:...*

Or scratching his arse, I thought, as Stan came out of the bathroom with that familiar preoccupied look on his face and his right hand behind him doing just that.

There are allusions to three Bruegel paintings in Auden's poem, and some nitpicking critic had once pointed out—though to what purpose I cannot recall—that in one of the paintings, "The Massacre of the Innocents," the horse that in Auden's poem "scratches its innocent behind on a tree" is not really scratching its arse on a tree at all, which seemed to me to be the critical equivalent of scratching your own arse on a tree.

"Do you want a coffee?" Stan said.

"Sure. When is the last bus?"

"Around twelve. Don't worry about that. I'm on the air at the midnight hour."

Stan had given all his records—over 500 of them—to an

alternative radio station, Co-op Radio, and he missed them so much he'd volunteered to do an early morning show.

"Make it a weak one," I said. "It keeps me awake."

"That's why I drink it," he said, heading back into the bathroom with the jar of coffee and the mugs. "Hope you don't mind tap water," he shouted. "I haven't got a pot in the place."

Not wanting to answer that, I began reading Auden's "Lullaby."

Lay your sleeping head, my love,
Human on my faithless arm ...

Someone had underlined "faithless arm" in guilty red ink.

Stan came out of the bathroom with the coffee. He laid one of the mugs on the table beside me, walked across the room and stood looking out the window at the city. He had an expression on his face of someone looking at something for the last time. He had lived in Vancouver, off and on, since the late sixties, when he'd gone out to study religion at UBC.

"What ever happened to that book you were writing on Thomas Merton?" I asked him.

"You remember that. Jesus, that was a long time ago. I guess I was miscast. I'm not a writer. When Merton died, it died along with him. I'd even arranged to talk to him—he was supposed to be coming here for a conference, but he was killed just a few weeks before it took place."

He sat down on the foam mattress and leaned back against the wall.

"Do you know how he died?" he asked.

"He was electrocuted, wasn't he?"

"Yeah ... in Bangkok ... turning on a stupid fucking fan. They found him lying in his own urine. One of the great souls of the age ... ends up dead in a pool of his own piss. Isn't that just the way it is.

"Who could monkey with metaphysics after that. And that's all I was doing, really ... monkeying around. Merton was the monk and I was the monkey.

"Do you know what the joke was going around about it?"

He lit a cigarette, took a mouthful of tap-water coffee, and screwed up his face. I was trying to drink mine, but it tasted like kerosene. He took a long drag on the cigarette and paused again for effect.

"What did the monks say when they found Thomas Merton dead?"

"What?"

"'Jesus, urine trouble, buddy.'"

We didn't laugh. He looked away and contorted his face again. Then he said, sadly and quietly, "You know, I cried when I first heard he was gone. It was like I'd lost a father or a brother and no one had even let me know. I had to find out from the fucking paper. I thought it was just an acorn—a big mother, mind you—but it turned out the sky was falling after all. Things really began to fall apart after that, and in the end I gave the whole thing up. Anyway, I was never convinced that footnote-infested piece of academic shit could be a book. A soul like that could never be bound in a book."

He looked around him, then gestured with open arms. "But here I am, after all these years ... back in the monk's cell after all."

He picked up his beloved concertina and began to play something from his vast repertoire of dirges. It sounded a bit like "Rock of Ages," but before I could place it, he went on to something else. Whatever sadness there was in him—and there seemed to be a lot more than usual these days—he squeezed out through that tiny instrument. When he played it, he showed a face that he didn't ordinarily show. And as I watched him now, with his body bent over it, he looked like a man trying to light a cigarette in the wind.

"I better get over to the station," he said, and he drained his cup. "It's just across the street. I'll show you where to get the bus."

"What are you playing tonight?" I asked.

"The Hummer. Glenn Gould doing Beethoven's Fifth on

the piano. It was transcribed by Liszt. He transcribed them all, even the Ninth. I wonder if anyone's recorded that. I don't know what else. I'll have to dig around."

He left me at the bus stop with a surly-looking man who kept looking my way and spitting fiercely on the sidewalk. It was hard not to take it personally. Behind me in the parking lot two men and a woman were arguing over the remains of a six-pack against a sonic backdrop of sirens, shouts, squeals of car tires, and the continuous ringing of a burglar alarm.

When the bus pulled up at the stop, the spitting man did not get on but stared up at the passengers sitting by the windows. As we drove off, I looked back at him through the rear window, and he bade us farewell with a great looping arc of spit.

We drove rapidly through empty streets of unlit buildings, past grim grills and cafes, desperate hotels, shops that looked so run-down it was impossible to tell if they were operating or not. We sped past the widely separated stops without so much as slowing down. When the bell *pinged*, and the driver finally pulled up at a stop, all the other passengers on the bus got off, as if this might be their only chance. Across the street was a long low building, perhaps an abandoned factory, with every single window smashed out; and on my side, the sad face of a mission-hotel, The Lord God the Almighty Creator and King of Heaven and Earth Hospitality Inn. "They stumble because they disobey the Word," read a line of Gothic script beneath the sign. The Order of Good Cheer, obviously, and a warm Christian welcome to it. The bus doors *hissed* shut, and we drove off into the darkness in our warm cell of light.

As I walked up the garden steps to Mrs. Dancey's house, someone sprang up out of the bushes and I jumped across the flower border on the opposite side and fell into a clump of ferns and nettles. Then, as I tried to get to my feet, a white-gloved hand reached in over the flowers to help pull me up. I ignored it and got up by myself.

"Sorry, I didn't mean to frighten you," a man's voice said. He removed a glove and extended his hand again. "You must be the new boarder."

"Roomer," I said, rubbing my hands.

"You probably got some bad pricks there," he said, stepping over the flowers on the other side and retrieving a white bucket.

Speaking of pricks, I said to myself, just who the fuck are you and what are you doing out here in the bushes scaring the shit out of people at this hour of the night?

"I was just picking a few shoots," he said, as if he'd heard. "You're going to need some of these. The only cure for nettles, as they say, is more nettles.

"I'm Rainer," he continued, leading me up the steps. "Come on in the house and we'll have a look at those hands."

Those hands were beginning to feel as if they were on fire.

"Are you staying here too?" I asked him. The porch light was backlighting his large wiry head of hair.

"Not really," he said. "Just over for tea. And you're in luck. It's just what you need for those stings."

"What kind of tea?"

"Nettle tea," he said, lifting the plastic bucket and swinging it by the wire handle.

We went inside where Mrs. Dancey was standing by the stove in a lonesome blue bathrobe. A black enamel kettle was on the boil. The stove clock said a quarter past one. She looked at us as if she had never seen either one of us before. Rainer was holding onto my arm, and I was wincing and holding up my hands.

Mrs. Dancey didn't even ask what was wrong. Like a doctor in an emergency ward, she immediately went into action. She put on a pair of gardening gloves, emptied Rainer's bucket of nettles onto the counter and began to pound them with a small wooden mallet and drop them into an iron pot on the stove. When the kettle began to whistle, Rainer put some of the remaining shoots into a ceramic teapot, filled it with water and covered it with a tea cozy—a red rooster with an enormous comb. And like an assisting intern seeking crucial information, he asked me my age, my birthday, the year I was born, and began to cipher what he called my "life-load"—from a numerological point of view.

"Heavy numbers," he said, shaking his head and stirring the teapot. "A lot of responsibility, a lot of duty, a lot of weight to be under. You've been given a load. How do you feel?" he asked, turning around to look at me.

"Itchy," I said, not quite sure if he was inquiring about my physical or my metaphysical health, but wanting to keep the conversation on the earthly plane. "I'm starting to feel itchy and hot all over."

"Most people think it's the spikes that do it to you," he said. "But it's the fine hairs on the leaves and stems. They release a venomous juice when you touch them, but when this juice is boiled up, it takes all the pain away."

As we drank our tea, Mrs. Dancey put the leaves from the iron pot in a piece of cheesecloth and wrung it out in a brown mixing bowl. The juice was an even blacker green than the tea we were drinking, which wasn't tasting half as bad as I expected, but wasn't doing anything much for the burning and itching in my hands. When Mrs. Dancey applied the nettle juice, however, it gave almost instant relief.

"That's why I like pain," Rainer said, reading the expression on my face. "I never feel better than when it goes away."

That night I was awakened by a thump against the wall between Mrs. Dancey's bedroom and mine. I had been dreaming about Anna. She had been given the part of Little Red Riding Hood in a school play and, to our dismay, Dorcas had made her a red décolleté dress.

"Marilyn Monroe was someone's daughter," Dorcas had said to Kate and me.

I'd had the not uncommon feeling that she was trying to teach us something, but I wasn't quite sure what. I was even less sure now that I was awake.

I raised myself on an elbow, listening for other sounds. The streetlight shone through the open curtain into the room. I remembered that Anna had not wanted to hear the story of Little Red Riding Hood since the one and only time we had read it to her. I recalled those titillating décolleté pictures of Marilyn Monroe that I used to look at in the old movie magazines that our next door neighbour, Rita, used to pass on to Mother. I could see her clearly in her low-cut satin dress held up by a single strap that doubled as a choker. Mother would snatch the magazines away from me and hide them if she saw me looking at them, so of course getting my hands on them became one of my teenage preoccupations.

I sat up on the edge of the bed wondering what time it was. I had given up wearing a watch since my old Gruen "Precision" had stopped living up to its name. It had stopped altogether, to be more precise. Mr. Kadinsky, the jeweler, had informed me that it was a mechanical watch, and parts for what he called "the movement" would be hard to find. He had placed it in the tiniest manila envelope I had ever seen, and then into a drawer that was to become its grave.

My hands and wrists were still covered in red welts that looked like the large hives I had been afflicted with as a child, but they no longer burned or itched. The glass of water on the night table was perfectly clear and still, and the water divided the tall glass exactly in half. I recalled Herb's hokey *Reader's Digest* psychologizing about the half-full and the half-empty glass, a personality test he would put me through at least once a month to determine my basic attitude toward life. He quizzed so many others that he probably couldn't keep track. To keep him guessing I would answer differently each time, perhaps leaning more often toward the pessimistic "half-empty" because that answer seemed to please him a bit more, as if he had expected as much, or had found me out.

In the half-light, or the half-dark, still half-asleep or half-awake, and, without my glasses, half-sighted or half-blind, I was startled by what looked like an envelope beneath my bedroom door. My dream clipped fast forward—it was a telegram and it was about Anna. The thought almost paralyzed me, but when I was finally able to walk over and pick it up, it turned out to be the thin rectangular block of wood that I had found in the closet and wedged beneath the door to keep the breeze from blowing it open. All the doors in Mrs. Dancey's house seemed to be leaning away from their jambs.

The next day Mrs. Dancey abandoned her principles altogether and was effusively attentive. She apologized several times for Rainer's behaviour, referring to him as her "ex-boyfriend."

"He lives on raw vegetables," she said, as if that might excuse him.

She insisted that I sit around the garden all day watching her work. It aided the digestion, she said, watching other people work. She continued to ply me with nettles. For lunch she served nettle miso broth and black soybean nettle stew on a glass-topped wicker table on the back verandah. She was wearing a revealing white halter top and faded jeans circa 1967, the Summer of Love. The seams were straining a bit now, and the bell bottoms were frayed beyond repair. Her long auburn hair was tied in a pony tail.

After a supper of nettle tofu casserole, we went for a walk around the neighbourhood and then sat on a bench in a little green-space overlooking the inlet. Mrs Dancey said it was called Meditation Park; it wasn't much bigger than a meditation mat. It would be difficult meditating here, however, because of the din rising from the wharves and the ships. A steep pedestrian stairway led down to the docks.

As we watched the sun sink below the western mountains, she removed a black notebook from her white canvas shopping bag and began to write. When she had finished, she handed it to me. It was a short paragraph, a sort of inflated haiku.

The cones spewing clouds o'er an inlet from the sea,
my soul a rusting hulk at the docks, my heart a heavy cargo
piled by rough longshoremen onto piers.

There must be something about my face that makes people want to bare their souls.

"That's a good poem, Mrs. Dancey," I said.

She smiled. "Call me Gale," she said. "How's your hands?"

"They're fine," I said. "The swelling's all gone, though they still feel a bit itchy."

She picked one up and looked at it, but made no comment. She held on to my hand as she turned her head to gaze beneath her visor at the last rays of the setting sun.

That night I shared Gale's bed—a waterbed with a low table of backlit flowerless green plants along the head. She said they helped her breathe better during the night. She turned off the plant light, and we lay side by side, naked under a single sheet. Wistful Hugh Auden lay in the space between us.

In the darkness I could hear the distant din from the docks, the huge cranes and rough longshoremen toiling away. The sound settled upon us like a woolen blanket. Gale noticed a crack of light from a street lamp and got up to adjust the curtains. When she got back in bed, she rolled over on top of me and slid her hands beneath my shoulder blades. She lowered her heavy heart upon my chest and laid her head upon my faithless shoulder.

We undulated; Gale, as it turned out, preferred a soft breeze and an absolute minimum of motion. The rusting hulk of her soul seemed more in need of a calm safe harbour than the rough and rocky seas of sex. But she felt very strong, and her skin exuded a pungent herbiness. My hands slid up and down her back: her skin was oiled as well as seasoned.

"Yes, yes," she sighed, after I had almost forgotten that this was the sex act we were engaged in. In a series of more urgent undulations, we rolled finally to the shore and onto the waiting sands of sleep.

On the day before I left I went to see the Dr. Sun Yat-sen Classical Chinese Garden, or "my garden," as Stan referred to it. He had lent me his pass and had been urging me to go. I'd read the descriptive brochure several times. It wasn't everyone who had the only full-scale classical Chinese garden ever constructed outside of China practically as his own backyard, with almost all the architectural components—hand-fired roof tiles, hand-carved woodwork, lattice windows, naturally sculptured limestone rocks, courtyard pebbles—shipped all the way from the People's Republic. Stan lived on the same street, and when he was on the night shift went there almost every morning to read and think.

I slid his Dr. Stan Yat-sen card under the half-moon opening of the wicket in the Entrance Hall and was relieved when the smiling young girl behind the glass barely glanced at it and then smiled all the wider at me. I went inside and strolled all alone through the covered walkways and courtyards, sat in the Water Pavilion and the Scholar's Study, and from the Lookout observed the authentic Ming Dynasty-style classical architecture of the pavilions and the Ting.

Returning to the Entrance Hall, I met up with a small group starting out on a guided tour and decided to go back round again. Just past the Main Hall, the docent, a disarmingly shy young woman dressed in a traditional Chinese black cotton suit, pointed out to "our American friend" what looked like a naturally sculpted image of the face of George Washington in the pitted limestone rock.

"Very interesting," he said, identifying himself, an elderly man in shorts with long spindly legs and a waxy red face.

She led us back along the route I had taken, pointing out the yin-yang balance of the Garden—light and dark, small and large, hard and soft, still and flowing; the plants and flowers symbolic of human virtues; and the intricate design of the eaves and roof that created a rain curtain during heavy showers.

She showed us the framed views-within-views, some "borrowed" from the adjoining Dr. Sun Yat-sen Park, which made the Garden seem larger than it was, and she remarked in a shyly philosophical way that all views were borrowed, in a sense, were seasonal, changing, "passing strange," there for the brief pleasure of our transient lives.

We sat sideways leaning over the Lookout, trying to see the pink and orange carp and the tiny blue bitterlings that she said were lurking beneath the milky jade water—deliberately cloudy so that we could not assay its depth, so that the pond would be permanently mysterious. She told us there weren't too many fish left because a crane was using the pond as his own private fishing preserve. A lone duck, a single mother, had flown in in the spring and hatched a brood of five ducklings, she said, as a harlequin couple sailed out from beneath a bridge.

At the end we stood on the terrace off the Scholar's Study and stared at the Ting, which the American called a gazebo in a tone so pronounced he gave the impression that he was discovering and naming it for us. It stood alone on a small island of manicured shrubs, "bookmark" grass, and sculptured limestone rocks, its multi-winged roof curving skyward to allow evil spirits to escape. After crossing the threshold into the study, we were told that in China visitors were judged by the way they stepped over the border into and out of another's house. Then she left us there to sit and reflect, but in a few minutes everyone else was gone, and I was alone with "The Three Friends of Winter"—the pine, bamboo, and winter-flowering plum, celebrating strength, grace, and renewal of life respectively—thinking about how I should cross the threshold on my way out.

It wasn't until the very last day of my trip that I discovered what my desultory wanderings in this sister city by the sea had been leading up to. I had been the unconscious agent of a most unlikely, a most serendipitous, match: Stan and Gale, both of whom had confessed to me that they'd stopped looking, had obviously decided to take one last look.

From the moment he arrived at the door this morning, wearing only hiking boots and cross-braced Swiss Alp shorts, looking like some large and hairy toddler, I could see that bonding had begun. He introduced himself to her by kneeling and kissing her hand, and followed that up by naming almost every flower and plant in the house, as if he were the Creator Himself. This impressed Gale even more than his saucy ironic chivalry.

And as we headed off to the airport in her smart blue Volkswagen Fox, Stan in the front seat beside Gale, and I in the back seat with only my knapsack beside me, they were busy exchanging glances and planning hiking trips to alpine meadows in the mountain air in search of the wild red Iceland poppy. When Gale pronounced "mountain air" the sound registered in my mind like one of those double images in which you can see only one thing at a time—now the climber or dweller amongst those solitary peaks, now the rarified elixir that he breathed.

We glided through the early morning traffic, and from the centre of the back seat I admired the masterful choreography of Gale's feet and hands as she operated the gas pedal, clutch, brake, and gears. Muscles rippled beneath the flesh of her bare brown arms and legs. True to the spirit of her name, she seemed to be dancing on the pedals. For someone like myself, who had trouble with just Drive and Reverse on an automatic, it was a most impressive display. Stan too seemed impressed. He hated what he called "motor cars" and had never driven one in his life. It was sometimes difficult even getting him into one. He had biked down to Gale's house from the post office after his four-to-eight shift, and his bicycle, with wheels removed, was now going along for a ride in the wagen with the volks.

As we had plenty of time to spare, we decided to stop on the way for coffee. Stan still hadn't eaten breakfast, so he took us to his favourite cafe, which he said served the best cappuccino in town. Gale, however, ordered camomile tea, as she didn't drink coffee; but she changed her mind and ordered a cafe au lait after Stan explained that Swiss Water Method decaff was the purest thing this side of the Alps. For breakfast Stan had no fewer than three bran muffins—what he called preventive medicine—and a cup of "skinny" cappuccino.

"Skim milk," he said, before we asked.

I ordered mine fat.

We were sitting at one end of a long pine table that had so many cigarette burns it looked like a pointillist painting. At the other end were two empty espresso cups and a pyramidal No Smoking sign. In the middle were coasters and ashtrays with pictures of flamenco dancers. On the walls were velvet paintings, posters, prints, souvenir plates, advertisements, movie marquees, bas relief sculpture, rugs, and puzzles—all devoted to the mythos of bullfighting. They depicted matadors in every noble and heroic pose and bulls in every stage of humiliation and defeat.

Although the cafe was cavernous, the space reserved for drinking coffee was actually very small, and was being encroached upon from all sides. There was a pool hall, an old-fashioned games arcade, and a dance floor with an old Rock-Ola. In addition to our table, there were about ten smaller ones, and a few more outdoors under an awning. A dusty unlit string of lights of a Christmas past, long past, ran along the colourless wall above the plate glass windows. A rubber plant, its sheen matted by dust, stood like a chastened child in a corner.

Even at this hour, there were more people in the entertainment enclaves than in the cafe proper. There was a lot of noise, and it was not easy to sustain a sensible conversation. Amidst the shouting and laughing, the *thwack* of billiard balls, the *blip-blip* and *flip-flip* from the games arcade, the hormonal angst of Paul Anka singing "Diana," and the 747 roar of the espresso machines, both Stan and Gale repeatedly reassured me that they were sorry to see me go, as if they were afraid that I hadn't heard.

"*We're* sorry to see you go," they kept saying; and I noted how easily and naturally they had adopted the conjugal "we," and how their lips in speaking it seemed to form a farewell kiss.

On the first morning after I arrived home, the mailman woke me early with a Special Delivery letter from Kate and Lydia.

They were in Greece. London had been wet and miserable, so they'd grabbed two cancelled seats on a one-week charter to the island of Mykonos. With the letter was a Polaroid snapshot of them posing with a creature Kate called "the Beeman," whose face and head, limbs and torso were entirely covered with bees. They were sitting at a table on the terrace of a taverna by the ocean. On the table were glasses of ouzo and plates of black olives and feta cheese. Dressed in shorts, halter tops, and white bandannas, their bodies pale and thin as filo pastry, they were squinting into the camera and grinning like fools. They looked like two sun-blinded creatures who had just awakened from an overlong hibernation. Just behind them, some squid and octopi were drying on a line; in the distance, a windmill tilted against a landscape of pristine white and blue. In the foreground, the eyes of the Beeman burned behind his dark and sinister mask.

P.S. to give you an idea of the elegant taste of this place the other
day, in company when I illustrated something by a quotation,
one of the company said with great simplicity, "Lord Mr
Haydon, you are full of *scraps*!"...
—B.R. Haydon, letter to John Keats

"You! hypocrite lecteur!—mon semblable,—mon frère!"
—T.S. Eliot, *The Waste Land*

SOCIAL WORK

The Wollenweiders brought their slippers with them, two
identical pairs of Hudson Bay sheepskins in the fold of Hilde
Wollenweider's huge burlap bag. In that tone of incipient
hysteria in which she nervously made small talk at parties, Hilde
told us that she used this bag for everything from a portmanteau
to a picnic basket.

Throughout the evening, Hermann, who was a geologist,
crossed and recrossed his legs, and in 2/4 time, tempo
geologico, tapped one shiny hide sole against the air and the
other in unison upon the hardwood floor as he described in
dreary and dreamlike detail his summer expedition to Portugal
on the trail of further evidence for his lifelong study of plate
tectonics and continental drift. Against the muted civilized din
of the dinner party, Hermann's foot tapping and measured
speech sounded like the solemn and timeless ticking of a
grandfather clock in a large and empty house.

One of his compatriots, a German weatherman named
Wegener, had proposed the theory of continental drift early in
the century, but as yet no one really understood the forces
underlying this convergence and divergence of great land
masses, this getting together and breaking apart, which had
been going on for hundreds of millions of years.

According to Hermann, a single supercontinent called

Pangaea had broken apart over 200 million years ago, and the separate continents were still drifting on huge plates of the earth's crust at the rate of about an inch a year. Pangaea had been the result of a convergence of the earth's land masses hundreds of millions of years earlier. Geologically speaking, at least, what God had joined together, He also rent asunder. Doubtless every pursuit had its occupational hazards, and geology was no exception. Dwelling for most of a lifetime on the slow facts of geological time had obviously done the trick on Hermann, to which fact the ponderous and oblivious pace of his interminable monologues bore painful witness.

The Wollenweiders were our neighbours, geographically speaking; we shared a street and the same green space. And because Anna and Gretchen attended the same school and had been classmates since kindergarten, Kate always invited Hilde and Hermann to our parties, infrequent though they were. They were much too frugal to have parties of their own, and rarely invited anyone to their house, though I had once been a guest at Hermann's squash club for the one and only squash game of my life. There I had literally felled him with my racket—or his racket, for he himself had lent me what was more or less a weapon in unathletic hands like mine—and as I helped him up off his knees, I heard him for the first time lapse into German—and what sounded like a very informal German at that. Ever the gentleman, Hermann Wollenweider, even in his anguish, had the courtesy to curse me in a foreign tongue.

Ruth came décolleté—a ruffled white taffeta with sequins as a backdrop for a perfect red tulip that she'd grown herself indoors from seeds ordered all the way from Holland. And she had taken to wearing her copper coils again, against doctor's orders. They were stacked from her collar bone to her chin, so that it permanently jutted out at you. Two small bunches of black ceramic grapes decorated her ears. On her face was the false smile of the socialite zealot—she was acting and having a wonderful time. Indeed, Ruth was so happy to be well again that she could hardly contain herself.

As our self-appointed performing hostess, she had completely taken over this Christmas dinner party—meeting guests at the door with that incredible smile, relieving them of their coats and their bottles of wine, showing them into the drawing room, introducing them to each other, and getting them their first drinks. Ruth felt that hosts never really enjoyed their own parties. There were just too many things to do. So she was relieving us of most of them and letting us relax.

Kate and I had prepared all the food well beforehand—a series of gourmet hors d'oeuvres and exotic mini-courses instead of a regular sit-down meal; and, as Ruth insisted on serving these as well, we were left simply to mingle with our friends—Kate's friends mostly, as it turned out—and chat. Unfortunately, this gave the loquacious bores and the conversationally challenged a field day. I had already been drawn into discussions of oak toilet seats, garborators, and oat bran, and had been given a complete consumer report on the new solid-disk electric ranges. I felt as if I'd stumbled onto the set of "Marketplace."

I was now listening to Maud the Beekeeper's ex-husband, Fred Bird, a stranger to me, casually drop details of his private life and tell me things I didn't want to know about cabinets. I was wondering if he was related to Mr. Bird of Bird's Family Restaurant fame.

"Fred's a cabinet maker," Kate had remarked offhandedly, throwing a conversational bare-bone between us and then casually strolling off, as was her way, carrying a tray of crab ramekins.

"So what kind of cabinets do you make?" I had innocently inquired.

I noticed for the first time that I had developed the habit of prefacing almost everything I said with "so"—a small air strip from which the tentative light planes of my conversational gambits took to the skies. I used it to change the subject, to get to the point, to turn the conversation back to something that had been left dangling—or simply to get my tongue working, to get a conversation underway. Formerly, I had restricted its use to the directly confrontational, as in *So?* or *So what!* But those had been my disputatious days. These days I hardly opened my mouth.

Fred Bird had become a recluse since the break-up of his marriage; he had that resigned and unkempt look that one usually associated with onlies and onliness. Like his ex-wife's bees, he was a workaholic, leaving the hive only to gather materials and supplies. And his solitary dialogues with wood, like Hermann's with rock, had seriously affected his conversational skills.

So, what kind of cabinets did he make? Not kitchen cabinets, not medicine cabinets, not filing cabinets—and certainly not commercial or industrial jobbies. No, nothing but exquisite, hand-crafted, hand-sanded, hand-oiled, one-of-a-kind, rare wood, objets d'art cabinets, with hand-carved friezes, scrollwork, and bas-relief tableaus. Which nobody wanted. For no one was willing or able to pay what he was asking, and few were even able to recognize their worth. So the cabinets were piling up and Fred was heavily in debt. He had started writing poetry.

"To help pay the bills," I said, trying to get a laugh out of him.

I was beginning to feel a little uneasy. Fred was a very serious man, and he was beginning to talk earnestly about his poems. He probably had them with him, in that hand-tanned calfskin pouch attached to his belt. In my unofficial capacity as Hypocrite Lecteur Emeritus, I could tell that I was about to be asked to read them.

Ruth was having trouble with the corkscrew, and I leaped to her aid.

"Excuse me just a second, Fred," I said.

I made a great show of examining the chromium corkscrew. I ran the ring up and down the spiral shaft several times and sized up the thread until I was almost cross-eyed. I rubbed it unnecessarily with a drop of Extra Virgin olive oil and ran the ring up and down the shaft again. It was amazing how much playing around you could do with this thing. Finally, I checked the cork in the wine bottle for dryness, emitted an audible mystified *uummm*, and plunged the sharp point of the corkscrew down into it.

Ruth had got bored watching me fiddling around and along with several others who had congregated in the kitchen had wandered off to other rooms. The kitchen had grown to the size of a barn and Fred Bird and I were all alone in it. He popped the question before I popped the cork.

"Maybe you'd like to have a look at them sometime."

"What's that?" I said, still working the corkscrew.

"My poems. Would you like to have a look at them?"

"Sure ... sure."

I cranked the corkscrew harder, and watched as its tiny arms rose through a time-lapse sequence in which the cruciform frame seemed to freeze. When they were raised in surrender, I grabbed them, forced them down to their sides, and heard a soft and satisfying pop. I lifted them again to reveal the cork and made a great pretense of examining it closely after unscrewing it from the shaft. Then I sniffed it almost carnally and laid it on the shelf. I peered down into the bottle and tried to get my little finger down there to remove some specks of cork. But Fred hadn't once taken his sad calf eyes off me. He was leaning back against the counter, holding his bottle of beer against his chest. I poured myself a glass of wine.

"I'll mail them in to you," he said, to my great relief. "I don't come into town that much."

"Maybe I'll pass them on to Kate's brother, Bill," I said. "He runs a little magazine called *news*."

He looked perplexed.

"'News that stays news,'" I added, quoting Uncle Ez.

Fred Bird sort of pecked at that; then a seed sprouted at one corner of his mouth, and a dandelion of a smile brightened the dark-set features of his face.

"Ezra Pound," he said, surprising both himself and me.

It struck me then that maybe I'd completely misjudged him—no hobbyist scrivener he, but a genuine artist who'd given up a safe place in the family's restaurant business; a true poet, perhaps, who had spoken only through wood, who had been working against the grain, so to speak, of his real inclinations, but who had now finally found his materials. I thought, What a cruel prejudging begrudging son-of-a-bitch you've become. That's what ten years of undergraduate English papers will do to you, not to mention the countless sheaves of juvenilia I had accepted as substitutes under the table in my vain attempts to encourage the more creative juveniles among them.

Every unfinished line in his sad face spoke, and a wave of empathy washed over me. Or perhaps it was just a lop from the Pouilly Fuiseé '79 I had just uncorked and which someone had quite generously contributed to this soiree, a glass of which, on top of several others of a rougher vintage, I had poured rather too quickly down my throat. But before I could throw open my welcoming arms and shout: "Bring me your artistes manqués, your weekend scriveners, your frustrated woodworkers, your poor post office poets" (someone had written a book on those, there'd been so many), I heard a huge commotion in the hallway—a crash, a heavy thump, and a great anguished roar.

I rushed out to discover my alcoholic ex-colleague, Bernie Oudette, and Kate's rotund legal acquaintance, D. Henley Arsenault, thrashing about on the floor in their overcoats like a pair of beached baby belugas. I noticed that both Bernie and Henley were wearing identical pairs of old-fashioned gaiters, which they were kicking furiously. Bernie had now got the upper hand and was on top of Henley and ... kissing him. Henley, for his part, was passionately resisting Bernie's rough amore and had grabbed two thumbs-up fistfuls of his lank grey hair, but to no avail. Bernie's arms were hooped around Henley's barrel-like torso, and his lips were stuck to his face like a barnacle.

They must have arrived together, unfortunately, but I knew there was no cause for alarm. This was just Bernie's way of breaking the ice at parties, of getting into the act, like a hockey player throwing his weight around in the early minutes of an important game. It was also his way of dealing with what he called "stiffs." Primly composed Henley could certainly be put in that category, but he had also unsuccessfully represented Bernie in a protracted divorce case, and maybe that was the real reason for Bernie's amorous assault.

Our guests had crowded into the hallway. Ruth was pulling on Bernie's gaiters and shouting at him. I restrained her and knelt down beside their beet-red faces.

"Henley, let go of his hair," I said.

"Get him off me, for Chrissake!" Henley sputtered, but would not let go.

"Bernie, let him go," I whispered into his ear. "Bernie, you're going to knock him up," I said. I could see him smiling into Henley's three chins.

He let me pull one of his arms loose, and Henley finally let go of his hair and pressed a protective palm against Bernie's forehead. I pulled Bernie to his feet, but he couldn't see a thing. His glasses were somewhere on the floor, but the plastic centrepiece had come loose and was embedded between his eyebrows.

"Jesus Christ, old man, you're a raving lunatic," Henley said, getting to his feet and trying to reconstruct his appearance. Bernie grinned blindly into Henley's face. Henley rubbed at a red blotch on the left side of his neck. I imagined him in court with a large purple hickey arguing a case in his blandly dispassionate tone.

"Your problem ... " Bernie said, faltering somewhat and blinking fiercely at him with the centrepiece of his eyeglasses still stuck between his eyes, looking like some enraged psychoanalyst who had finally reached the end of his tether with this patient and was going to go for broke, to risk it all, to do the unthinkable and hurl the horrible truth unearthed from the psychic murk right at him, spit the irritating bit of grit which he'd discovered at the heart of his pearly life right in his face,

"... your problem," Bernie repeated, more emphatically, but looking unexpectedly vulnerable without his glasses, "is that you can't even go camping without a hair dryer."

It was not the sort of remark that one readily had an answer for, even the polished and articulate Henley, with years of experience in the adversarial forums. I suddenly remembered that he and Bernie actually had gone camping together to discuss their case during a break in the trial. Perhaps it was simply to calm Bernie down. Henley just gave him a baleful look and kept on brushing and smoothing his clothes. Ruth handed Bernie his gray glass-bottom spectacles and smartly led him into the living room trailing a line of guests.

Exeunt with trainer and train.

Kate and Henley and I were left centre stage, and without any lines.

"I think I'd better leave," Henley said finally, directly to Kate, who had invited him.

"Oh, Henley, please don't," she pleaded, not really sincerely, I thought.

"I'm sorry about this, Henley," I said, but he ignored me.

"Marion couldn't come, as you know," he continued, "but she asked me to thank you all the same. She's eight months now and she feels a bit uncomfortable. I should go back and see how she's getting on."

In that large and oddly proportioned body of his, Henley had always looked pregnantly uncomfortable himself, like a seal out of water. The only time I had ever seen him at ease was in the courtroom, at Bernie's divorce trial. Bernie, at least, had always referred to it as a trial; Henley, more neutrally, as "proceedings."

The quixotic Bernie had contested his divorce, and had invited all his friends along for moral support. There, on the witness stand, Bernie had proceeded, as the judge remarked, in a "highly irregular" way—reciting no fewer than six Shakespearean love sonnets to his wife, Eunice ("the Dark Lady on our left, Milord"), to whom he was still fatally attached. After an evening's drinking, he would tell you all about it.

Throughout the recitation—even during the noble and moving "Fortune and men's eyes"—she had sat nonchalantly filing her nails, as if she had heard all this before. She was not asked to take the witness stand, did not, so Bernie told us, speak a word during the three-day trial, and did not, in fact, on the day that I was there, even raise her eyes to look at anyone in the room. Her lawyer, a short woman with close-cropped silver hair, stood by her side and presented Eunice's version of the cold cruel facts of her and Bernie's life together.

But though it seemed to be his natural element, Henley once told us that he avoided the courtroom whenever he could. He was the provincial art gallery's legal counsel—the "arts counsel," as he jokingly called himself. It was the only joke I had ever heard him make. He saw himself as a specialist in arts-related matters—obscenity charges, copyright claims, publishers' contracts; but, legal and political coward that he was, he had backed off when he had been faced with a really sticky case.

This had involved a complaint by an anonymous patron that led to the seizure by the Royal Newfoundland Constabulary of an "obscene" painting. But, as the work in question was in the gallery's permanent collection (though it had never before been displayed) and was therefore owned by the provincial government, Henley had advised against pursuing the matter as the government had, in his opinion, merely seized its own property. The curators (Kate included) had been opposed to this, for they felt that an important principle was at stake and they wanted to make a political point. In the end, however, Henley's purely legal view prevailed.

Kate continued to offer apologies to Henley as she followed him to the door. Back in the living room, Hermann Wollenweider's foot was still tectonically tapping. The lonely continents drifted on their tectonic plates through time—separating, converging, then diverging once again. In some places, Hermann said, the plates neither diverged nor converged, but simply ground continuously against one another, causing earthquakes.

I thought that I could hear a grinding going on right then and there. Beneath the civilized chatter of this dinner party, we were all desperately grinding our teeth; or perhaps it was only my own teeth that I was hearing; or Bernie's, who seemed to be moving his own plates around.

Think of tectonic plates as giant jigsaw puzzle pieces of the earth's crust, Hermann was saying; or as rafts, 60 miles thick, floating on a molten sea. Think of the continents as sailors timelessly adrift, or as sealers lost on giant ice floes.

I recalled a large black and white photograph that I had saved as a child, one of hundreds cut diligently out of old magazines. In it a man dressed entirely in black, wearing a black beret and holding a black umbrella, was floating on a solitary white ice pan in a still, black sea. Years later, coming upon this photograph again during my own sartorially black days, I was to discover that it was a picture of Jean-Paul Sartre, or perhaps some existential stunt man, a Sartre stand-in.

As Hermann droned on, this image of Jean-Paul Sartre existentially adrift on his solitary ice pan, bug-eyed lonesome, refused to leave my mind. I had obviously reached that pitiful point in the evening when I was starting to feel sorry for myself. I began to drift away on my own ice pan, and without even the hell of Jean-Paul's company.

Where were all my friends? I thought. Why had I let Kate talk me into throwing this silly social, this desperate diversion on a large scale, this joint conspiracy to keep us from being alone together? For Kate disliked parties as much as I did, her attitude toward them more like that of a moralist than a socialite.

"We owe it to them," she kept saying, laying out a social spreadsheet of credits and debits as rigorous as a moral account. We owe it to ourselves, I thought, to sit down together some evening before it's too late . . . but perhaps I already felt that it was too late, so I said nothing.

Your problem, I said, strictly to myself, is that you can sit here all night and listen to this crap—that in some strange way you find it comforting—instead of jumping up and rationally freaking out and shrieking some Bernieism into their faces. And what would I say at that fateful moment, my arms hooped around that quivering social mass, my wild eyes staring into their anxious faces? But at my back I always hear Time's winged chariot hurrying near? That would certainly get Dorcas back on my case.

Better to nod over my drink along with Bernie. Now that he had gotten the kinks out of his system, he was sitting quietly and listening to Hermann drift on and on. He would concentrate on drink now for the rest of the evening, and would stay on long after the others had gone. Then we would both sit quietly drinking in those late hours, chatting warmly about old times, as relaxed as watchmen listening to the late-night stations. Then he would pass out on the sofa and I would cover him with a blanket and in the morning Kate and I would wake and find him gone. Within a week I would be gone along with him.

Acting on the strength of my convictions, I transformed myself into a nightingale. Since neither the reason nor the resolve necessary for this sort of action lies within the realm of the ordinary, I think the story of this metamorphosis is worth telling.

—Wolfgang Hildesheimer,
"Why I Transformed Myself into a Nightingale"

"None of your magic nonsense here, mind! We want explanations. Who broke the guitar? And how? And why?"
"None of your scientific nonsense here ... None of your scientific nonsense, now! Just magic explanations!"
"Let's have a drink first ... Afterwards, I'll put you to sleep with a more or less coherent disquisition on the cutting, pricking, bruising, crushing, smashing uses of human language and perhaps of the language of birds, but let's have a drink first."

—Rene Daumal, *A Night of Serious Drinking*

PART III—*AMONG THE NIGHTINGALES*

And first, truly, to all them that professing learning inveigh against Poetry may justly be objected, that they go very near to ungratefulness, to seek to deface that which, in the noblest nations and languages that are known, hath been the first light-giver to ignorance, and first nurse, whose milk by little and little enabled them to feed afterwards of tougher knowledges.
—Philip Sidney, *An Apology for Poetry*

And surely, in the end, as we all know, poetry is one thing and life is another.
—Graham Swift, *Ever After*

THESE ARE OUR HORIZONS

There's nothing like a scent to bring back memories—a neuro-newsflash up the olfactory channel. In my shower-reverie on Christmas morning, the astringent antiseptic smell of Lifebuoy soap, pure carbolic acid, brought the image of Mr. Bungay's bulbous face—wholesome Lifebuoy shine and all—onto the blinding needlepoint dot matrix shower-screen. It flashed back across light years of the past like light from a dead but still bright star.

In my absence, Kate was using Lifebuoy again, a holdover from her childhood days. Knowing her weakness for "cold cream," I'd managed to supplant it with Camay. I even would have settled—then and now—for that scentless and latherless organic lump that she once brought back from the health food store. But though I could have done with a good penitential cleansing, I didn't want to be disinfected with pure coal tar.

Mr. Bungay, Grade VIII, English and religion, home room, All Souls Boys' School; Mr. Bungay, whom we all called "Bunga," after the African Pygmy yam digger of Grade IV geography fame; Mr. Bungay, religious fanatic, who had converted English and religion into one subject.

His *régime pédagogique* involved reading a poem to us from *These Are Our Horizons*—the book of lessons disguised as literature we were using that year—and then writing the title of the piece on the blackboard along with its theme or moral. I had a scribbler full of morals, which I was expected to memorize. Mr. Bungay dug for themes as diligently as Bunga dug for yams. Bending over our desks to check our themes, he smelled just like a Lifebuoy factory.

His head looked like an outsized bulb of garlic. His eyesight was poor, and he squinted a lot, but for some reason he never wore glasses and had to bend over our desks until his large nose was almost in contact with our scribblers to make sure our themes had been what he called "inscwibed." I never even knew what the word meant, let alone how perfectly appropriate it was. Scwibes we were, and not mere scwibblers, as we received the Laws of Life from Moses Bungay.

His readings were one part affected orations, another part fire and brimstone homilies, and a third part unintentional up-the-'arbour-and-down-the-shore parodies. He was a stand-up evangelical declaimer, an ersatz Dylan Thomas-in-tongues from Carbonear; and he orated, narrated, and berated us into a sort of resigned trance.

No one ever asked any questions; we never discussed the poems. He just told us what they meant, what the message was. Every poem had a theme, Mr. Bungay said, just like every life. "If you could be a poem," he once asked us, "which one would you be?" He would be "Invictus," he said. "Unconquered."

> *It matters not how strait the gate,*
> *How charged with punishments the scroll,*
> *I am the master of my fate:*
> *I am the captain of my soul,*

Mr. Bungay claimed and declaimed, thumping his chest. And the THEME ? "Life is hard. It will test your mettle. Don't give up." He underlined the "Don't give up," using the whole length of chalk to form a thick rhomboid line. He recited this poem whenever he had the chance; and he wrote the theme on the board after every recitation, always underlining the "Don't give up."

During one reading buck-toothed albino retard Norbert Neary let out a fart forte—*leripzzzzzrjam*—which literally lifted him up off his seat. Mr. Bungay began to club him on the head with his teacher's edition of *These Are Our Horizons*, a thicker version than our own, and kept right on reciting, not missing a beat.

> *I am the master of my fate;*
> *I am the captain of my soul,*

he repeated, drubbing poor Norbert iambically. He was the undisputed captain of all the souls at All Souls. I could see him now cheerleading the class with his pointer.

> *Life is hard;*
> *Don't give up;*
> *Rah,rah,rah;*
> *Go team go.*

Though I didn't know it at the time, he'd probably been trying to convince himself as much as us.

We heard "Invictus" almost as often as the Glorious, Joyful, and Sorrowful Mysteries of the Holy Rosary, which we recited in the morning before school began, before lunch, after lunch, and at the end of the day, down on our knees on the cracked hardwood floors with the sickly sweet smell of Dustbane in our nostrils. And he had a sharp eye for anyone trying to insert a soft moral-padded scribbler beneath his knees. He would bend down and pluck it out like an offending eye, telling the young miscreant to suffer the discomfort like a man for the suffering souls in Purgatory.

Sometimes he would dramatically interrupt our prayers to send one of us out to the water fountain in the hall to fill his teacup; but he would always call us back just as we reached the door, saying, "No, no, never mind, I'll bear the thirst for the poor suffering souls in Purgatory."

The souls in Purgatory never had it so good. All the suffering souls in Grade VIII certainly knew what they were going through. By the end of the year I was sure that our collective agony, combined with Mr. Bungay's hair-shirt histrionics, had earned every last one of them a place in what he called "That Greater Kingdom."

The poem I had always wanted to be was "Leisure," by poet-supertramp William Henry Davies. I had always pictured him as a sort of nineteenth century beatnik, a man a hundred years ahead of his time.

> *What is this life if, full of care,*
> *We have no time to stand and stare.*
>
> *No time to stand beneath the boughs*
> *And stare as long as sheep or cows.*

A world-weary philosopher even at thirteen, I spent most of my time away from school standing and staring up in one or another of several tree houses I'd built in the tall spruce woods not far from our house. I would listen to my mother calling me for supper, or to friends shouting for me to come down to the meadow to play baseball or football, but I wouldn't answer. I'd just stand and stare beneath the boughs like old Mr. Davies, listening to the birds singing and the wind sighing in the branches of the trees, breathing the sweet scent of evergreens, and pondering Mr. Bungay's THEMES.

Sometimes I would stay there till well after dark and risk getting a flick from the old man. I felt safe in the knowledge that I was loved and wanted, but what I wanted most of all was to be by myself. I was happiest when I knew that no one knew where I was.

> *So runs it in thy blood to choose*
> *For haunts the lonely pools, and keep*
> *In company with trees that weep.*

From William Henry's "Kingfisher," as I recall.

Undoubtedly, Dorcas would say that I was still up there, dreaming away, leaving the cares to someone else. And maybe she was right. Maybe at thirteen this lifeboy had already set in his mould. Perhaps even long before that. Maybe it does run in the blood to choose . . . to be whatever it is we end up being . . . and after childhood none of us change all that much. And some of us have to haunt the lonely pools and keep in company with trees for good.

But back then Mr. Bungay was leading the real lonely life—a gossip-plagued bachelor's existence, moving from one boarding house to the next. He carried a suitcase of peculiar habits and eccentricities, which made it hard for any family to take him for any length of time; a lasso wrapped around his shoulder, which he said would allow him to escape from any house in the event of fire, but which everyone else said he planned to hang himself with; and a whole trunkful of books and crucifixes. The crosses he insisted on hanging in every room in the house, including the bathroom. What vampires Mr. Bungay tried to keep at bay, none of us will ever know.

We got most of our gossip that year from Norbert Neary, whose mother ran the boarding house where Mr. Bungay stayed after Christmas. But only until the spring, when he'd been evicted once again, this time for persisting in his habit of trying to get the whole unholy Neary family—all eight of them—down on their hands and knees for an hour after supper to recite all fifteen decades of the Holy Rosary, the very hour of Don Jamieson's "News Cavalcade," a show Mrs. Neary had watched religiously since it came on the air in 1955. Television itself had come on the air only a couple of years earlier.

If Mr. Jamieson had got his way, Mrs. Neary had once told my mother, we'd have had TV long before that. As it was, she was the first person in the neighbourhood to have a TV set; it had been sent to her from Boston by one of her brothers.

In the 1950s and 1960s Don Jamieson was the undisputed

don of Newfoundland TV news anchormen; and though he was but a grey and ghostly graven image in those early days of TV transmission, being regularly denied the opportunity to worship at the flickering feet of her idol proved to be too much for Mrs. Neary, and she exploded hysterically one evening in the middle of one of the Glorious Mysteries and ordered Mr. Bungay out of the house.

During the Confederation debates and referendums of the late 1940s, the smooth-talking young broadcaster Don Jamieson had sowed his political wild oats by advocating the idea of union with the United States, a third and not unpopular alternative to political independence or confederation with Canada. The idea seemed eminently sensible to Mrs. Neary, for most of her brothers and sisters (and, some said, her wayward husband) had left Newfoundland long ago for what she called the "Boston States"; and there, she was fond of telling her boarders and everyone else she came in contact with, they had been watching television since the 1930s.

Though Mrs. Neary had little interest in politics, and probably thought of union with the United States more in terms of a family reunion than anything else, if she had campaigned for Mr. Jamieson she would have offered the voters a TV in every living room instead of a chicken in every pot. She seemed to regard it as some sort of talisman, a harbinger of great things to come; and, with a certain prescience, she seemed to know instinctively that in most people's minds TV would become inextricably bound up with the whole idea of America and the Good Life, a kind of holy or unholy trinity, depending on how you looked at it.

In retrospect, the way I looked at it was that the military bases that the Americans established all over Newfoundland in the 1940s were nothing compared to the television bases that appeared in the '50s, '60s, and '70s. What American comics, magazines, and movies had started, television would relentlessly finish. It was a second colonization, ubiquitous this time, and much faster and even more deadly than the first. It was

Entertainment America Inc., and we would be turned into dazed and vacant blobs. Though we had joined Canada in 1949, our minds and souls would forever belong to the States.

Reports that Mr. Bungay had finally used his rope to take his life rather than to save it reached me every now and then even after my university years; but, as I found out for myself one cold winter morning, the reports of his death—to borrow a quip from Twain—were just an exaggeration.

I was driving to work up Military Road around eight o'clock. As I rounded the Basilica, about to turn up Bonaventure Avenue, there he was coming straight towards me on the crosswalk in the early morning slush. Heading for early Mass at the Basilica, no doubt.

I braked to a quick stop, and, as he walked past, he actually tipped his hat and gave me a crazy sideways grin—though I seriously doubted that he had recognized me. He was dressed in an old fur hat with bald spots like craters, a ratty beige raglan, and mud rubbers—sans shoes. Inside the shallow rubbers he wore a pair of grey work socks, and inside these he had tucked his red-striped pajamas.

It was the sort of miserable sight that would make any errant spouse disregard even irreconcilable differences and keep him at home and hearth forever.

The host with someone indistinct
Converses at the door apart,
The nightingales are singing near
The Convent of the Sacred Heart. . . .
—T.S. Eliot, "Sweeney Among the Nightingales"

Is she kind as she is fair?
For beauty lives with kindness.
Love doth to her eyes repair,
To help him of his blindness,
And, being help'd, inhabits there.
—Shakespeare, "Who Is Silvia?"

NEW MAN WITH OLD BLUE GUITAR

By late afternoon I'd already drunk three or four unmeasured Glenfiddiches on an empty stomach and was resigned to spending Christmas Day with Mr. Bungay and other ghosts of Christmas past. There was not even a poor old mother to visit this year; she was in Vancouver spending Christmas with Ruth. I had given her Stan's and Gale's phone number and address. Perhaps by now they had the same one and Ruth would take her over for a visit.

Among my friends, Stan had been Mother's favourite. He had always been able to make her laugh, something I had not been inclined to do. She liked his hearty good nature—in this he was a lot like Ruth—much in contrast to the reserve and politeness characteristic of most of the friends I brought home. Not that Stan wasn't polite. But he could put away a salt herring, two large plates of fish and brewis, two helpings of rhubarb pie and ice cream, three cups of tea—and still be polite. It made Mother happy to see someone really eat what she cooked. She had often lamented the fact that we were a family of pickers.

I was vaguely considering what remaining crusts of bread and rinds of cheese I might assemble for a traditional ploughman's Christmas dinner, when who should appear at the door but our friend Sylvie—Our Lady of Perpetual Help, of the House of Sylvia and Byron, with the long raven hair and perpetually astonished, but sorrowful, eyes. I'd forgotten all about the note Kate had left for her on the kitchen table. She had come to nourish Miro, but there was still a mound of dry cat food in the brown dishpan, and the stainless steel bowl was filled to the brim with water. Miro preferred to wet his whiskers at the toilet bowl.

I was sitting at the kitchen table in the dark, looking out through the window at the bunches of berries still hanging on the dogberry tree, when I heard the key turn in the front door. From the table I could see straight down the hall, and I watched Sylvie turn on the light, sit on the landing of the stairway, and unlace the pointed fairy boots that barely covered her ankles. Then she stood up to remove her scarf and ankle-length coat, revealing that tall lissome shape, that long lovely body, that was always clad entirely in black, a body that I confess I had once lusted after, though Sylvie clearly saw me as a living example of that post-modern manifestation of the Zeitgeist known as "the New Man," and beyond such basic and victimizing things as lust.

And though her spirit had been trammeled at a tender age, Sylvie too had been moved by the spirit of the times. She worshipped Kate and saw her as the very template of the New Woman, whose coming had been foretold by Rilke when the century was but a few years old. The emergence of this "womanly person," according to Rilke, would transform the relationship between the sexes and would, in fact, transform love itself. This New Love would be a meeting of "two solitudes," who would "protect and limit and greet each other." But the trouble began, it seemed to me, when these two solitudes began living under one roof.

Having lived with me for ten years, Kate, for her part—and just as clearly—did not see me as a template for the New Man; and though this sensitive and caring creature had been well documented in the sociological literature, and sightings had been widely reported in the popular press, I think she felt that, when all was said and done, he might well turn out to be the sociological equivalent of the Piltdown man.

But my feeling for Sylvie was not sexual, really—it was just the way she looked at me with those dark dolorous eyes; though I knew that she looked at the whole world that way.

Sylvie and I, however, had vicariously partaken of lust and its uproarious satisfaction on the night we first met—thanks to the uninhibited couple in the third-floor apartment of the house she and Byron had just moved into. She had been taking painting lessons from Kate at MUN Extension in the evenings—Byron, who was an artist himself, had told her she had talent—and had invited us over to their place one Saturday for supper. They had rented the second-floor apartment of an old run-down house on Military Road that had three apartments joined by an open stairway.

The upstairs couple's passionate moans and groans garnished our aperitifs and our hot hors d'oeuvre, and this joyful noise continued all the way through our entrée of tandoori chicken and basmati rice. It punctured our struggling speech balloons. At one point, an actual orgasm seemed to be in progress, but if *longevity* could be used to describe an orgasm, then this was the one. Even with the hall doors closed, the sounds seemed so loud and close that it felt as if we were sitting round their bed instead of at our beds of rice. When Byron, who had a low-key sense of humour that was seldom evident in his work, surmised that it must be the low cloud cover, he finally released our pent-up hilarity. Coffee cups and dessert plates in hand, we all got up laughing from the dinner table and followed him out onto the balcony where Sylvie told me about her life and Byron told Kate about his art. As the balcony was very small, I found myself listening to both.

"Anyway, it sure helped break the ice," Byron said as we were leaving. "It feels like we been socializing for years. And his name is Randy Dicks, I kid you not." He shook his head. "Randy and Delores. Put that in a book and who would believe it."

About six months later Byron tried to put them, and a replica of their bedroom, in a gallery. "Sex in Public," he called the show, and Randy and Delores had agreed to go on, but no gallery owner in town would risk it. Byron planned to construct a doorless, windowless bedroom with no ceiling, which visitors to the gallery could preview during the day. In the evening Randy and Delores would enter the bedroom through a basement hatch. Then Randy would enter Delores. Two-hour performances, thrice weekly. Adults only. No cover charge. Byron felt that we were all too hung up about sex.

Sylvie Mercer had spent about half her young life in an orphanage. When she was six, she and her younger sister had been abandoned, first by their mother, who left her alcoholic husband and simply disappeared, and then by their father, who perhaps decided that he couldn't look after the children. Or maybe the authorities had deemed him unfit and taken them away. Whatever the reason, Sylvie had never seen her mother or her father again. And Fate, in its sometimes unmerciful and ironic way, had passed her on from one mother inferior to another, the last one cleverly disguised as a Mother Superior of the Sisters of the Sacred Heart. Among the many acts of motherly love Sylvie could recall, the worst had occurred at the age of fourteen when this heartless mother had had her head shaved for touching a boy from the neighbouring school through the orphanage's high chain-link fence.

All of this was still there in Sylvie's sorrowful eyes, which nonetheless mirrored an astonished kind of light that other eyes never seemed to catch; but they also reflected a tearful fragility that both drew you to her and, at the same time, made you keep your distance. Oddly enough, it was Sylvie who had once remarked, in her offhand poetic way, that she had always thought of *me* as a "blue man." She was in my arms at the time, and she was trying to make light of the fact that we were dancing to a blues band at my wedding.

There's a long story behind that, but who wants to hear it? It's like a rumour about someone that you want to believe is true; that you don't want to hear anyone earnestly discount; that is somehow more fundamentally true, even if false, than any parading fact; that should be true, even if it isn't. So I won't bore you with explanations.

Ah, what the hell, I'll tell you anyway.

Dorcas the meddling mother-in-law, and the most unmusical person I've ever known, but, as we've already seen, a hyperactive member of the St. John's Symphony Guild, decided that it was her job to book a band—or an orchestra, as she called it—for her daughter's wedding and hired the number one schmaltz group in town. Fortunately, however, they cancelled at the last minute, had an "overriding commitment," and we were left to sweep up with a band called Dust My Broom. A little downbeat, maybe, but that's the blues. And the lads could play it—I even strummed along with them on "The Thrill Is Gone." But let's not read too much into that.

Kate didn't mind this mix-up at all; she wanted a very informal affair. But it got things off on the wrong foot for Dorcas and me, and we never did learn the steps of the dance we had to do.

"Hi," I called to Sylvie out of the half-dark kitchen, and she jumped and let out a squeal and pulled open the front door.

"Sylvie, it's me," I said, standing up so she could see me.

She stood with one foot in the porch below the threshold and the other on the hall carpet. She held the doorknob as if poised to slam the door.

"Sylvie, it's Will," I said, and turned on the kitchen light.

"Jeezz, Will, what are you doing here?" she said.

"Home for Christmas—'I'll be home for Christmas,'" I crooned, and gave her a hall-length grin. I was feeling a bit giddy-headed for sure. This made her relax somewhat, but she still didn't come in out of the porch.

"You scared the daylights out of me," she said. "I thought you were living downtown."

"I am," I said, still grinning like a fool.

She finally came back in and closed the front door. I walked out to greet her. Her eyes looked even wider and more amazed than usual. They shone coal black in the dim hall light. She ran both hands through her long wavy hair, then shook it and ran them through again. God, she was beautiful. I'd forgotten just how beautiful she was.

"You scared me," she said again. "There was a rape just last week, over in the park. It wasn't even reported in the papers. Kate asked me to come by and check on the house and make sure the cat had enough food. She asked Bill too, but you know what he's like."

"I was talking to Bill ... and I saw the note. Everything's okay. Come on in and I'll make you a Christmas drink."

"Are you ... ? I mean ... Kate didn't ... "

"No, no ... I just wanted some peace and quiet. I can't get any sleep in the place I'm living in. I've been here a few days. Come on in and sit down. I haven't seen you for so long."

"No, I can't, really, Will. I told Byron I'd be back in ten minutes. He worries about me walking around after dark."

"Ahh, he won't even know you're gone. I bet he's down in the workshop right now, even on Christmas Day, buried in something or other."

"He is, actually. He's got an opening right after New Year's. And he's only got about half the work done."

Byron worked in Styrofoam and papier-mache—on a large scale. He had once installed a seal hunt in all four rooms of the provincial gallery. The papier-mache hunters, holding real gaffs, and the Styrofoam seals and ice had all been splattered with real seal blood. The installation was complemented by actual sounds of the hunt—gaffings and clubbings; squeals, shouts, and barks; boots scrunching on ice. Bloody flippers and ugly hunks of seal carcass hung in airtight plastic bags on the walls.

Byron's notion of Art was that nothing should be left to the imagination—and not just the viewer's. In his view, artists who nattered on about *The Imagination* were just trying to hide the fact that they didn't know what they were doing. In my view, what was wrong with Byron's work was that not only Byron but everyone else knew exactly what he was doing, and many of us were wont to wonder why he was doing it.

If it had been possible, I'm sure he would have installed "The Hunt" in a freezer compartment, where he would have been able to use real ice, where visitors would have suffered some of the same privations as the sealers. Perhaps he should have gone all the way and installed his viewers on a sealing ship and packed them off to the ice and saved himself a lot of time and trouble. There were some, and perhaps I was among them, who would have liked to install Byron ... but never mind. We liked Byron—he was driven, and we wanted him to succeed; but he had succeeded only in driving us to detraction.

"What's he working on now?" I reluctantly asked Sylvie.

"Two shows, actually," she said. "One's called 'The Barbershop Quartet.' He's reconstructing the four oldest barbershops in town—papier-mache and knotty pine. Three of them are gone now, so it's mostly from memory, and from a lot of photos that he took years ago. He doesn't like to work that way. He's going to use a carpet of real hair on the floors that he's collected from barbershops all over town, and the owner of the only shop left open, who's almost 80, is going to cut Byron's hair at the opening."

"Wow," I said.

"He's also reconstructing the smallest taxi stand in town. Cabot Cabs. Have you ever noticed how tiny they all are? The lots are small enough—but the teeny little houses they wait in! He's building it in that little gallery on the waterfront. People will actually be able to dispatch a cab—he's going to install all the electronic stuff. There'll be one waiting outside the door every day."

"Wow," I said again, and thought that maybe Byron should be driving it—and not just to complete the artistic picture. If you're going to drive a cab, artistically speaking, you might as well get paid for it. All Byron needed to do, it seemed to me, was set his meter running.

"So what've *you* been up to?" I asked. We were still standing in the hallway. "I haven't seen you since our party last year."

"Oh, you know, looking after Sam mostly. He's in Kindergarten this year. And I've been spending a lot more time at the Light. They've given me a part-time job."

Sylvie had a degree in Social Work. She had given up her government job when Sam was born, but she had continued her volunteer work at the Harbour Light, the Salvation Army's rehabilitation centre downtown. Over her office door, instead of the Army's shield and motto, "Blood and Fire," I imagined a heart-shaped plaque, a tole painting, perhaps, with Keats's famous line: "I am certain of nothing but the holiness of the heart's affections and the truth of imagination"—or at least the first part of it; for the Harbour Light was the sort of ideally realistic place that Byron might one day get a notion to do.

I imagined them with an outreach program for adrift and despairing husbands and wives, with Sylvie as their most conscientious field worker, their warmest, wisest and holiest heart, out in the field now even on Christmas Day, to comfort, nurture and console. But she wanted to make sure I really needed her help.

"Come on in and have that drink," I said, for the third time.

"Okay, but just a smallish one," she agreed, and I motioned her ahead of me into the kitchen. Her long black hair fell in curly locks almost to her waist. As it trailed past, the hall lamp timer switch clicked on and the light struck it like a small flash of lightning. I thought, Christ, this is the hair that has been foretold. *Oh where are you going with your love-locks flowing?* She sat down at the kitchen table and watched me as I poured her a drink. I was careful to make it a smallish one. She lit a cigarette, then passed the pack to me.

"You look so different," she said. "You've grown a beard."
I felt my face and raised my eyebrows as if I hadn't known
it was there. It felt as dry and stiff as a wire brush.

I turned off the harsh overhead light and turned on the
small reading lamp attached to the cookbook shelf. I sat down
and poured a largish drink for myself. I was feeling sort of
lightheaded and unsteady. An hour or so earlier I had been
really hungry, but I had gone beyond hunger to a feeling of
hollow fullness.

Across the table Sylvie was playing with her cascading curls,
pulling them straight and letting them spring back into shape.
This was not a frizz or a perm, but a natural feature that many
women these days spent long hours in the salons trying to
duplicate. She began to wax nostalgic about Kate and me, how
our sudden separation had broken her heart and pulled the rug
right out from under her.

"Not so much the *perfect* relationship," she was saying,
pouting the word at me like a bubble or a mock-kiss, "not so
much a model, but we really thought you guys had it all
together. You were . . ." She was struggling to find just the right
word. "I think you were a *consolation* for the rest of us."

Sylvie not so much pronounced the word as exhaled it,
breathed it rather than spoke it. It was the way I had always
heard it in my head. And there was the bond between Sylvie
and me—we lived not by our deeds, our loves, or even our
desires, but by the cold blue flames of our consolations. We lit
a cigarette every time we wanted to touch someone.

One summer day, just before Anna was born, Kate and I had
walked with Sylvie through the leafy lanes and parklike
grounds of what once had been the caged compound of the
Sacred Heart Orphanage, the old stone buildings now converted to offices. On that day she had relived the pain and
humiliation of her lost childhood, describing the cruelties of
her warders as tears streamed from her dark eyes. The brief
Newfoundland summer was at its height, and Sylvie's sorrowful

memories filled our green cup of sadness to overflowing. A late afternoon breeze stirred the leaves and branches of the tall trees, carrying on it the distant echoes of children's voices.

Kate, who was eight months pregnant at the time, and who often cried seemingly for no reason whatsoever, sat on a bench with her arms around Sylvie and tears streaming down both their faces. It would have been impossible for a passer-by to tell who was consoling who. I leaned self-consciously against a tree wondering why no dark cold day of February or grey rainy November afternoon ever stirred in me the kind of sadness and longing I sometimes felt on a summer afternoon watching the aspens shimmering and trembling in the breeze and the yellow bells of the laburnum silently tolling.

I got up from my chair and stood beside Sylvie. She looked up at me and I touched her cheek. I leaned over, rather unsteadily, and gave her a fatherly kiss on the forehead. I kissed her hair, the beautiful black hair that had once been mercilessly shaved from her head. She placed her long fingers around my wrist and rested her face in my palm. Her large eyes shone like dark moons in the half-light of the kitchen and seemed to be in orbit around her tilted head. She stood up, put her two hands upon my chest and laid her head upon them.

I put my arms around her, and something began to well up in me, something I had always wanted to say to her and had never had the chance. But, quite unexpectedly, she said, "Will, what happened with you and Kate?" and before I had time to recover and offer some vague half-truth, Sylvie's body began to shake and she started to cry. As I held her close, her hands and head still pressed against my chest, I felt tears fill my own eyes. Now it was Sylvie and me on the bench beneath the laburnum, with Kate watching us from the shadows; or perhaps just strolling past, a stranger now, a passer-by, noticing two other strangers crying.

The reading lamp flickered in the dark glass of the kitchen window. Through the glass, high above the reflected light, I could still see the silhouetted clusters of berries on the crown of the dogberry tree: sustenance for the birds that had stayed behind and a conspicuous source of food for those rare bewildered exotic visitors that sometimes got blown off course on their way to more hospitable climes. Through Sylvie's blouse the thin sharp bones of her shoulder blades felt like the wings of some small frail bird, left behind in a cold but familiar country.

After Sylvie left, I ordered a pizza. It was hard to get away from bread and cheese. Delivery within 12 minutes—faster than the police, an ambulance, or the fire brigade; certainly faster than the plumber, the furnace man, or the telephone repair man. Market forces, as they say; it was a race to get to your door. Pizza peddlers were proliferating, growing ten times faster than the general population; faster even than weed men, yard men, and lawn doctors, who over the past few years had multiplied even faster than their number one enemy, the dandelion.

I browsed through the Yellow Pages. Besides Gino's 12-Minute Pizza, there was Miranda's Half-Price, No-Name 2-4-1, and Pizza Pete's 3 for 2; Pizza Experts, Pros, and Pals; Pizza Supreme, Delight, Deluxe, Perfecto; Tower of Pizza, Pizza Hut; Venice, Roma, and Napoli Pizzeria; Pavarotti Pizza—did Pavarotti's impresario know about this? Delivery men in tuxes singing " 'O sole mio!" perhaps, with glass-covered gourmet pizzas on miracle-metal hot platters.

Dorcas had actually spoken to Pavarotti's impresario on the phone in a vain attempt to lure Pavarotti to St. John's for a ballpark concert. The symphony crowd had been quite impressed with the turnout for the Pope, who had conducted a ballpark Mass the year before, but had abandoned the idea after getting a ballpark figure for Pavarotti's performance fee.

I abandoned the idea of a Pavarotti Pizza. I might have enjoyed being sung to, but I was starving to death. I chose the 12-Minute Pizza, jumbo, all-dressed: pepperoni, salami, ham, bacon, and Italian sausage; green and red pepper; green and black olives; cheese, onion, tomato, mushroom, pineapple, and anchovies ... I asked for it all. I might miss the turkey, but I'd get my share of dressing. I ordered the 14-inch garlic fingers on the side, though I wasn't really sure what they were. I was in a festive mood. Seeing Sylvie, strangely enough, had raised my spirits, or perhaps it was just the multiple Glenfiddiches.

The pizza clerk sounded suspicious. I felt like Scrooge giddily negotiating with the young lad on Christmas morning to go and buy the giant turkey hanging in the window of the butcher shop for Bob Cratchit's family. He took my name, address, and telephone number. He enunciated the price, then told me I wouldn't have to pay it if the pizza was late. He even gave me the correct time before he hung up. I imagined a throbbing Formula One waiting outside the door, a helmeted delivery man already at the wheel.

He arrived in *ten* minutes driving an old Volkswagen Bug. It was the pastry chef-taxi driver with the perfectly cold hands who had driven me to Mother's apartment last Christmas. He was wearing the same black watch cap, greatcoat, and dark glasses. For a moment I couldn't believe my bleary eyes. As Byron said about Randy Dicks: Put that in a book and who would believe it.

"No anchovies" was all he said when I opened the door. He removed the pizza box from its insulated wrap.

"That's all right," I said. "I don't really like them anyway."

I looked at the receipt taped to the top of the box, and I gave him my last twenty dollar bill. He made no motion to look for change, just looked at me with eyes that I was unable to see. I wondered if he recognized me, and why his cold-handed expertise was not being used on the production end of the operation.

"That's okay," I said, and he raised the bill and tipped his head toward it.

"Merry Christmas," we said in unison, and smiled, two strangers who had met again, two Christmases in a row, brought together by market forces, with not a lot to say.

How many wretched Bards address *thy* name,
And Hers, the full-orb'd Queen that shines above.
But I *do* hear thee, and the high bough mark,
Within whose mild moon-mellow'd foliage hid
Thou warblest sad thy pity-pleading strains.
O! I have listen'd, till my working soul,
Waked by those strains to thousand phantasies,
Absorb'd hath ceas'd to listen!
   —Coleridge, "To the Nightingale"

Poetry must work out its own salvation in a man.
—Keats, *Letters*

THE LANGUAGE OF BIRDS

Around noon on Boxing Day I found myself in the windowless basement of the Topsail Plaza. I was sitting in an indoor field of stylized chanterelles—orange brown, mushroom-shaped stools and tables—sipping black coffee from a Styrofoam cup festooned with holly leaves and berries. I was the only customer, and Mr. Coffee was one of the few shops open in the Food Court, a semi-circle of ubiquitous burger and pullet take-outs whose overly festive facades seemed only to add to the dreariness of the place. On top of my moulded plastic mushroom table sat an inedible bran muffin that was a mirror-image of its host. I had walked here all the way from Mooney Terrace, where, on Bill's invitation, I had tried to pay my one and only Christmas visit; but it appeared that Bill and Dona were still not up.

Every fall before Anna was born Kate and I used to look for chanterelles on our walks along the Gallows Cove trail in Logy Bay. Besides the psilocybin Magic Mushroom, for which Anna was to become a more than adequate substitute, the chanterelle was the only edible fungus we really knew how to identify. We were always on the lookout, however, for a rare gourmet mushroom, the morel, which a friend had once described in detail; but we soon gave that up when we found out that there was a poisonous look-alike called the false morel.

Like birds that came back to the same nesting sites each spring, we returned to the same spots every fall. Beneath the spindly misshapen branches of some aging spruce, we harvested our secret crop of chanterelles. And as soon as we got home we would wash them in a large stainless steel bowl and slice them and fry them up with onions in a well-seasoned cast iron pan. In another pan I would prepare a pizza-size omelette—or "momelette," as Anna was later to christen it, charmingly and innocently typecasting her mother. Kate, however, didn't like to cook at all, ate raw food whenever she could, and would probably revert totally to stalking and gathering wild fungi, roots, herbs, and berries given the opportunity.

Into the Food Court rolled a small detail of dedicated consumers pushing shopping carts and baby carriages overflowing with Boxing Day bargains. One toddler had been displaced from her carriage by nothing less than a TV set. She followed gamely behind it, one pale plum of a fist clasping the drooping pink canopy, which was filled with plastic bags of bargains. More bags were stuffed into the seat around the TV, and tall tubes of Christmas wrapping, like multiple antennae, shot up in all directions behind it. Her mother carried several more purchases, along with a multicolored snowsuit and a brocade bag. Slowly they made their weary way to the fast food counters.

When Anna was a toddler, Kate and I took her out here one winter afternoon to show her the fountain. The water shot up past the railing on the second level; but that day it had been turned off for maintenance, and there wasn't even a puddle for her to throw a coin in and make a wish. There was just a thin rivulet winding its way through the silt. Anna, however, had got inside the brick enclosure to play with the coins and debris scattered on the floor.

About a week after that, around eleven in the morning, the skylight above the fountain had collapsed under the weight of a thick crust of silver thaw, sending an avalanche of glass, snow, and ice down upon the fountain, the stairs, the escalators, and the few shoppers who happened to be about at that time of the day. No one had been seriously hurt and, after the usual investigation, the building had been declared structurally sound. But Kate had refused to take Anna out there again.

This was a different kind of sick building, according to Kate. For some unknown reason it had a permanent tremor, perhaps due to a constructional flaw—an undiagnosed congenital defect. We had noticed it before, but like everyone else had paid it no mind. You could feel it through your feet as you walked around the second floor.

The fountain was off again today, and it had a desolate look, as if it had been defunct for years. The sparsely scattered coins were hardly visible beneath a dry reddish brown silt; in places, a yellowish green algae was forming. A bedraggled bagman, with no less than three gloomy-looking garbage bags at his feet, was sitting on the fountain wall reading a paperback called *Night Fighter*. He lifted his chin to scratch underneath it every now and then and, as he did so, he moved his head ticlike to take conspicuously casual glances over his shoulder at the coins on the fountain floor. With an enormous curly grey beard, a puffy red face, and a nondescript faded brown overcoat that blended with the silted floor of the fountain, he looked like a Santa Claus for existentialists.

Before leaving the Food Court, I went over to look at Mr. Coffee's Christmas display. With a small scoop I filled a red paper sack with a mixture of Viennese, Columbian, and Jamaican coffee beans—a Christmas gift for Bill and Dona. I poured the beans into the coffee grinder and set it on Fine. As I waited for the paper sack to fill with coffee, I felt someone breathing heavily behind me. I turned and looked into the eyes of a man whose Christmas spirit had obviously long since departed, and who had me set on Extra Fine, if not Espresso, as he waited impatiently for me to finish.

It took me a long while to find my way back to Mooney Terrace. The day was cold and clear, with a hard blue sky. A fine dusting of snow lay on the pale frozen grass along the sidewalks, untouched by the weak sun that hung close to the horizon.

There had been no distinguishing features, no landmarks, to etch themselves on my memory during the ride there in the cab, or on my meandering walk downhill to the mall. On my way back I went astray in a maze of row houses in bad repair, with surly Trans Ams and rusting Pintos and Chevettes parked in oil-stained driveways. The scrapped remains of other cars sat on blocks or lay grounded in the frozen dirt behind them. In front of one house, in rabid defiance of the Upholstered and Stuffed Articles Act, an orange sofa was turned upside down on the grass, its shredded foam stuffing ripped out and strewn halfway up the street. In tiny treeless backyards crouched all manner of abused, broken, and discarded things: wheelless box campers with tattered flapping tarpaulins, rusting oil drums, charred dismantled barbecues, handmade swings with tires attached to fraying ropes, torn mattresses with their coils sticking out. There wasn't a soul in sight, and though it was early afternoon, most of the curtains were still drawn. It was as if some disaster had just occurred; a smoking oil drum was the only sign of life.

I followed a road that wound steadily uphill to a newer development of look-alike bungalows with lawns of frozen mud. There wasn't a tree, or even a shrub, anywhere to be seen. I found Mooney Terrace almost at the top of the hill, an arc of larger bungalows and two-storey houses with two-car garages, flagstone walks and driveways, and pale lawns with small trees wrapped in brin bags and maple saplings guy-wired to the ground.

In the basement apartment of number eleven, a back-split with a front, rear and side entrance and a shameless view of the whole sorry suburban sprawl, Bill and Dona were about to sit down to an anthill-size mound of French toast coated with the largest oat flakes I'd ever seen. I saw no point in telling them that I'd come by earlier. From a large cassette player on top of a gleaming pine bookshelf came the sound of bird-song and a feathery formal voice announcing the names of the singers.

"The chipping sparrow," said the voice, and then, right on cue, came "*chip chip chip chip.*"

"A present from Ruth," Bill said. "There's a book along with it. A nice change from all that Christmas twittering in the air."

There was, in fact, a dearth of all signs of the season in Bill and Dona's apartment, at least in the dinette and the large living room, which Bill was obviously using as office space. There wasn't even a Christmas card on display, as far as I could see.

It was a very roomy place, as basement apartments go, but no flat surface was left uncovered. There was a dizzying disarray of books, magazines, newspapers, opened and unopened letters and bills, personal letters on display for all to see, stacks of army green file folders, and large manila envelopes filled with submissions to *news.*

Three white boxes with WRETCHED/OUT scrawled on their sides were stacked against a wall next to a drawerless pine desk with a black goose-neck lamp clamped to the top. Above it was a bulletin board with so many overlapping sheets of paper pinned to it that it resembled the ruffed chest of some great white bird. Alongside the desk stood a presentation easel and a huge writing pad with about half the pages draped over the top. It straddled a small stack of manuscripts with a yellow slip of paper taped on top, which said, emphatically, YES YES YES ... *and yes I said yes I will Yes.* Beneath this slip were the few favoured slips, the unrejected slips, clipped from the great proliferating plant whose tendrils worked their way through the mails to Bill's post office box, a plant he had tended half his adult life. But perhaps these were the last few slips that he would plant.

"The black-capped chickadee ... *phoebe phoebe phoebe.*"

Bill did most of his magazine work at the easel, but this was not just an affectation of his. He had problems with his circulation and could not write sitting down for very long. First his toes went numb, then his feet and legs; even his arse froze, he claimed, if he sat there long enough. He said he had to save his legs for his real work. Standing at the easel, he would nod his head continuously and lift his feet up and down like a tethered horse. I had spent a fair bit of time with him over the years slogging through submissions. He liked to use me, and other friends, as a sounding board, which was as close as he wanted to get to an editorial board.

Close to another wall were two identical love seats covered with sheepskins. A coffee table laden with more manuscripts sat between them. The walls were beige and bare, except for a single god's-eye watching from above a bookcase; but, as Bill once said to me in another apartment of his, where this same woolen icon dangled in lonely decorative splendour over his bed, one god's-eye was enough.

Scattered throughout the living room were small oases of potted plants set on top of round wicker tables and wooden kegs. They seemed huddled together, as if under siege, though they looked remarkably green and healthy. The carpeted floor was hardly visible; here and there patches of rusty brown showed through, and the overall effect was of some dormant brindled beast.

A beast was indeed what Bill's magazine had become. It had taken over not only his apartment but his entire life, literary and otherwise. Leaning stacks of back issues, going back ten years or more, were piled against every wall.

"The mourning warbler. . . .*chory chory chory chory.*"

Thanks to Dona's parents, who owned the house but now lived in Florida, she and Bill had the apartment rent free for ten months of the year. Dona's sister and her husband and their three children lived on the main floor. Every summer, when her parents came back to St. John's, Dona and Bill went traveling for two months, usually camping around the island. They had spent all of last summer at Windmill Bight, on the northeast coast. On their very first day there, Dona, a registered masso-therapist with several years of clinical experience, had helped an ailing octogenarian pass a kidney stone the size of a marble. She used what Bill called "deep massage techniques"—but no pounding or chopping or wrenching. News of the tender healing power of Dona's hands had spread quickly through the small campsite, which for two months of the summer was taken over completely by seniors with huge house trailers and even larger trailers of time. Dona had been moved by both the needs of the campers and the quiet beauty of the place and stayed there for the entire summer as a sort of camp mother, quieting chest spasms, relieving migraines, asthma and gout, freeing seized muscles, and generally attending to all the assorted ills that aging flesh is heir to.

"The hooded warbler," the birdman said, as Bill began to pour syrup from a plastic Aunt Jemima bottle over the French toast. *"Tawit tawit tawit tee too."*

"Jesus, look at this," he said, pointing to the label. "How can they still get away with this stuff? Dona, what are we doing buying this racist syrup?"

Standing by the coffee maker, Dona turned toward us and simultaneously raised her arms, her shoulders, and her eyebrows in a well-choreographed shrug, but the only sound came from the speakers.

"The yellow warbler, yellowbird, or wild canary ... *sweet sweet sweet sweet sweet.*"

Dona began to fit an unbleached filter into the plastic cone. Coincidentally, they had run out of coffee the evening before, and Dona was about to reheat some old coffee left in the carafe when I arrived. They were as delighted as orphans when I pulled their gift out of my sack.

Dona herself was dressed in a hooded sack, a sort of combination cowl and caftan. It covered her body from her chin to her feet, and a piece of rope was tied loosely around the waist. The shoulders peaked close to her neck and seemed to be supporting it like bookends. Her overlong sleeves partly covered large sinewy hands with very long fingers and short nails. Everything yielded to them, claimed Bill, from backache to heartache. Her rather severe haircut—almost a brush-cut—was softened by a kind face whose features seemed set in a permanent warm smile.

Though she appeared to be a large woman beneath her loose-fitting clothes, and was fairly tall as well, she ate, as they say, like a bird. I'd read somewhere, though, that some birds ate up to half their body weight each day, so I guess it was Bill who was the bird in the family. He attacked his stacked plate with just a fork, furiously stoking his fast-burning metabolic furnace. On his six-foot frame there may have been 150 pounds at the most, and that at the end of a good day's gorging.

"The yellowthroat . . . *wichity wichity wichity wichity.*"

Maybe because we had just met, but also perhaps to counteract Bill's totally unselfconscious and over-exuberant display, Dona and I, knife and fork politely in hand, cut off bite-size pieces of toast on our plates and presented them neatly to our mouths. My eyes were drawn to her long firm hands, and I imagined them kneading my flesh and bones after a long day's travail; and perhaps because I hadn't had sex in over a year, and my poor inert neglected organ would probably have to start crawling again before it learned to stand, I also imagined them gently coaxing me back to life.

Dona didn't say a word all through the meal. When she finished eating, she wiped her hands and mouth distractedly with her serviette and sat back in a sort of shallow trance with her hands in a prayer-like position at her lips. And at the top of the middle finger of her right hand, as if it had just risen along with the splendid lunule above it, I was surprised to see a small perfect wart; but what surprised me even more was that it had never struck me before what a remarkable resemblance it had to a nipple.

What I needed was a massage *parlour*, not a clinic.

"The black and white warbler . . . *wesee wesee wesee.*"

When Bill finished his toast, he refilled our cups and then sat down and began to rock back and forth on the hind legs of his hardwood chair, turning sideways slightly so that his right hand could clasp one of the wooden knobs at the back.

"Great toast," I said. "I won't need any supper after this." I laid my knife and fork upon the empty plate.

"That's Dona's Seven Grain, from the *Seventh Day Adventist End-of-the-World Vegetarian Cookbook,*" Bill said, laughing loudly. "Dona's mother gave it to us. It beats the hell out of the *Enchanted Broccoli Forest* and all those other high-priced tomes. What I like about the Adventists is that they look after their stomachs as well as their souls. Build up their strength for the big event."

He was about to say something else, but the cassette player clicked off. He got up and turned the tape over and stood next to the bookcase waiting for it to begin. Dona took some dishes over to the sink.

"The starling... *quirk quirk quirk.*"

"You know, there's not even a starling around here any more," he said, as he sat down again. "There's no place for a bird to nest, or even perch ... no trees, no poles, no wires ... not even a clothesline. There's an unwritten law out here against hangin' out your clothes. Spoils the look of the neighbourhood, gives away your lower-class roots. All in all, I think I'd rather live with that Trans-Am tribe at the foot of the hill.

"We got chastised by the woman next door not long after we moved in. Not in person, mind you; she pinned a note to the makeshift clothesline I rigged up. By-laws this and by-laws that. Jesus, there can't be a by-law against hangin' out your clothes. What the fuck is the world comin' to? I went over to talk to her but she wouldn't answer the door, so I stuck a note under her wiper blade telling her there was a CRTC by-law against sending messages over the clothesline. Christ, if I owned this house I could stir up some shit, I tell you. I'd wash out our condoms and dry them outdoors. Dona could recycle her Tampax."

He looked over at her and gave her a big grin, but she was standing at the sink with the water running.

"The savannah sparrow... *tsip tsip tsip tsip tse-wheeeeeee-you.*"

"I think I'll go in and do some work," Dona said when she'd finished with the dishes. "I'd like to get started on that table."

She gave us a small wave as she walked off and disappeared through a door at the far end of the hall. She was a woman of few words; she seemed content just to let Bill gab away.

"What a woman," he said, shaking his head and looking genuinely proud and amazed.

"She doesn't talk much, Dona, " I said.

"Well, she's got a lot on her mind. Her daughter, Jesse, at this very moment—as we speak—is speeding down from Toronto on icy roads on a motorcycle with some lunatic boyfriend. And then there's the psychotic father, the ex-husband, that Jesse's staying with in Toronto while she goes to school. Such are the joys of motherhood."

"I thought she looked uneasy," I said.

He spit out his coffee.

"The white-breasted nuthatch . . . *tew tew tew tew.*"

Bill lit a cigarette, an unfiltered Camel, closed his eyes and took a long deep drag. He exhaled with a contented sigh. I was convinced every time I watched Bill smoking that something that gave someone that much satisfaction could not possibly do him any harm. I lit one of my own, a Matinee mild.

"She's got a workshop in the furnace room. She built that desk over there . . . and all the bookcases . . . and this table," he said, giving the gleaming pine an appreciative thump. And when she's not making tables she's heaving me up on one and getting my blood moving again if I've been sittin' too long on my arse. She transformed the spare bedroom into a clinic. I've seen people go in there stiff as light poles and come out loose as chimpanzees.

"Course she's just about useless in the kitchen," he added, laughing and exhaling smoke simultaneously. "I can hardly trust her to turn out some toast and tea. But Jesus, it must be great to be able to work with something like wood—wood and flesh. Make no wonder she's so together and the rest of us are so fucked up. You can't get more down to earth than that."

"How about earth?"

"Well ... yeah ... but we'll be into that soon enough. But wouldn't you rather be doing something like that than at this wretched depressing stuff?" He looked round the room. "And when we're not writing it we're reading it ... or talking about it. When I get through this load, as I told you, that's it for me." He flung out his hands and looked straight at me. "I'm willing it all to you," he said.

"How can I ever thank you," I replied.

"The white-eyed vireo ... *chick! widdo-weo chick!*"

"This used to be a woods," Bill said, as if on cue. "Dona's father used to play here when he was a boy. Now you can't see a tree for miles. The developers didn't leave a bush, and now people are paying hundreds for scrawny little tucks that can't even make it through the winter, though they're wrapped up tight as caterpillars.

"I'm lookin' forward to the summer, when we hit the road again. Spend a month or two out by the ocean. Maybe we'll go back to Windmill Bight, and Dona can take up her old job again. That was a great summer, except for the icebergs. We lived on fresh cod, trout, salmon, moose, caribou, rabbit ... and home-made bread and jam made from every berry you could name. People dropping over day and night with fresh supplies, and all for the laying on of hands.

"Hardly anyone goes up there, and we had all those great white sandy beaches to ourselves. You can walk for miles along those beaches and over the dry mossy barrens above them. No one seems to know the place exists. You certainly never see any of the locals. And the old folks spent most of their time playing cards in their trailers—until the bakeapples started to ripen, and one morning they swept down over the barrens like lemmings."

"The least bittern ... *coo coo coo coo coo.*"

I excused myself to go to the bathroom, trying to step only on the exposed patches of carpet in the paper jungle that was the living room floor. Walking down the hall, I stopped in front of an open door and saw a massage table set in the centre of a small white room filled with a cool light from the weak solstice sun shining through white sheers at the windows. I stepped inside. The table was long and narrow with several pillows at one end and a doughnut-shaped cushion at the other. On a smaller table were several bottles of herbal oils in various sizes, fragrances, and colours. They glowed with a warm translucent light. White towels hung from wooden racks along the wall beneath the windows. A thin canvas mattress, like a wrestling mat, lay upon the parquet tile floor. Along another wall was a narrow table with plants and a cassette player with relaxation tapes—"Mozart with Ocean Sounds," "Desert Winds with Chimes," "Seabird Symphony," "Algonquin Park," "Rivers and Waterfalls." Two small lamps were set on wicker tables in the corners.

The room was luminous and serene. It was not the sort of room you expected to find in a basement, but of course this basement was well above ground and at the very top of a hill. It had an austere elemental look, like a monastery cell—a room for the soul—though it had been specifically designed for the body. It seemed a place where small miracles might be performed, simply with oils and the laying on of hands, a place for healing or purification, even acts of contrition.

In my mind I could see a cool white room in a whitewashed stone house on a tiny island in the Aegean, the tip of a long-dead volcano. From a distance, the small house looked like a sculpted cube of light. It was a place where estranged lovers, as far away from the world and all its cares as they might ever hope to be, might feel their burdens mysteriously lift, a place where even departed lovers might meet again. On the small Greek island of Santorini, more than ten years ago, Kate and I had spent one of the happiest months of our lives.

Farther down the hall, there *was* a room for the soul—a windowless writing room, little more than a closet, really, with nothing in it but a manual typewriter, table and chair. Bill had yet to use an electric typewriter, let alone a word processor, which he spoke of with much disdain. It was the word "processor," not the word processor, which bothered him, I think, with all its mundane domestic and commercial connotations.

About the size of a piece of commercial equipment, Bill's typewriter *occupied* the room. I'd seen it before but I was always newly impressed. It was an old coal-black British Imperial—with "British Right Through" stamped proudly in gold letters on the front. Set into its sides were two rectangles of glass, which allowed you to look right into its cast-iron British guts. This lightened its opaque mass, its solemn solidity, somewhat—but not much. Hunkered down on its four rectangular rubber legs, it still looked inimically black and squat. I thought of Philip Larkin's oppressive toad, *work,* to which he became reconciled, in his way, in the end.

> *What else can I answer,*
> *When the lights come on at four*
> *At the end of another year?*
> *Give me your arm, old toad;*
> *Help me down Cemetery Road.*

It was a severe- and fearsome-looking thing: a machine, indeed, for working souls, and would obviously tolerate no dilly-dallying. I approached cautiously, ran my fingers lightly over its circular yellowed keys and then, more intimately, pressed the Tab key. The carriage flew across the top—light on his feet, as they say, for a heavy man—its bell making a businesslike sound at the end, like a shopkeeper's.

When I returned to the living room, I found Bill down on his hands and knees foraging among his files.

"The editor at his noble task," I said.

"Your editor's typical dignified pose," he replied. "Nosing around for the udder of subvention ... for all those mother fuckers of invention out there. I was trying to find that grant application that's due next week."

Instead, beneath the coffee table, he found half a bottle of Fundador, a Spanish brandy that he fancied, and we had our traditional Boxing Day drink.

"To the Don," he said, and we clinked our whisky tumblers. When I was leaving, Bill bawled out to Dona to come and say good-bye. Her eyes were bloodshot and she blinked a lot. With her hood up she looked almost monklike. There was a fine dust all over her sack dress, which was now held tightly at the waist by a wide black leather belt, and at the wrists, by thick elastic bands. She now looked trim and wiry instead of ample. She surprised me with a hug and a kiss on the cheek, and I was back on the massage table once again.

"It was nice to meet you, Will," she said, and though she had hardly said a word to me, I knew that she meant it.

They invited me out again for the weekend. I said I'd be out for sure, but I knew that I didn't mean it. It was a struggle these days socializing with myself.

I walked down the hill to the bus stop at the front entrance of the mall and stood among some shoppers waiting for a bus back to town.

That I might drink, and leave the world unseen,
And with thee fade away into the forest dim—

Fade far away, dissolve, and quite forget
What thou among the leaves hast never known,
The weariness, the fever, and the fret
Here, where men sit and hear each other groan; . . .
—Keats, "Ode to a Nightingale"

A slow singer, but loading each phrase
With history's overtones, love, joy
And grief learned by his dark tribe
In other orchards and passed on
Instinctively as they are now,
But fresh always with new tears.
—R. S. Thomas, "A Blackbird Singing"

THE BUSY GRIEFS (I)

Tasker Murphy pulled sad songs out of the air like trap lines out of deep blue water—hand over hand, line after line, song after song after song after song. Some men were tattooed "Born to Run," "Born to Be Wild," "Born to Kill." Tasker's tattoo said "Born to Sing," and he did so whenever he had the chance. And the blueprint wasn't just on his arm or chest; it was stamped right on his double helix. He was programmed to sing and weep and moan like his whole troubled tribe, the Irish diaspora.

At my kitchen table at nine o'clock on New Year's Eve, Tasker, with hands and eyeballs rolling, was singing and sobbing his way through his "Molly," "Mother," and "Kathleen" song cycles; and as I sat across the table listening to him, I recalled all the NO SINGING signs I'd seen in the pubs in Ireland. You might as well post signs on beaches telling capelin not to spawn.

He was now singing "Molly Bawn."

Oh! Molly Bawn, why leave me pining,
All lonely, waiting here for you;
While the stars above are brightly shining,
Because they've nothing else to do?

He stopped suddenly and grabbed the band of his grey wool stocking cap with both hands, as if he were about to pull it down over his eyes. Loose strands of wool hung over his ears. Tears were streaming down his face.

"I'm sensitive, you know what I mean," he rasped. "Kit don't understand me ... and Jerry ... O Jesus ... Jerry Jerry Jerry."

Jerry was the youngest of Tasker's five grown sons, and he couldn't mention his name without crying. He was an aircraft mechanic in the Armed Forces and had been home again from Cold Lake, Alberta, for Christmas. The others were working on the Mainland as well, but none of them had been back for years. Tasker and his wife, Kathleen, or "Kit," were now spending their twilight years alone, though Kathleen was probably the lonelier of the two, for Tasker inhabited a twilight of his own. Since he'd "come in off the water," as he put it, he had taken seriously to drink, and left her alone almost every evening.

For most of his life, Tasker had worked on the water, and on every kind of boat, from a dory to an icebreaker. The name Murphy actually meant "sea-warrior," and was the most common name in Ireland according to the old man's favourite browsing book, *Family Names of the Island of Newfoundland.* Perhaps the legendary St. Brendan himself had been a Murphy. He had ventured across the North Atlantic four hundred years before the Vikings with seventeen monks in an oxhide boat in the vanguard of our emigrant brood. And considering Tasker's capacity for drink and song and sorrow, he might have attained some sort of mythic or generic status himself, had he been christened Mick or Paddy.

After he'd retired and had lots of time on his hands, Dad had begun to trace our family history. In *Family Names* he had been most perturbed to discover that someone way back may have been calling us names; Wiseman, his beloved cognomen, which, as far as he was concerned, needed no further explanation, may have been an ironic appellation. And there may have been tricksters, wizards, sorcerers, conjurers, enchanters, and diviners in the ancestral mix as well. These he could have let pass, but his brows had permanently darkened and knit at the book's suggestion that we might have been descended from a family of fools.

Tasker now worked part-time at the dry dock as a longshoreman, and spent the other part at the Harbour Inn, where he probably sang songs to Kathleen like the one he was singing to her now, while she waited and worried at home alone.

> *So, my Kathleen, you're going to leave me,*
> *All alone by myself in this place,*
> *But I'm sure that you'll never deceive me,*
> *Oh no, if there's truth in that face.*

I began to cry a few tears myself and my own spirits sank as I watched the level of my new bottle of Glenfiddich sink lower and lower. It was an extravagant purchase, made just a few hours before with my last few dollars and all 846 cents from Anna's Canada Post mailbox piggy bank. (Tell that to your officious social worker.) This irreplaceable resource—at least for the next thirty-six hours—was now in danger of being rapidly depleted, and the darkest part of this evening of totalitarian joy was still ahead of us.

Tasker threw the exquisite single malt—made from barley dried in peat-heated kilns and fermented in Douglas fir vats, matured for ten years in double oak casks—straight down his throat without even tasting it, and threw himself up on the beach of song, exuding notes and tears like milt. I imagined him in his heyday sailor days, before this family anguish had settled upon him, commanding his crow's nest like a priest his pulpit, high above the saltspray, singing to the wind and the waves.

I now regretted my decision to let him in, but I'd watched

him pacing up and down the other side of the street in the cold for over an hour, afraid to go home; so when I heard the mild-mannered knock and saw the pitiful stubbly face topped by an unraveling stocking cap in the oval window of the front door, looking like some sad old daguerreotype, I unwisely opened it and invited him in. He had probably been drinking since early morning; some bars opened their doors at nine.

Though our houses shared a wire fence at the back, Tasker's house was around the corner on the intersecting street. But he would usually stop outside our house on his way home from the Harbour Inn and pace up and down on the sidewalk. Then he would walk across the street and sit for a spell on the bus stop bench, his elbows on his knees and his head in his hands, unable to take the last few steps home. Though Tasker had sailed the Seven Seas, he could not navigate evenings like oceans.

Though I'd been gone over a year, it was more than likely that he was completely unaware of it. In the five or six years that we'd been neighbours, he'd been in our house no more than a half dozen times, usually around Christmas, and each time it seemed that he hardly knew us. He would re-introduce himself, thinking that we didn't know him, and announce that he'd just dropped in for a cup of tea. Kit would kill him, he'd say, if he came home like this. Kate would put the kettle on and leave me alone with him, for she had a fearful aversion to people who were drunk. And I had seen him lapse into the indecipherable singsong dialect of the permanently shamelessly hopelessly drunk.

Sometimes he would sit in silence for a while, staring at the kettle as it rumbled to life, looking thoughtful, or perhaps lost, squeezing his eyes as if trying to focus them and turning his cap in a circle on his head. Then all of a sudden he would blurt out that he had to sing, as someone else might jump up and say that he had to leave. Did I mind?—he just had to sing. And once he started singing, his big voice rolling, it was clear that no cup of tea would ever do, no matter how barklike you could make it. You felt almost ashamed to serve it. And so, of course, you'd offer him whisky, or whatever else you had in the house. It mattered not a tad to Tasker.

"After he spoke o' the knife," he once shamefully confessed to me, referring to the doctor he'd consulted about his bad back, "I lost a whole week o' work because of the drink."

Of course he'd never ask for a drink, just sing for it—breaking into the lines with shouts and moans, questions, entreaties, apologies, tears.

"*She WHEELED her wheelbarrow* ... t'row me out, t'row me out, if I'm boderin' you, me son, t'row me out ... *t'rough STREETS broad and narrow* ... do you like me singin'? ... *crying COCKLES and MUSSELS, alive, alive, oh!* ... she's gonna kill me, Jesus, Jesus, she's gonna kill me ... you're OK, b'y, you're OK ... I know I'm a nuisance ... you're OK ... I'm sensitive ... you know what I mean ... do you like me singin'?"

"Yes, b'y. Have another drink," I said to him.

I was falling into it now from trying to keep up with him and get my share of that precious Scotch, bought to shore me up against New Year's Eve. It was now approaching the bottom of the bottle, and I'd hoped to nurse it along through New Year's Day. I was even taking on Tasker's brogue, as rooted in the Old Sod as Scotch in the Highlands.

"Would you be knowin' 'Carrickfergus' now?" I said, trying to get a rise out of him. The first time I'd asked him that he'd not been quite this far gone.

"'Carrickfergus'! Jesus, I'm from Carrickfergus," he'd replied, referring, I guessed, to some distant ancestor. He'd told me before that his family was from Cork, which was where the old man's forebears had shipped out from, though I'd kept that to myself.

But he didn't respond this time, just lit right into it, and when he sailed off into the stratosphere with a bellowing chorus, I let out a harmonizing shout or two myself, and was surprised to feel myself filling up, as they say. Sensitive ... you know what I mean.

But the sea is wide and I can't swim over,
Nor do I have the wings to fly. . . .

It was a song that seemed beyond hope and despair, its roots sea deep in an inexpressible grief. A man could drown himself in *aqua vitae*, the water of life, as the Scots liked to call their national drink—their Glenmorangies, Laphroaigs, and Old Fettercairns, their Lochnagars, Balvenies, and Laga-vulins—without reaching this *taedium vitae*.

I'm drunk today, but then I'm seldom sober—
A handsome rover from town to town,

Tasker sang, with, as you would expect, real feeling.

The old man, who knew more than a few Irish songs himself, also had a real feeling for "Carrickfergus," and he would sing it at Christmastime or whenever he'd had a few too many. Otherwise he just whistled, or tinkered with the accordion. But though he sang Irish, he drank Scotch, which was how I'd developed a taste for the stuff. His taste, however, ran to the more robust and pungent varieties—the peatier and brinier the better. His favourite was Laphroaig—"peat and seaweed and tears," as he described it—from the Isle of Islay, where, coincidentally, our Carrickfergusian rover had been marooned, in a place called Ballygrant. Islay, according to the old man, had more whisky makers per square mile than any place on earth, which might account for the undertone of meditative content, of crooning consolation, in the song.

It was almost eleven by the time Tasker left, though he would have stayed on to wail out the old year like a drunken banshee if there had been another bottle of whisky. With a final dramatic flourish he got up from the table and walked off taking everything on it: the oversized but still overloaded ashtray, the sugar bowl, butter dish, and honey jar, the unused cups and saucers for our tea, the empty glasses and the empty bottle of whisky. All went crashing to the floor in a startling cascade, the Glenfiddich bottle smashing upon the radiator on its way down.

Tasker had tucked the checkered tablecloth into his belt, mistaking it for his longshoreman's plaid. He just stood there awestruck for a moment, blinking hard at the mess at his feet with the tablecloth hanging from his waist like a failed breechcloth. Then he slumped down on his knees in the ashes and butter and butts and glass and made a sort of pantomimic motion with his arms, as if he were about to use them to sweep it all up.

Seeing him there on his hands and knees in the ash-covered mess, I thought of his namesake, Sam Beckett's Murphy, whose ashes—"body, mind, and soul"—had been scattered upon a barroom floor and, at closing time, had been swept away with the other dust and ash, the vomit and spit. His earthly remains had been thrown angrily at another bar patron by a man whose honourable task it had been, following Murphy's written instructions, to flush the packet of ashes down a toilet at the Abbey Theatre—and during a performance, if possible.

Tasker had managed to make one sweep with a right arm whose hand had been pulled up inside the sleeve of his shirt, gripping the cuff inside with his fingers and making a sort of stump-mop at the end. I took hold of his other arm and tried to pull him up, but his body was stuck to the floor like a limpet. It took him a while to straighten up after I finally got him to his feet. He pulled the tablecloth from his belt, held it up in his fist and gave it a puzzled look; then he dropped it upon his feet on the floor and burped.

"You're all right," he said, blinking hard at me and offering his hand. And with my hand still in the cast of his longshoreman's grip, and my arm around his shoulder, we staggered out of the kitchen and down the hallway toward the door. In the porch he surprised me by pulling a mickey of Screech out of his coat.

"Doch-an-dorris," he chimed, but he didn't offer it to me, though he did wish me a Happy New Year before he stumbled out the door.

I left the mess on the kitchen floor and went out for a walk to clear my head. I even considered going down to the waterfront to mingle with the crowd and listen to the ships toot in the New Year, but the thought of being swallowed up by thousands of people, all filled with a desperate irrepressible joie de vivre, seemed a daunting if not downright joyless prospect, even though I was well fortified for the occasion.

The New Year's Eve waterfront soiree had once been a much smaller, more casual, affair: just a few people strolling the docks with mickeys of rum in their overcoats. On a few occasions Kate and I had been among them, singing "Auld Lang Syne" and kissing and embracing strangers at midnight. But, in less than a decade, it had festooned into a "tradition," a raucous media-whipped affair with radio station ghetto blasters on wheels and a City Council fireworks display.

People poured down the steep hills, head over heels for the harbour and a tryst with tradition and good cheer. The DJ's in the mobile studios provided on-the-spot coverage and music for dancing and assured the revelers that this was where it was all happening, this was THE New Year's Eve event, and they were right in the thick of it. They could dance and sing and shout and hear the sounds of their own voices coming through the speakers as friends were being interviewed by the announcers. It was almost as if they needed to hear themselves on the radio in order to believe that they were there and that all this was really happening. Like some huge bio-feedback device, the mobile ghetto blaster confirmed that they were having a heart-thumping good time.

This year or next it would probably be on television; then there would be barricades and a cover charge. And as more and more people stayed home out of the usual wind and cold to watch the scene on TV in the comfort of their living rooms, the whole thing would gradually subside until there was nothing much to broadcast any more. And then, thankfully, back to a few people casually strolling the docks....

With these sour and unfestive thoughts, I made my way up

Military Road and sat for a spell on the Basilica steps high above the harbour. Through a luminous fog I could hear the radio music and the cheers of the waterfront crowd; the smell of the salt air was sobering and sad. There were probably ten thousand or more down there this year, for it was the mildest New Year's Eve we'd had in quite a while.

I walked on up Harvey Road through the vinegary air of the fish-and-chip district, then down Lemarchant Road to Barter's Hill. Walking down the hill I began to feel the powerful bass of the ghetto blasters pounding in my chest, supplanting the beat of my still-hedging heart. Perhaps one of the reasons for its apprehension was that I had once crawled up this hill on New Year's Eve—or New Year's Day, to be more exact—after a night of serious drinking downtown. The heart remembers, though the mind wants to forget.

I had been living in the attic of an old house on Lemarchant Road at the time, a room that had a great view of the harbour but was always filled with nauseating medicinal smells from the dentist's office below. At the top of Barter's Hill, which was even steeper than the almost vertical Signal Hill, whose narrow winding road at least allowed you to tack, I had risen to my full height like *Homo erectus* for the first time only to double over a minute later and disgorge the entire contents of my stomach onto the street. When I lifted my head again, I was confronted by the ghostly face—doubtless mirroring my own—of a garish plastic clock that had been installed on the front of the funeral home on Lemarchant Road. It said three o'clock, a time that seemed more wrong than right, or, as Sartre once put it, an hour that was either too early or too late for anything you wanted to do. But perhaps he'd been talking about the afternoon.

I could see the moon-face of this same clock right now, rising over the crest of the hill. Its hands were almost folded at twelve o'clock. I was leaning over an iron railing on Livingston Street, which crossed Barter's Hill about halfway down, when the ships' horns began to sound. A huge cheer went up; the crowd began to sing "Auld Lang Syne"; over the Southside Hills

219

fireworks lit the sky.

I wandered the streets for another hour or more, avoiding the crowds of people downtown, but even on back streets I kept running into small bands of revelers moving from one house party to the next. Three women dressed more for Halloween than New Year's, with spangled faces and glittering capes and caps, surprised me rounding a corner on Victoria Street, and all three of them kissed me full-square on the lips and wished me a Happy New Year. I felt a great rush of guilt and gratitude and stood there on the sidewalk as their laughter trailed away in the dark.

Back at the house, tired but still restless, a bit edgy and raw-eyed, I set to sweeping up the mess on the kitchen floor, and then sat in the sunken well of the leather smoker, smoking. To distract myself, I switched on the TV, and there before me like a vision appeared the radiant face and looming honeydews of my teenage heartthrob, Kim Novak, last of the silver screen goddesses. *Kimmeee,* as she liked to sign her love notes, was playing the part of *Carrleee,* an American innocent in London falsely accused of murdering her husband.

We were in Carly's kitchen, with the innocent jar of arsenic on the counter, and, in that old black-and-white, soft-focus celluloid print, she glowed with a translucent sensuality that brought back all my adolescent love and longing, made even worse now by the knowledge that I would never have her, and that her painful beauty had now faded.

The Notorious Landlady, circa 1962, also featured two dueling American diplomats—a boyish and boisterous Jack Lemmon and a very spare Fred Astaire, hopping like a sprite through the London fogs. It was directed—*auteured,* in fact, when *auteuring* was just a silver gleam in most American directors' eyes—by none other than Kim's former lover, Richard Quine.

A strange film, in more ways than one. Jack Lemmon had said that he didn't understand it at all, that its befuddled plot had completely confounded him, even after watching it years later on television. And though he had delivered his lines with absolute conviction, he had no idea what they meant. Kim had said that it confused her as well, and that she was sick and tired of playing the role of Kim Novak.

All this and more in *Kim Novak: Reluctant Goddess* — "Told for the first time ... the shocking love affairs ... the shocking photos ... her flings ... her fights ... her tormented liaisons ... a story that reveals the tortured heart of a woman trapped by a world of greed and power, who dared to break free and live."

I had read it over Christmas, along with *The Life Story of the Fish: His Manners and Morals*, one on each bedside table. (I had taken to sleeping on both sides of the double bed.) As I used to tell my students, Comparative Lit serves to broaden the mind. Needless to say, when all was said and done, it was the fish who had flopped up on the high moral bank when compared with the venal callous lot who had created Kim Novak and other vamps to activate the lapping reflex, to salivate the Pavlovian dog, in us all.

Poor Kimmeee had been just another entranced victim of the Hollywood star machine—or, at least, that's how she was portrayed. But perhaps Chicago's "Snow Queen" and "Miss Rhapsody in Blue," the USA's "National Trade Show Appliance Queen"—"Miss Deepfreeze"—of 1953, back when the Thor "Freezer Chest" had been more famous than her own, had played some small part in creating herself. But all of us had played our part, and though my desire had once been pure and sweet, I looked at her now with only a pure lust stirring and thoughts of self-love on my mind.

And as I stared at Miss Rhapsody in Blue, like some mesmerized French peasant schoolboy at Lourdes, it was revealed to me what the film was really all about, and why Lemmon and Novak had felt so confused; for in the shots of Kimmeee—in the kitchen courtyard now, helping Lemmon put out a barbecue fire that had caught an awning and making orgasmic moans as she struggled with a garden hose, and later, inside the house, soaking wet and tousled in front of the fireplace, her natural charms even more in evidence—our *auteur*'s painful longing filled every frame. Having lost *her*, how could he have been expected to keep his mind on something as trivial as a plot.

I thought of the empty bottle of Glenfiddich in the kitchen, "Stand Fast" emblazoned on its broken neck. Not even the dregs remained to anoint my tongue—ten golden drops I'd squeezed from the last one. In the end it always came down to this: the empty bottle, the empty bed, evenings like oceans, onlies and onliness; even after the walk abroad among your fellow men, the long walk back home to your bowl of gruel and your ghosts.

Fred Astaire, dancer extraordinaire, confined in the role of embassy official like a foot in a shoe two sizes too small, came striding down a gleaming embassy corridor—a dance floor, really—twirling his umbrella like a tap dancer's stick and looking straight into the camera with a mischievous glint. You were sure he would break into a dance at any moment, click those taps on the hard waxed floor. But he never did, he never did. The prick was only tantalizing us.

DANCE YOU SILLY FUCKER, DANCE. IT'S NEW YEAR'S EVE, I shouted at him. I switched off the TV, grabbed my jacket and walked out the door.

Where are you now? Long, long ago
Ashes. But your "Nightingales" still
Live. Death snatches everything, but
He shall not lay his hand on them.
—Callimachus

The flesh is sad, alas, and I have read all the books.
—Stéphane Mallarmé, *Brise Marine*

THE BUSY GRIEFS (II)

A woman named Kerry followed me home from the bars. It
seemed she had nowhere else to go. She reminded me of Jenny,
my first love, who had opened her wonderful long legs for
poetry—and stuff for which the term "juvenilia" was high
praise. Even the Commissariat of Enlightenment would have
rejected it. But these days I had trouble even *reading* poetry, and
here was a woman trying to force herself on me.

"I'd rather read than *fuck*," she said to me, in the middle of
recounting her personal history. "Sometimes I think it's all I
know how to do."

She said it like some final shameful judgment of herself, as
if for some emotional deformity. And she was reading, even as
she said it, in a George Street walk-through on New Year's Eve,
among strangers desperately rejoicing. This was where the urge
to walk abroad among your fellow men could lead you.

Though fashionably outfitted, in a perennial sort of way,
with clothes that looked as if they'd been handpicked with a
discriminating casualness at antique clothiers specializing in
sullen black, Kerry looked wrapped or bandaged rather than
clothed, her long scarf and ankle-length coat and skirt enfolding
some fragile self, cocooning some old sorrow. She had a "Belle
Dame sans Merci" look about her. If alone and palely loitering
in a dark corner of a bar on a late winter afternoon when the

light outside was quickly fading and the lights inside were just being turned down for the evening, you were to raise your head out of your book, she would be there looking back at you over the pages of her book from another dim smoky corner.

Rather read than fuck. I think I knew what she meant. I recalled a dream in which I was visiting my doctor with what seemed a rare or secret or even shameful complaint. There was this sense of my carrying a heavy weight. The burden seemed to be that I was having trouble sleeping, or perhaps even getting a certain bodily part to awake. But when she posed her usual question, "Well, what do you have for us today?" what I said was, "I'm having trouble reading." I can't recall what she said after that.

We had been sitting elbow to elbow at the bar with a crush of belching and bellowing bodies at our backs. Over our heads, and between our heads, arms holding paper and plastic fenced with arms passing change and drinks. But Kerry was bent over her book, in another world altogether.

"What are you reading?" I asked, innocently enough.

She straightened up and glanced at me, then turned the book over on the bar for me to see. Posthumous Hemingway. *The Garden of Eden.* Then she took out a handkerchief and blew her nose several times.

"It's the smoke," she said. "I've got allergies."

I douted my cigarette and we introduced ourselves.

"What do you do?" she asked.

"I used to teach Papa," I said, tapping her book and sounding pompously jovial. She looked at me again. A smile seemed to be hiding inside her mouth. I half expected some sort of rejoinder, such as, "You did a piss-poor job," or, "You must be older than you look."

Instead, she said, "I thought you looked familiar. The university, right?"

"That's the place," I said. "A clean well-lighted place."

Her attention became sidetracked by a man in a hound's-tooth check suit who was doing a flailing spastic kind of dance whose purpose seemed to be to get out of it—the suit, I mean; he himself was already out of it. The anima of the place, perhaps—or maybe just the animal—he was thrusting his arms and legs like foils, and thrusting his load at one of the load-bearing posts that was holding the roof over our heads.

Something was stirring beneath the bar stool. I looked down, half expecting to see some red-eyed reveler clinging to the rungs and looking up at me; but it was another animal—Kerry's dog—a coal-black, miserable-looking mutt of indeterminate species wearing a red kerchief, a New Year's Eve touch perhaps, or maybe permanently tied on to brighten him up. As I looked down at him, with my two hands clamped on the black vinyl seat, he began to lick one of them.

"Down, K.," she said. K.? I didn't ask.

A permanent structure of arm scaffolding now seemed to be in place around our heads, and I invited Kerry to a table, a few of which, surprisingly enough, were empty. She led her stowaway along by the kerchief and installed him under the table between our feet. Then she went back to get a large canvas knapsack.

As Kerry was soon to reveal, she had been a stowaway herself—on the Queen E. II, the mother ship of the university line. As she explained it, she'd lived for years in the stacks of the Queen Elizabeth Library, but though she looked familiar, too, I couldn't recall ever seeing her there. She had read whatever took her fancy, she said, while working not very seriously on an Arts degree. But each term she managed to pass enough courses to avoid being academically dismissed and to enable her to get her student loans. She had never got the degree, but she had, as she put it, garnered enough useless information to fill a grain silo.

She used a lot of prairie imagery, though she'd grown up around the Bay—Trinity Bay, to be exact—where the only thing resembling a great plain was the ocean. And she'd been off the island only once—a trip to New York City—which, as we all know, doesn't have a lot of prairie either. But then she began to tell me about Nat, who had left her—and not for another woman, but for another place.

An ex-folk singer and late-blooming back-to-the-lander from New York City, he had been unable to convince her to move with him to St. Brendan's, an isolated fishing community on an island in Bonavista Bay that Nat had discovered 500 years after Cabot. St. Brendan himself, she said, would have had more luck getting her to go across the ocean with him in his leather boat. On the island Nat had rebuilt an abandoned house and started an organic garden. In the summers he fished and indulged his obsession with sunflowers.

Having grown up on the cold northeast coast, Kerry had been adamant about going back. Her parents had moved to St. John's when she was thirteen, and, before long, her father had built a bungalow in Mount Pearl. She liked the soft city life, where she could spend whole afternoons in bookstores and libraries, and evenings drinking at the Ship Inn downtown. But the Ship was where she and Nat had met, where all their friends still hung out, and she found it hard to go there any more. I told her I avoided the place for much the same reasons.

"Sometimes it's easier to talk to strangers," she said.

"You're right," I said. But I didn't talk, and she didn't ask.

She talked on. About Nat, about her lost job, her lost father, her crazy mother. After Kerry had lost her job, she'd had to give up her apartment overlooking the harbour and move back into the bungalow with her mother. But she lived out of her knapsack whenever she could.

"She hasn't slept in years—not since Dad left," she said. "She's up all night banging things around, dropping dishes on the floor, slamming doors. She plays the organ in the middle of the night.

"Her name is Vi," she said. "For violence."

We left George Street around three o'clock and strolled down a laneway and across Water Street to the harbour. We walked in silence along the waterfront looking at the ships braided to the fluorescent gumps on the dock. The pavement was still completely bare; we had made it into the New Year and were still waiting for the snow. We nosed our way through a thickening fog, the salt air clearing the smoke from our heads. Kerry, carrying that heavy-looking knapsack on her back, kept turning around and calling out to K., who was lingering over the New Year's Eve post-party trash.

On Duckworth Street we stopped for coffee at a small cafe where the only other customers were leaving. We sat in silence for a while, reading our place mats and feeling the petals of the plastic flowers.

"What did he do, Nat, before he came down here? What did he do in New York?" I asked her. It seemed to relax her to talk about him.

"He isn't from New York, actually. He's from Saskatchewan. He went to live in Greenwich Village. He was a supervisor," she said, laughing.

I smiled back. "Supervising what?"

"Plants," she said. "It was a family joke. His old man was a real mean bastard. He wanted all the boys to stay on the farm. But all Nat wanted to do was play the guitar. He went to high school with Joni Mitchell. And when she went off to New York, he did too. Nat's job on the farm was to look after the animals—the cows and pigs and hens. His older brothers looked after the crops. 'Animal supervisor,' Nat used to call himself—he even put it on his resume. His old man used to tell him he couldn't supervise a plant. The funny thing was, in New York he actually got a job looking after plants, in a high-rise complex with atriums and offices full of exotic vegetation. At night he played in the Village folk clubs. But he got sick of that life pretty fast—or maybe he was just sick of New York. Anyway, he drove down here on a holiday one summer to get away from the heat and, like a lot of people who come here, he loved the place and stayed."

Though it was New Year's Eve, it soon became clear that

we had overstayed our welcome. Our cups had been refilled and our check had been delivered. It lay in its small plastic tray like an eviction notice. The tables had been cleared and set for the next day. The plastic red roses in white vases had been replaced with plastic yellow roses in blue vases. The Open sign in the window now faced in instead of out. One of the waiters, jauntily dressed in a black beret and a long red scarf, had already left, intoning a loud sing-song "Good Night" to his partner on his way out the fire exit door. In a far corner behind the counter the other waiter's face appeared and disappeared in the dim light as if he were swiveling his head like an owl in the green shadows of a tree. There was nothing left but the vacuum cleaner, which I was sure would soon be deployed. But we were lingering, not wanting to go out into the uncertain night.

K. was waiting outside tied to a parking meter. I invited them back, and offered to carry the knapsack.

As we walked past the regimental row of old houses that shouldered one another erect along our street, all of them only a few feet from the sidewalk, Kerry trailed behind me collecting sample packets of tampons that someone had hung on the doorhandles. Ahead of me the long line of plastic rectangles glimmered beneath the streetlights like the pages of some half-forgotten book. I thought about the poor souls whose desperate job it was to go hiking up and down the steep hills of St. John's hanging tampon samplers on the doorhandles of people's houses on New Year's Eve. Magnanimous humanitarian though you might be, you had to admit that it made all your own burdens just a little lighter.

Miro welcomed us at the front door, but on spotting the dog drew back and hissed an electrifying current of air that shot through her longhaired body and transformed her Persian perm into a cartoon fright. Kerry left K. on the mat in the porch, and we closed the inside door and removed our boots in the hall. Miro remained frozen, puffed up on all fours, her feet together like a furry pedestal, poised like a fur balloon ready for flight.

Kerry discovered a leg on the plaster ceiling of the bedroom. On her back on the bed, among a pile of paperbacks, her head propped up on several down pillows, she happened to glance up from a crumbling copy of *Immortal Poems of the English Language*—the "Introduction" to which contained a testimonial to the effect that every poem therein had given the editor an "immortal wound"—and her eye caught the shape of a woman's leg in the plaster. She pointed at it and laughed with a childlike glee.

I'd never noticed it before, though I'd slept in that bed for seven years. There was something unsettling about it. It had a severed, an amputated, look—foot extended in the attitude of pulling on a stocking, rippling varicose veins in the calf, bent knee, leg ending at mid-thigh. But for some reason it really caught her fancy; indeed, it soon induced an astonished hilarity that might have inflicted an immortal wound on the mere mortal male ego, had I, and not the *Immortal Poems*, been in her arms.

But at least there was no worry about that. She'd gone straight for the bookshelves when she came in the door, and was delighted to find one in almost every room. She was an avid, if not a downright rabid, reader. Reading with her could be as unsafe as sex.

"I've never seen so many books," she said, and I could only agree. I'd been collecting them since I was six, and I'd never parted with a single one.

She'd found the *Immortal Poems* right off, after only a few minutes foraging. I'd bought it a long time ago, at John D. Snow's secondhand shop downtown, among the cake tins, candlesticks, and coffin handles. She said she'd once owned a copy of it herself. It had been given to her as a teenager by her mother, who had worked at home as a seamstress and had secretly written poems. Kerry had discovered them one evening in her mother's sewing basket when she'd been looking for a pair of scissors.

Besides the *Immortal Poems*, she had found *A Little Treasury of*

Modern Poetry and *A Pocket Book of Modern Verse*—part of what I thought of as my fifties collection, mostly from secondhand shops, where my first serious browsing and book collecting had begun. She'd brought them over to the bed, along with volumes of Keats, Blake, and Dylan Thomas.

In her knapsack were ... God, what else ... books. *The Book of Nightmares, Paris Spleen, Modern Man in Search of a Soul.* She'd dumped them all out on the bed while trying to find her brush.

She kept asking me if I actually lived here, and I assured her that I did. I was restless and was walking around picking things up and looking at them. I stared at the pictures on the bedroom walls as if I were at an opening in an art gallery. Sitting in a large bamboo chair, Leo Tolstoy, looking surly and messianic, glared out of an old hand-coloured photograph dated 1908. He was dressed in a blue peasant's smock, green breeches, and black boots. I was always amazed to rediscover that he had actually lived ten years into the twentieth century.

I stared at Kate's self-portrait a la chiaroscuro—"Self-Portrait After Rembrandt #23." "Shadow husbandry," she used to call the technique. But here the shadows seemed wild and out of control and were gnawing at the obscure outline of her jaw and head, her wide mouth, her high cheekbones and brow, her large dark eyes. She'd done dozens of these, but this was the only one that she'd framed and hung. She would surpass the Old Master—at least in quantity—if she kept at it. He was supposed to have done sixty or more.

"Is that your wife?" Kerry asked, and I turned around to see her looking at me over the pages of her book.

"She has a beautiful face," she said, without waiting for a reply. "But it's sad, it's awfully sad."

"It's just Art," I said. "Nothing to worry about."

She gave a cautious little smile. She had brushed out her long dark hair, and it hung down over her face like a veil.

"Actually, she still lives here," I said, "but she's away for Christmas. I'm just looking after the house.

"I came back to see Puss," I added. "I have visiting rights."

She gave an uncertain laugh.

"You're strange," she said, adjusting her pillows. She fell silent and bent her head over her book. Her face darkened and almost disappeared behind her curtain of hair. She used a book as a skilled actor might use a prop, her long fingers marking several pages.

"Are you peeved at me?" she asked, suddenly looking up. "Did I say something wrong? Maybe you don't really want me here?"

"Oh no," I said, much too quickly.

I felt an increasing sense of unease. Had I unthinkingly brought an emotional Trojan horse into the house from which some old sorrows were going to emerge—to disarm me, to unmask me, to bare all my horrible weaknesses and transgressions, to remind me of every failure and unkindness?

It seemed that there was an emptiness inside her that my own meagre spiritual resources could never fill. I was equipped only to look after an emotionally healthy cat, and I was lucky that Miro fit the bill. If nature abhors a vacuum, I wondered how it felt about two—alone together on a cheerless New Year's Eve in a house full of ghosts with not even the cold comfort of sex.

"Would you like a cup of tea?" I heard myself say.

"Do you have herbal?" she asked.

"We probably have nothing but herbal," I said.

"I'll make it," she said, and threw her black leotarded legs over the edge of the bed onto the hardwood floor. She had taken off her skirt, and her stockings were so worn that patches of flesh were visible. She spotted a pair of grey socks rolled into a ball next to the night stand and quickly pulled them on over her thinly covered feet. Watching her do this so offhandedly, without a second's thought or hesitation, somehow confirmed so poignantly Kerry's fragility, her lostness, that orphan quality that hung about her, that easy willingness to be drawn into another person's life, her need to be cared for, to be looked after by someone else, that I felt a familiar dark anxiety stir in me, combined with a sense of numb hopelessness that seemed to double the weight of every bone in my body.

I followed her out to the kitchen and sat down at the table. She didn't ask where anything was, she just set to work. She put on the kettle and then began poking around in a cupboard behind cans of Ovaltine, Inca, and Fry's Cocoa, as if she were the one who lived here and I was the guest, as if she knew more about the inside of this house than I did myself. She examined several packages of herbal teas.

"How about Sleepytime?" she said. "Chamomile flowers, spearmint leaves, lemon grass, tilia flowers, passion flower leaves, blackberry leaves, orange blossoms, hawthorn berries, and rosebuds." Her voice sounded especially pleased with rosebuds.

"Fine with me," I said.

She found two teapots on the shelf next to the fridge and settled on a white one with a blue cover and a yellow equator. She filled it with warming water from the tap and then sat down across from me at the table. She looked at me quizzically, then put her hand to her face and began to raise and lower her top lip with the knuckle of her index finger in an innocent sex-kitten-type gesture. The kettle began to emit a low rumbling sound, and I let out a sudden laugh, which startled her.

She jumped, then stood up and said, "I don't really know what you want," as if to someone with whom she'd shared a life rather than a night.

"What do you mean?" I said.

"Why did you ask me back here?"

"I thought you wanted to come back."

"I did, I suppose," she said absently, and tilted her head sideways like a bird. Her gaze fell on the plastic packets of tampons that she'd laid on the kitchen table. She reached out her hand and ran her fingers along the crimped edge of a packet.

The kettle began to whistle, and she went over and took it off the burner. Then, with what seemed like four arms moving all at once, she turned off the stove, emptied the warming water out of the teapot, removed two tea bags from the box, dropped them into the pot, filled it with boiling water, fitted it with a tea cozy, and set it down in front of me on a ceramic coaster on the table.

She sat down and put her hands around the tea cozy to feel the warmth of the teapot coming through.

"Let's take it to bed with us," she said. "Is there a hot water bottle?"

"I'm sure there's one somewhere," I said.

Though I'd turned on the rads, it took a long time for the hot water to warm their old cast-iron bones. I was so preoccupied most of the time that I was unaware of just how cold the house really was.

The hot water bottle was nowhere to be found. Kerry and I sat up in bed with our clothes on, reading and drinking Sleepytime like an old retired couple, the patchwork quilt pulled up to our chins, Miro curled into a ball between us.

She read me to sleep—all her favourites from the *Little Treasury*, the *Pocket Book*, and the *Immortal Poems:*

> *When I see birches bend to left and right*
> *Across the lines of straighter darker trees ...*
>
> *somewhere I have never travelled, gladly beyond*
> *any experience, your eyes have their silence ...*
>
> *It's a warm wind, the west wind, full of birds' cries ...*
>
> *It was my thirtieth year to heaven*
> *Woke to my hearing from harbour and neighbour wood ...*
>
> *I will arise and go now, and go to Innisfree ...*

And for Nat, completely from memory:

> *Ah, Sun-flower! weary of time,*
> *Who countest the steps of the Sun;*
> *Seeking after that sweet golden clime,*
> *Where the traveler's journey is done;*

Where the Youth pined away with desire,
And the pale Virgin shrouded in snow,
Arise from their graves, and aspire
Where my Sun-flower wishes to go!

I nodded off in the middle of "Dover Beach":

Ah, love, let us be true
To one another! for the world, which seems
To lie before us like a land of dreams . . .

For poetry makes nothing happen: it survives
In the valley of its making where executives
Would never want to tamper, flows on south
From ranches of isolation and the busy griefs,
Raw towns that we believe and die in; . . .
—W.H. Auden, *In Memory of W.B. Yeats*

THE BUSY GRIEFS (III)

In the morning Kerry asked if we could drive out to Cape
Spear. Though there was a touch of frost on the bedroom
window, there was a sun of sorts peeping in through the slats
of the mini-blinds. She had come in to wake me up around
eleven o'clock, and was now peeping back and quietly scratching at the frost with one of her well-bitten fingernails. After
reading me to sleep last night, she had gone off to Anna's room
and slept in the bunk bed.

The spare key to Kate's Lada was still where it used to be,
and so was the car, parked halfway up the street with an old and
tattered ticket under each wiper. "Offender remove this stub,"
I read along the perforated edge. Though I was not the guilty
one, I obeyed, and the thing separated into two pieces. I tried
reading the rest of the washed-out text, but I couldn't make out
what the offence was.

I pumped the gas pedal a few times, and to my great
surprise the car started on the first turn of the key. If the
Russians can make vehicles to penetrate the frozen wastes of
space, why can't they make one that can get us through a
Newfoundland winter? I had said to Kate one morning as we
sat freezing in the Lada listening to the battery lose its last
ounce of strength.

As I didn't like driving, or even being driven, Kate had

always been the family chauffeur; the Lada's feints, jerks, and outright stalls now betrayed my unpracticed art.

In her ongoing, but now quiet, protest against the U.S. for its atrocities in the Vietnam War, Kate bought only European cars; but in the early stages of the St. John's anti-Vietnam War campaign, she had been on the front lines, actively engaged as a placard painter and marcher. She used to stand on street corners handling out leaflets that said, "Stop the War." She had even come close to getting herself arrested one evening in the fall of 1969.

At the height of the war, when there were over a half million troops in Vietnam, and major protests were sweeping the United States, we had taken part in a demonstration at the American Consulate on Kings Bridge Road. Rocks had been thrown and windows had been smashed; one of Kate's friends had been carted off in the paddy wagon by the police. She had held on to his feet so tightly that she'd been left holding one of his work boots after he'd been dragged away. Then she'd thrown a flour-bag bomb at the paddy wagon as it went past.

It had been twenty years since we had a country of our own, and we were lucky, perhaps, to still have an American consul with an official residence to throw rocks at. And though it was a mere consulate with only a lowly consul—not an embassy with an ambassador extraordinary and plenipotentiary—it had been in the country since the 1840's; in the 1940's, during the Second World war, the Americans had set up military bases here. And they took even longer to withdraw from Newfoundland than they did from Vietnam. We were trying to tell them that they'd outstayed their welcome here as well. Withdrawal, as one memorable placard had read, was something we wished Richard Nixon's father had practiced.

Kate had owned, of course, the ubiquitous Bug and the socialist Volvo, but both third- or fourth-hand and ready for the scrap heap by the time they had been handed down. Then she had fallen for a Czech Skoda, a love, unfortunately, unrequited.

After that there had been a French car, a Simca, and then the Russian Lada, the automotive version of Socialist Realism.

It was at least ten years since I had been out to Cape Spear, a favourite haunt of ours in the late sixties, along with Motion, a small but spirited cove just up the shore in Logy Bay. But the Cape had had a real spiritual hold on us, and, indeed, the trek out there at that time was not unlike the road to Calvary. A few years ago I was painfully reminded of just how much the place had meant to us when a friend of ours who had died in Ontario had directed that his ashes be brought back and scattered over the ocean there.

In the late seventies the bleak and beautiful Cape had been declared a national historic site and had been developed into a federal park. But, long before this, it had been the site of some historic highs. In the sixties you could light a fire there as well as a joint, though wood was hard to come by, and we had cooked up some great scoffs on warm summer nights. Motion had also become a park—a private one—the Waldenian preserve of a local broadcasting magnate who had bought and fenced all the land around the cove, but was reported to have built nothing but a solitary meditation hut on its secluded and densely wooded oceanfront acres.

Long before the tortuous ten-mile stretch of road to Cape Spear had been paved—indeed, long before there had been a road, for what we had driven over was worse than a cart-track—we had made our way out there in Kate's various vehicles, the last time in that petite curvaceous voiture, or voiturette, the Simca. Able to hold its own, perhaps, in the lunatic laneways of Paris, it had a hard time on the rugged road to Cape Spear—a rift or rent through wooded hills steep as towers, diagonally rutted by roaring rivulets that sent cars veering toward the ditch. It was also crisscrossed by broken trees and pitted with potholes which, when filled with water, were more like gullies or small ponds.

Once we got out of town, and I didn't have to keep changing gears, the Lada sped out the paved road like a sputnik. Now there was a paved parking lot as well, and even asphalt walking trails over the marshy ground. There were stairways on the hillside, lookout platforms for whale watching, a restored nineteenth century lighthouse, an Interpretation Centre, and *conveniences.*

After parking the car we tried using them, but the building was locked up for the winter. We climbed the steep wooden steps to the new lighthouse and the lighthouse keeper's cottage, which shone like cut and polished stones, white and immaculate in the midday sun—not even light housekeeping required. We knocked on the doors of both buildings but nobody answered.

We walked on out to the restored lighthouse, on opposite sides of which we had a quiet and restorative pee. K. probably would have enjoyed this part of the excursion, but Kerry had left him back at the house. He loved to swim in salt water, she said, and when he did that at this time of year he developed chilblains.

A sign on my side of the lighthouse informed me that the light for this historic edifice, originally built in 1836 and now the oldest surviving lighthouse on the island, had come from an old lighthouse in Scotland. I wondered if this very light had once guided our lovesick Irish rover through the fogs and firths of the craggy Scottish coast, a bleating foghorn echoing his longing for Carrickfergus and his lost love.

We walked back along the cliff and down the steps, looking up over our shoulders at the revolving light, which was hardly visible against the sun. Kerry was of the opinion that the lighthouse was unmanned, as practically all of them were these days. At the foot of the steps we took the paved trail to the first lookout platform, with its plastic-covered Azimuthal Equidistant Projection map of a Newfoundland-centred world, *le monde vu de Terre-Neuve,* and Kerry checked the distance to fabled European ports. From here, North America's most easterly point, it was about 3500 km to Lisbon, to Reykjavik, to Waterford, from which her ancestors had sailed some two hundred years ago, and about twice that distance to Murmansk, from which a more recent immigrant, the Lada, had embarked.

Kerry told me that Nat had once made a mock azimuthal map of a Ship Inn-centred world, *le monde vu de Ship Inn*. It was where they had met, where Kerry had spent nearly every Friday night of her adult life; and though Nat had lived only a year in St. John's, he had spent most of it at the Ship Inn. It had been the centre of their social universe, and Nat's map had gone beyond the earth to the immediate physical universe, with grid lines not just to New York and Saskatoon, but to the moon, to Mars, to Venus, to the sun.

The sun was about as close to it as some of us now wanted to be, for if half the town drank on the George Street Strip, the other half drank at the Ship Inn, and this half included everyone you knew, among whom, of course, was everyone you didn't want to see. Pity poor John Keats, out for a quiet pint of an evening, a man who professed to have no self, no nature, no identity—at least as a poet—and when in a roomful of people felt the identity of every one of them press upon him to the point of annihilation. He would not have stood the chance of the proverbial snowball in Hell in the agonistic crucible that was the Ship Inn.

Kerry jumped down off the lookout platform and began to walk off over the tawny red ground along the cliff. She stooped down every now and then to pick a frozen cranberry or partridgeberry, which she popped into her mouth, or to examine some small brave green-growing thing. There were no trees, except for a few tuckamores, which were as spread out and low-lying as clumps of berry bushes, for the wind and the sea were usually relentless. Today, however, there was barely a breeze, though the waves were still foaming on the rocky shore below. Every hundred feet or so there was a Parks Canada DO NOT GO BEYOND THIS POINT sign on the edge of the cliff, reminding us of the federal presence here, even in this most isolated spot, its purpose not just heritage preservation and conservation, but the actual saving of lives. Care Canada, determined to keep us from drowning ourselves, calling us back from the precipice. Part of the unwritten "Terms of Confederation," I guess.

But the park was officially closed for the winter, as another sign had already informed us, and with no one watching or caring Kerry lunged past a sign and down the cliff like a lemming, as if she *were* intent on drowning herself. I followed behind, down the sloping cliff to the large flat rocks that stretched all along the shoreline. Farther down, a slablike stretch of stratified rock sloped out into the ocean. It was heaved up at a 45-degree angle, and its long wide mouth gaped at us and frothed and roared. Some rocks were white with frozen spray, some algae-green. I came to a faded sign that said DANGEROUS SURF. Surf? I thought. You'd think this was Waikiki. The smallest grain of sand on this beach was a boulder. Beyond the sign, a line of sharp rocks jutted straight upward.

I turned my head and caught a glimpse of Kerry disappearing into a deep cleft of rock; then she reappeared and clambered up the other side. In her long, crazy-quilt, hooked-mat sweater, black leotards, and yellow boots, she looked from a distance like some large exotic insect roaming the rocks. She raised her arm and waved me onward, then vanished around a prow of rock. She seemed to know exactly where she was going.

I found her lying on her back in the lund. In the shadow of the rock her face was wearing a smile that was close to a grimace. Her long black legs were drawing the weak solstice sun, now at its zenith but barely above our heads. Here there was no wind at all, and the sun was comforting, if not warming. It was a lund within a lund, a natural alcove, a high-walled recess of rock in the shelter of the cliff.

Kerry sat up and unfurled her long scarf. She shook her hair loose and tied it in a ponytail with a red elastic loop, which itself was looped with ridges and looked like a worm. Her ears revealed, I noticed for the first time that her tragi were unusually hairy. Her lips and fingers were still red with berry juice, and she was pressing her lips together like a woman evening out her lipstick before an evening out.

"Nat and I once made love here," she said, looking longingly out over the ocean, her gaze set north-northwest, past the Narrows, the Gut, Motion in Logy Bay, the blueberry hills of Cape St. Francis, the cliffs of Baccalieu; past her resettled childhood home of Ireland's Eye and round Cape Bonavista to St. Brendan's, now Nat's island home in Bonavista Bay. Farther to the west, the road back to town cut a perfect "S" through the green wooded hills.

I looked at the water closer to us: *The moving waters at their priestlike task/Of pure ablution round earth's human shores* ... in the words of John Keats in his last poem on this earth. I looked at Kerry, who was still gazing off into the distance. She pressed her lips together again, her lips red with the earth's blood, and I felt the waters move in me and saw my hands move and come to rest on her shoulders. She turned her face to me and I kissed her. It was a kiss for every one of us, for all our weary and wary hearts, but in this place—her bower, her refuge, her elfin grot—to which, it seemed, she had been summoned, it was clearly not enough.

She freed her arms from inside the long loose sleeves of her oversized sweater and, beneath it, began to peel off the black skin of her body suit, her yellow duck boots ending up trapped inside the hollowed stocking feet. Against the dark rock her legs were white as milk. She worked her arms back inside her sleeves and then put them around my head. The heavy wool dampened the sound of the sea. We kissed again, more passionately this time, then eased ourselves down upon the smooth warm stone. When all my senses returned again, the sea rushed back into my head with a roar.

This is the Hour of Lead—
Remembered, if outlived,
As Freezing persons, recollect the Snow—
First—Chill—then Stupor—then the letting go—
  —Emily Dickinson, "After great pain, a formal feeling comes"

My great blue bedroom, the air so quiet, scarce a cloud. In peace
and silence. I could have stayed up there for always only. It's
something fails us. First we feel. Then we fall....
—James Joyce, *Finnegans Wake*

SNOW

White with salt, the road from the airport wound into town
like the scar of an old wound; but this part of the road was new,
and had been blasted through a hill of solid rock. Though the
wind was raw, it was at my back, and the shoulder of the road
was hard and dry. Under my arm was a copy of *Goodnight Moon*,
which I'd bought as a Christmas gift for Anna.

It was the sixth of January, Old Christmas Day, the Feast of
the Epiphany. Acting on some epiphanic whim, I had taken a
cab out to the airport to meet Kate's flight. It had been
scheduled to arrive at noon, but had been delayed; then it was
rescheduled for three, and finally canceled altogether. A heavy
snowfall on the west coast had grounded all flights; but as the
sun, albeit a weak one, was still shining here, and all the roads
were bare, I decided to walk back to the city.

To the north, the airport road led out to Windsor Lake, the
city's main water supply. It was five hundred feet above sea
level—as high as Signal Hill—and the water reached St. John's
by the force of gravity alone. As a boy I had been told that the
lake was five hundred feet deep. On Sunday drives I had stared
through the rear window of my father's car as we drove along
the lakeshore into town and imagined a rainfall so heavy that

the lake burst its banks. The water rushed downhill behind us—a wave-wall of water gathering strength as it rolled down a five-hundred-foot incline—and my father tried to outdistance it in his new push-button Dodge Dart; but it finally overtook us and swept us down a river-road into town. Seeking its own level, as they had taught us in school, the water filled the twin valleys of St. John's to the steeples, rising, finally, to the top of Signal Hill and carrying us on past Cabot Tower out to sea.

In the distance, I could see Cabot Tower and the Southside Hills, set against a pale grey-blue sky. Out of that sky, almost a century ago, had come the first wireless message from across the sea, a *pip-pip-pip*, the letter S, soon to become the first letter of the international code of distress; for Marconi, though, it was a note of joy.

In a low building below the tower, the old fever hospital, he had waited—in a fever all his own—by a crude receiver in a small dark room furnished with only a table and chair. Good and faithful servant that he was, he had never doubted that the message would arrive, that the curvature of the earth would be no obstacle, as his many detractors had predicted. Outside his shelter a howling wind with freezing rain threatened to uproot his kite and its 600-foot aerial wire, as it had done with his balloon the day before.

Beyond the deep cut of the Narrows stretched the ocean's cold battleship grey. Signal Hill and the Southside Hills, still without snow, displayed their tawny and purplish autumn hues. I couldn't remember a winter with so little snow; but the storm that had canceled the flight was tracking east, and now the snow was finally on its way.

As I came to the end of the tunnel of rock, I saw a pale mottled white moon low in the eastern sky. In the west, a cold January sun laid its tired head on the horizon. On that high white road, with a pale disc in the corner of each eye, I felt like a tightrope walker with outstretched arms and a planet in each palm for balance; or a figure in some distant constellation, holding a planetary pendulum or a celestial scales of justice. I fixed my eyes on the far horizon, where the sea met the sky. Never look at your feet, I once heard a tightrope walker say.

My feet led me back to my rooming house, where I hadn't been for two weeks or more. In a corner of the front porch, next to the peeling white radiator, was a large shapeless package in plain brown paper with my name and address in heavy black ink on the side. On top was a smudged Gaze Seed Company stamp and a Christmas sticker that said, "Merry Christmas! Love, Sis." Ruth was being more conscientious than Santa Claus this year.

The package was heavier than a sack of nails. I lugged it down the hall to the door of my room and laid it against the wall as I searched for the key. The hall was cold and damp, but the doors to all the other rooms were open. I walked up to the second floor to turn up the heat. The thermostat had been turned off, and the doors to the second-floor rooms were ajar as well. The house appeared to be completely empty. I guessed that Mr. Priddle had sold this one as well.

My own room felt even colder when I walked in. I laid the heavy package on the bed and began to open it.

Inside the thick brown paper was a three-story, pagoda-style plastic bird feeder and a 20-kg plastic bag of bird seed—Special Mix—with a faded cardinal and a pale blue jay on the front. As it seemed to be warmer outdoors than it was inside the house, I decided to set it up right away. With a pair of scissors I cut a corner off the plastic bag and stood it against the wall.

The feeder was ingeniously designed, with a green pyramidal roof to keep the birdseed from getting wet, and a chute running down the inside that let you fill the three compartments from the ground floor up. On each level there was a small opening that looked like a cartoonist's mouse-hole. Beneath it was a lip to catch the seeds as they came out, and a perch for our peckish feathered friends.

I sat on the bed with the bird feeder between my knees and

poured the seed down the chute until it rose to the third-story ceiling. When I pressed the roof back in place, seeds of various sizes, shapes and colours slid out through the mouse-holes and over the plastic lips onto the floor. There were sunflower, sesame, and watermelon seeds, and kernels of millet and corn. Holding the bird feeder by the four pieces of green plastic wire that were attached to the corners of the roof, I carried it upstairs and out through the fire escape door on the second floor. I stood on the landing listening for birds and looking out over the untended back garden. It was filled with dead grass and weeds, mostly the decaying stalks of mile-a-minute. There was a wavy wooden fence on each side, and an unpainted lopsided shed next to the laneway at the back.

Not far from the house was a large bare maple, or perhaps two maples, whose grey bark looked like elephant hide. As a mere sapling, it seemed, its two selves had diverged, and about two feet from the ground its trunk forked toward the sky. It looked like ... *the thing itself ... unaccommodated man ... a poor, bare, forked animal ...* but with its legs pointing toward Heaven and its head and torso accommodated in the earth.

On the other side of the garden was a sprawling lilac whose branches and trunk were all cracked and split. Farther down, the fence rested against a large white birch, a "paper birch," which, true to its name, was shedding papyrus-like sheets of bark. At the back, beside the shed, was an enormous dogberry, its crown still laden with fruit. I walked down the rotting steps into the garden and twist-tied the four strands of green wire around the lowest branch of the maple. They formed a truss for another pyramidal roof.

I went inside and sat in the bay window with my coat on, looking out and beholding my handiwork, waiting for my first avian visitors to arrive. I sat there a long time, but not a single bird appeared, not even a starling. I waited for the moon to show its face above the Southside Hills, as it usually did, but it must have been tucked in behind some cloud. There was still a thin winter light in the evening sky.

I must have drifted off, for when I looked out through the window again, there was a large flock of birds in the garden—not at the feeder but on top of the dogberry tree, beneath the streetlight in the laneway at the back. I had never seen anything like them before. They were large crested birds, mostly yellowish brown, but with black-masked faces, black wings with a line of red droplets, like blood, and black fanlike tails with yellow borders. There must have been thirty or more, all eating avidly, but ignoring the bounty of seeds beneath the maple tree. They seemed on display, freeze-framed beneath the streetlight, but then they rose suddenly, like a single silhouetted shape, and disappeared over the rooftops into the fading light.

I walked over to the front window, where I noticed some starlings warming themselves on the chimney pots of the house across the street and some pigeons moving about under the eaves, upon the rounded crowns of the dormers. A fine snow, barely visible, was beginning to fall, like seed or dust motes or a manifestation of atoms. Little snow, big snow, as the old man used to say. It was falling upon the flat tarred roofs of the houses, drifting down through the haloes of the streetlights, swirling in small eddies upon the sidewalk, seeding the bare frozen ground.

The heat still hadn't come on in the house, so I lay back on the bed against some pillows and pulled the sleeping bag up over my coat. I opened Anna's copy of *Goodnight Moon*, a large-format, 40th-anniversary hardcover edition of a book that had appeared before I was born, that had been read to me as a child and that I, in my turn, had read to Anna. Though she was now well past its simple incantatory phrases, she would perhaps one day read it to children of her own.

I thought of all the times I had read it to her as she watched me, wide-eyed and sometimes fearful, through the bars of her crib—the ribs of a wooden shoe in which she sailed off to sleep every evening; the skeleton of a barque that had been a-building since the day she was born, and in which one day she would sail away for good.

In the great green room there was a telephone and a red balloon and a picture of the cow jumping over the moon . . .

Through the tall bay window at the back I could see the silhouetted shape of the bird feeder swaying in swirls of snow beneath the branches of the maple. I could hear the wind picking up—tugging at the eaves, scattering the pigeons. Impatient now, the storm was gathering strength.

Goodnight room goodnight moon goodnight cow jumping over the moon goodnight light and the red balloon . . .

Soon it would descend upon us in all its fury. The snow had held off long enough. It would block our doors and shroud our windows, fill the streets and gardens to the roofs of the houses. As we slept it would sweep down upon us like the waters of the lake.